AN AJ DOCKER & B

FAULTY BLOODLINE

GARY GERLACHER

Black Rose Writing | Texas

First printing

ISBN: 978-1-68513-383-2
PUBLISHED BY BLACK ROSE WRITING
www.blackrosewriting.com

Printed in the United States of America
Suggested Retail Price (SRP) $21.95

Faulty Bloodline is printed in Minion Pro

*As a planet-friendly publisher, Black Rose Writing does its best to eliminate unnecessary waste to reduce paper usage and energy costs, while never compromising the reading experience. As a result, the final word count vs. page count may not meet common expectations.

For the real life CJ, who understands friendship
and loyalty better than most.

For Katy Paolini, who started me on a writing journey in 6th grade
with 500 word essays on why I should pay attention in class.
I paid attention.

FAULTY BLOODLINE

CHAPTER 1

Sunday, April 10
2:38 p.m.

Stalking his prey, the man slid silently from tree to tree. With each step, his excitement grew as the hunger for his next kill consumed him. Kills, not kill. There would be two bodies this time, a first for him. One of them would be a woman, another first. Anticipation thundered through his veins as he narrowed the distance between them.

Blissfully unaware of the danger behind them, the couple held hands, laughing and flirting as they hiked along the trail. Dappled sunlight filtered through the trees, and a moderate breeze kept the air comfortable and soothingly rustled the aspen trees. They moved off the trail and found a clearing to have lunch.

The killer watched as they slid their backpacks off and laid out a blanket. As he approached, the man wrapped his arms around the woman from behind, squeezing her breast with one hand while kissing her neck. The woman turned around, standing on her tiptoes to return the kiss. The long, passionate kiss led to the couple reaching for each other's clothes.

The killer moved back into the trees to watch. The couple struggled out of their shirts and shorts, revealing well muscled bodies of seasoned hikers. They rolled onto the blanket, with the woman ending up on top of the man, riding him energetically. The killer watched in fascination, the scene further arousing his emotional state. The hunger inside him grew as their intensity increased, and when they climaxed, he could contain himself no more. His heart pounded as he walked toward their naked bodies. Every sense tingled as he neared them. Time to kill again.

The woman noticed him first and screamed as she sat up and tried to cover herself with the blanket. Her partner froze with fear. They saw before them a man waving a large handgun between them with a cruel smile curled across his face. The man tossed two shovels at their feet.

"Put your hiking boots back on and start digging." The killer could not hide the excitement in his voice as he gave the order.

The couple stared in stunned horror as their heads swiveled from the shovels to the gun. Finally, the man spoke. "Now wait a minute, we…"

The gun shot sounded like a cannon at close range. Flame darted from the barrel of the gun as the .45 caliber slug fired into the ground between them. The killer spoke slowly. "I said, get your boots on and start digging a fucking hole."

The couple slowly stood up, still covering themselves with the blanket. The woman started reaching for her clothes, but the killer had other ideas. This was going to be his best kill yet.

"No clothes, just the boots."

The woman sobbed as the man looked on helplessly. Resigned to the inevitable, they reached for their boots and laced them up.

"Good job. Now I need you guys to dig a hole about three feet deep and wide enough for two bodies."

The woman sobbed uncontrollably, and the man trembled in fear, but found the courage to speak. "We have money. What do you want?"

The killer approached him and saw the man's trembling increase. The killer's anticipation was nearly uncontrollable. "All I want is for you to dig that hole. If you do that, I promise you a quick and painless death. If you make me dig, I'm gonna gut shot you and throw you in that hole and bury you alive. I suggest you take the easy way out and dig a nice hole."

The man cautiously reached down and grabbed the shovels, handing one to the woman. Timidly, they dug through the tears.

The killer could barely contain his emotions. The helplessness of the couple was more stimulating than all of his other kills combined. They pleaded for mercy, not realizing the pleas were fueling his desire for the kill. It was the longest, most satisfying thirty minutes of his life.

Finally, the hole was deep enough, and he ordered them to throw out the shovels and get on their knees. The couple turned to him one last time. Dirt and sweat covered their naked bodies, and all attempts at modesty were long gone. The woman made one last appeal.

"Please, we'll do anything. Just let us go. Please."

The killer barely heard her as the blood rushed through his body. His muscles twitched, and his breathing became shallow as the moment approached. He eagerly pointed them to their knees.

With all hope lost, the couple turned and knelt, leaning on each other and holding hands, whispering words the killer could not hear. It was perfect. The killer had never felt such a high. He floated into the air, watching from above as he pulled the trigger twice, and their twitching bodies slowly collapsed on each other.

It was too much, and the killer fell backward, his vision narrowing, as the adrenaline rush peaked. He sat there until his heart and breathing returned to baseline, then stood up and admired his handiwork. The woman landed on top of the man, their bodies and blood entwined forever. He took out his phone and snapped a few pictures to add to his collection.

Full of energy, he threw their belongings on top of them, grabbed a shovel, and quickly filled the hole. With each scoop, he replayed the moment the bodies fell forward on each other. In no time at all, he finished. He carried his shovels with a smile as he hiked toward his car, the memory of the kill playing over and over.

CHAPTER 2

Monday, May 2
2:42 p.m.

"Banshee, driving from Houston to Montana has to be the stupidest thing we've ever done, which is saying something, because we've done some really stupid things."

I was not expecting a response, as Banshee had his head out the window, exploring all the smells in Wyoming, tongue blowing in the wind. Apparently, Wyoming smelled different than Texas. It certainly looked different. The prairie rolled endlessly to the horizon in a bleak landscape devoid of trees or signs of life. The vast expanse was beautiful for its openness, but depressing for its emptiness.

My traveling companion was a Belgian Malinois, who always stayed at my side. A former police dog, Banshee, understood over two hundred verbal and visual commands. He was sixty pounds of pure muscle and brains who spent most of his day as a friendly pet. On command, he turned into a war machine. His dark brown coat shimmered in the sunlight, and his black eyes missed nothing.

We pulled into a truck stop for some snacks, exercise, and gas. My Mercedes G wagon was an impressive vehicle, but did not get the best gas mileage, especially when accelerating its 600 hp engine, but it was big enough for Banshee and all of our stuff I would need for the next three months.

Banshee eagerly leapt out and ran to some grass to do his business and explore unfamiliar smells. I lost sight of him, but didn't worry. Banshee knew how to stay out of trouble, or cause trouble, as needed.

As I finished pumping the gas, I turned to find two guys approaching me. I hate to stereotype the locals, but I immediately thought of them as Cletus and Other Cletus. Big, dumb guys with beer bellies hanging out of a t-shirt that might have fit forty pounds ago. Soap and laundry detergent did not appear to be priorities. Whether cousins or brothers, I was confident the Cletus family tree had a few inappropriately intertwined branches. It took dedicated inbreeding to produce these two.

Cletus smiled and showed off his favorite three teeth. Clearly, toothpaste was a rare commodity as well. I briefly wondered how he would eat corn on the cob. Would he nibble a single kernel at a time, or would he move the ear sideways a row at a time? They stopped three feet away, close enough to intimidate, but not close enough to threaten. Yet.

"Mister, that's a pretty fancy car. You might want to pay me to protect it while you go inside the store," Cletus mumbled.

"Yeah, we're pretty good at watching cars like this. Cost is $100 for each of us to make sure nothing happens to this pretty car."

A shakedown from some country bumpkins in the middle of Wyoming annoyed me after an already long day. I am sure they looked at my six-foot-one inch, 195-pound frame as an easy target. In my shorts, plain gray t-shirt, Oakley sunglasses, and comfortable sandals, I must have appeared to be a typical tourist easily intimidated by their bulk. I took off the sunglasses to reveal my controlled anger radiating from my icy blue eyes.

"Thank you, kind gentlemen, for the offer, but I respectfully pass."

"Pretty sure something bad gonna happen to this car without a guard," Cletus threatened.

"Sorry, let me clarify. I didn't mean I would leave it unguarded. I meant I didn't need you two to guard it. Banshee will guard it."

"What the fuck is a Banshee?" Other Cletus asked.

"Turn around and find out, but I recommend you do it slowly."

They turned to find Banshee sitting at attention two feet away from them. He had approached silently when he saw the men approaching me and now awaited commands. I tapped two fingers on my right forearm, and he had his command, "GROWL."

Banshee bared his teeth and erupted a low growl from the depths of his being. They both took a step back, but quickly recovered.

"Mister, that damn dog ain't gonna protect your car. We got plenty of dogs scarier than him around here. Now give us our money," Cletus demanded.

I knew nothing about Wyoming dogs, but I was confident there were no scarier dogs than Banshee. Other Cletus stared at Banshee, who patiently growled as he waited for a new command.

"FACE," I said calmly.

Instantaneously, Banshee powered off his back legs straight into the air five feet, which meant his head was about seven feet off the ground and looking down at Other Cletus. When he reached the apex, Banshee was almost a foot above Other Cletus' face, and he let out a bark and snapped at his face. He didn't make contact, as the command was only to intimidate, not to attack, but Other Cletus didn't know that. Other Cletus only saw a demon dog that had levitated in front of him and was now descending on his face to eat him alive. He fell backward and probably pissed his pants, although it would be hard to tell through all the other stains.

Banshee landed gracefully in his previous location and calmly awaited his next command. Only four seconds of activity had the desired effect, stunning the two Cleti like a Jeopardy question.

I patted the hood of my G wagon. "UP," I commanded and Banshee sprung onto the hood. "GUARD," I commanded, and turned to the Cletus twins. "Gentlemen, I'm going to run inside and use the restroom and grab some snacks. Banshee has guard duty and your services are not needed. Have a nice day." I turned my back and walked into the store, confident that Banshee had me covered.

When I returned five minutes later, Banshee was still on the top of the G Wagon and Cletus and Other Cletus were nowhere to be found. I opened the door and Banshee hopped into the copilot seat. "Good job, boy," I said as I handed him some jerky. "Let's get out of Wyoming and head over to our new place in Montana."

Banshee was too busy working on the jerky to agree or disagree with the plan.

. . .

Dusk fell as we finally approached Waterford, Montana, my home for the next three months. I chose Waterford for its small size and proximity to the mountains. A town of 28,000, it rested at the base of the Beartooth Mountains with easy access to Custer Gallatin National Forest, near Yellowstone. It offered a pleasant combination of rustic heritage and modern convenience.

Waterford had a large hospital for a town that size, but it also served the regional area as well. Bozeman and Billings were the nearest cities, each over 90 minutes away. The nearest tertiary care center was in Salt Lake City, over 500 miles away. I was a long way from my Level 1 trauma hospital in Houston.

I reached the outskirts of town and slowed my vehicle when the dreaded blue and red flashing lights bounced off my mirrors. A police car approached rapidly and turned on its siren in case I did not notice him two feet off my bumper.

"Well, Banshee. We made it 1,830 miles with no ticket, but now it's time to meet the locals." I gave him a reassuring pat on the head. "FRIEND," I commanded, and pulled over.

An officer approached, and I rolled down my window. "License and insurance." The cop was all business.

I handed over my license and insurance, as well as a copy of my concealed carry permit. "Good evening, officer. Here is my concealed carry permit. I currently have two handguns and a shotgun in the car, none within reach." I kept my hands on the steering wheel.

The officer looked at my papers and then back at me. "Sheriff. I am the Sheriff here, not an officer. Why are you speeding in my town?"

"My apologies, Sheriff. I thought I was going the speed limit."

"You weren't. Now, what are you doing in that fancy car in my town? It ain't tourist season, and we don't want no trouble."

"Well, sir, I am moving here to start a new job at the hospital. I am AJ Docker, the new ER doctor at the hospital." I held out my hand as a peace offering.

The Sheriff's demeanor immediately softened. "Apologies for the rude welcome. We get a lot of disrespectful rich folks tearing through our town, and we like it quiet here. Welcome to Waterford," as he handed me back my documents. "I'm Sheriff Stein. Can I help you get anywhere?" Before I answered, he held up his hand as his radio crackled.

"Sheriff, are you available?"

The Sheriff responded into his microphone. "This is Stein. What do you have?"

"If you are in the area, can you stop by Esther's house? The poop bandit has struck again, and she called 911 as usual."

The Sheriff laughed. "I'll head over there lights and sirens. Stein out."

I looked at him questioningly. "Poop bandit?"

"Yes, the great poop bandit of Waterford is on the loose. Esther is a nice old lady who likes her yard and calls 911 whenever someone's dog leaves droppings. We stop by each time to keep her happy. The joys of a small town Sheriff. That's a good looking dog you got there. Is it a Belgian Malinois?"

"Yes, sir. He used to be a police dog, but got injured in a gunfight. Lost a kidney and had to retire from active duty. So now he hangs with me."

"Brave dog."

"You got that right. He took a bullet for me. Little guy saved my life." I scratched his ears, and Banshee beamed at the attention.

"Hopefully, we won't have any excitement like that around here."

"That's why I left Houston and took a job here. Looking for a little calm and quiet in my life."

"You came to the right place. The poop bandit is our most wanted criminal these days. Now, can I help you get anywhere?"

"I am supposed to meet an attorney here in town to sign some papers and pick up my house keys. Name is Travis something."

Sheriff Stein's smile tightened. "Travis Foster. I know him well. Follow me, and I'll show you the way."

The Sheriff led the way into town. We passed a few commercial fast food restaurants and hotels on the perimeter, but the central area of town contained all home grown businesses, including a barbershop, boot store, clothing boutiques, a diner and a gun store. Large trees shaded the sidewalks, which were full of families. The center of town housed the county offices in a magnificent three story stone building. An expansive park across the street hosted playful children and dogs. Banshee had his head out the window, working overtime to observe everything.

He stopped in front of a small storefront with "ATTORNEY" written in faded letters above the door. I waved thanks to the Sheriff for leading me here, but he was already pulling away. Banshee and I hopped out of the car, stretched, and entered through the battered glass door.

Foster's office looked like it had not been cleaned within the last ten years or decorated within the last thirty. An enormous desk dominated the center of the room. Three mismatched chairs at obtuse angles cowered before it. Shelves and file cabinets lined two of the walls. Binders and papers were scattered everywhere. I wondered briefly how many trees had died to provide all that paper. A well stocked and well used bar comprised the third wall.

A heavy musk of cigar smoke pervaded the room and had to be overwhelming poor Banshee's nose. The source of that acrid odor puffed on his cigar as he lounged behind his massive oak desk. He immediately stood. "Good evening, sir. Travis Foster, Esquire, at your service," he said with a rehearsed flourish. "I presume you are the distinguished Doctor Docker. Please have a seat. Can I get anything for you or your companion?"

"Nice to meet you, sir. Please call me Doc. Dr. Docker makes it sound like a stutter. Nothing for me or Banshee. We ate a little while ago and are looking forward to resting at the new home."

"Of course. Of course." He walked over to the bar and refilled his bourbon glass before sitting down. He moved agilely for a man in his sixties who was no stranger to drinking and smoking. His svelte frame suggested he was in better shape than his lifestyle might indicate. Shocking white hair in a disheveled mess covered his head and drew attention from his nose, which showed significant evidence of past drinking and fighting. His sharp eyes were a clear blue that did not appear to miss anything. Attorney Foster was nobody's fool.

"Let's see, I have the lease agreement and keys right here," as he pulled an envelope from one of many piles on his desk. "Looks like three months at the old Werner place. Nice piece of land. About five acres and magnificent views. Here are the keys. Sign here, and you are good to go."

I signed the papers and handed them back. He threw them in the copy machine and then turned to face me. "So is there anything else I can do to be of service this afternoon?"

"I assume you know a fair amount about this town."

He leaned back and laughed, which turned into a coughing fit. He pointed to his right. "Son, I was born about a half mile down that way 64 years ago, and I'm going to be buried about a half mile down that way," pointing to the left, "in the not too distant future. Except for school, I've spent my entire life in this town. I know the good, bad, and the ugly of this place."

"I've only been here for a short while and have seen none of the bad or ugly."

He pondered that for a moment. "I saw the Sheriff led you here. I assume he pulled you over for a ticket on the way into town?"

"Yes, sir, but he gave me a warning, not a ticket."

"Sounds about right. If you met the Sheriff, then you have seen some of the bad and ugly in this town, but I won't bore you with gossip. You're only here three months, and you'll hear more than enough gossip in the ER. Lots of good folks in this town, but like any place, a few rotten apples are mixed in."

"Like the poop bandit?"

Travis laughed uproariously at that. "Waterford's most wanted. Poor Esther." He stood up suddenly, indicating our meeting was over. He came around the desk to shake my hand and to scratch Banshee behind the ears. "Pleasure to meet you, Doc, and you too, Banshee. Here's the copies of your lease and my card. I doubt you'll need it, but if I can be of any help while you are here, please let me know. Let me walk you out. I need to get down to Tully's before happy hour ends. If I miss happy hour, they'll probably file a missing person's report on me. Enjoy your time here."

"Thank you, sir. Enjoy your happy hour. Banshee and I are going to get some much needed rest."

. . .

We drove north toward the edge of town as I idly replayed the conversation in my head. Mr. Foster played the part of a doddering old drunk, but clearly he had a sharp mind and a keen understanding of the workings of this town. His distaste for the Sheriff was palpable. I would keep my eyes open, but hopefully, my time in town would be unremarkable.

I pulled up to the property and was pleasantly surprised. Recent updates on the sixty-year-old house were evident, as it rested on five acres of lush green land. A slight rolling of the terrain supported hundred-year-old trees. Mountains rose into the starry skyline in the distance. The almost complete isolation from the neighbors felt perfect for me.

The comfortably modern house was way bigger than I needed, but the land and privacy were worth the extra money. I headed to the back of the house to make sure it had the one mandatory feature I had requested. A new dog door gleamed in the light of the back porch. All Banshee needed to be happy.

I walked outside and closed the door. "Banshee, here," I whistled, curious to see how long it took him to figure out the dog door. He pawed at the clear plastic, and when it moved, he pawed harder. When it opened enough, he pushed his head through and launched his body. He looked up at me, waiting for his praise.

"Smart boy," as I scratched his ears. "As a reward, I want you to 'EXPLORE'," as I waved my hand out over the landscape.

Banshee took off like a rocket, bounding from tree to tree. It would take him a while to categorize all the fresh smells and mark his territory. I went back inside to unpack. I would start my first day of work in the morning.

CHAPTER 3

Tuesday, May 3
7:51 a.m.

Felton Memorial Hospital, a medium sized facility only four stories high, provided breath-taking views of the surrounding mountains and forests. Composed of stone and brick, the exterior looked more like a resort than a hospital. The hospital offered only 74 beds, eight of those reserved for critical care. With four operating rooms and fifteen ER beds, it more than adequately served the community. The Feltons had donated a serious amount of cash to build this complex.

I parked in the half empty tree-lined lot and put Banshee on a leash. He wasn't happy about it, and neither was I, but people felt more comfortable around him on a leash when they first met him.

We walked into an open, well lit lobby with a waterfall, pond and plants everywhere, without a single metal detector, definitely a different feel from the big city hospitals I was used to.

I followed the signage to find my way to the emergency room where I found another clean, well lit, and empty waiting room, another difference I would enjoy getting used to. I introduced myself to the receptionist and she brought me back to main ER area, where fifteen exam rooms surrounded a nursing station. Bright, modern, and once again, nearly empty with only two rooms occupied, I was going to have to remember to bring a book to work.

A friendly voice called out, "Dr. Docker, so nice to meet you in person, finally! And this must be the famous Banshee as well. Welcome to the ER."

Dr. Christina Johnson, Director of the ER, Chief of Staff for the hospital, and hospital spokesperson, and I had many calls prior to my taking this job. Dr. Johnson, or CJ, as she liked to be called, was a colorful character known for her positive energy she brought to work each day. She always had a smile, a kind word, and a colorful outfit. Today she sported black pants with a leopard print blouse and matching leopard print pumps. The number of shoes she owned remained unverified, but betting under a hundred pairs would be a mistake.

She had trained in Washington DC, and moved to Montana about fifteen years ago to get away from urban stress. She loved hiking, fishing, golfing and skiing in her free time. Well respected for her medical knowledge, she frequently informed the public on social media and news programs. It was unclear how she easily managed all that and still had time to raise two happy teenagers and a dog.

"Good morning, CJ. Say 'HELLO' Banshee."

Banshee stood up on hind legs, then bowed his head forward and gave a polite woof. The effect was a bow and a brief hello.

The staff loved it and applauded Banshee's performance. Everyone except one person. "What is that damn dog doing in my ER?"

CJ rolled her eyes and turned to the humorless voice. "Good morning, Lois. This is Dr. Docker, our new physician, and his service dog, Banshee. Doc, this is Lois. She's the charge nurse for the ER."

I made eye contact with Lois, and the experience was not pleasant. Lois was an angry woman with a stern countenance that had not broken into a smile this decade, and probably would not in the next decade, either. She crossed her arms in front of her and firmly planted her feet as if looking for a fight.

"I repeat, what is that damn dog doing in here?"

I decided to see if charm would work. "So nice to meet you, Lois. I've heard only good things about you and look forward to working with you. Banshee is my service dog and will be here with me on shifts. He's well trained and won't be a problem."

Immune to my charm, her frown deepened, and she looked from me to CJ and back to me. "If that dog pisses or shits on this floor even one time, he's out of here. And so help me God, if he bites someone in here, I will drag his ass down to animal control myself. Do I make myself clear?"

"Perfectly clear," I said with a smile still on my face.

After a moment of more staring at me and then at Banshee, Lois turned to the staff and yelled, "Back to work, everyone!"

CJ got my attention. "Lets head back to my office and go over orientation." We walked back to the administration area and CJ waited until we were out of earshot before she spoke. "Sorry about that. Lois struggles with people skills. She's been here for thirty years and is kind of set in her ways. She's difficult, but gets better once she gets to know you."

"No worries. Not the first charge nurse to bust my balls on day one."

"I'm sure not. Did you get all settled in okay?"

"Yes, ma'am. Unpacked both suitcases last night and ready to get to work."

"Only two suitcases? I take that on a weekend trip. Plan is for you to work with me on the first three shifts, and I'll show you the ropes and teach you the documentation system. We're a slow ER with only forty to sixty visits a day, depending on the time of the year, but we cover regionally, and see some trauma from people making poor decisions. Hiking accidents, falls, and drunk driving accidents top the list of acuity. We can do a lot locally, but major trauma and strokes need to be airlifted out to Salt Lake City. It's a good crew, and besides Lois, everyone is real friendly. Ready to get started?"

"Lead the way."

. . .

The day proceeded without drama until early afternoon, when EMS notified us of a motorcycle accident coming in. The ambulance arrived with a young man who was awake and alert thanks to his helmet, but in obvious distress. The paramedic's report was succinct. "This is a previously healthy 22-year-old male who put his bike down while doing some tricks. Fortunately, he was wearing a helmet. Unfortunately, his right leg got all jammed up between the bike and the curb. He is moving three of his extremities, but not much good happening on the right leg."

The report was a definite understatement. The right leg had basically compressed like an accordion and deformed from hip to ankle, the kind of injury that led to amputation.

CJ and I began our examination with ABC, as always. Airway was patent. Breathing was good. Circulation was good everywhere except in the right foot. The extensive injuries had compressed and injured the vessels that provide blood to the leg. To save the leg, we had to restore blood flow quickly.

I looked up at CJ at the head of the bed, where she was getting some history from the distraught man. "What is our ortho situation? I have no pulses down here."

CJ turned to one of the techs. "Call Dr. Jenkins and have her get down here immediately, please." She turned to one of the nurses. "Let's set up for rapid sequence intubation. We need pain control and immediate reduction, and ortho will want him in the operating room as soon as possible. And get radiology over here to see what we have."

The rest of the team already worked at collecting blood samples, establishing a second IV, and pushing some fluids and much needed fentanyl. It would take the edge off the pain, but full pain control would have to wait until after intubation.

Luckily, his injury was localized to the leg, and CJ was able to clear his cervical spine from injury. The patient was given 100% oxygen to breathe while preparations were made. When everything was ready, CJ called for the medications to be given.

The first medication given was etomidate, used to calm the patient and give him amnesia for everything about to happen. Next came fentanyl to help with pain control and to sedate the patient. Last, we added rocuronium, a quick-acting paralytic to relax all the muscles in the body.

The nurse pushed the medications through the IV, and the patient immediately became sleepy and then unresponsive. The respiratory therapist assisted breathing by blowing air into the lungs through the use of a bag and a mask tightly sealed on his face. Within thirty seconds, the patient was sedated, paralyzed, and unaware of what was happening.

CJ positioned the patient and then slid a laryngoscope into the mouth and down the throat with her left hand. The scope had a bright light which illuminated the back of the mouth and throat. She advanced the scope until she visualized her target, the vocal cords, two pearly white vertical structures with a small opening between them. Without taking her eyes off the cords, she held out her right hand, and the respiratory therapist placed a breathing tube in it. She advanced the semi-rigid tube into the mouth until the tip was at the vocal cords, and then slowly advanced it through the cords. She continued to advance the tube until the two lines printed on the tube were at the vocal cords. Then, she removed the scope and held the tube in place.

The respiratory therapist confirmed the correct placement of the tube, taped it in place, and hooked the patient to the ventilator. The patient was now safely sedated with pain control, and the leg could be splinted without further pain.

X-rays were back in under ten minutes and confirmed the extent of injuries. The right hip was dislocated; right femur was fractured; right knee cap was dislocated; right tibia and fibula were fractured; and the right ankle was dislocated. His previously straight leg was now a set of switchbacks with no pulses.

"Good afternoon, folks. What do you have for me?" The petite, athletic figure in her thirties had jet black hair pulled back tight, highlighting her warm, dark brown eyes. Her manner was all business as she surveyed the room. "You must be the new guy. I'm Kirsten, orthopedist. What do we know?"

"Nice to meet you. I'm Doc. Everything from hip to ankle is dislocated or broken with no pulses in the foot."

She scanned the X-rays as I spoke. She turned to me with a smirk, "Doc, huh? Original." She turned back to CJ. "Has he had pain meds?"

"Plenty of fentanyl so far."

"Good. Give him some more. I'm about to do some cavewoman shit on that leg before we go to the OR."

The type of "cavewoman shit" she was about to perform intrigued me.

The nurses pushed another dose of fentanyl into the IV, and then she called me over. "Doc, hold down his pelvis and don't let it move at all, no matter what."

I leaned over the patient and placed both hands on the pelvis to stabilize it. Kirsten hopped up on the bed like a gymnast mounting a beam. She grabbed his right foot and put it on her shoulder. She delicately placed her left foot in his groin, avoiding the family jewels. She looked me dead in the eye. "You ready? This works only if the pelvis doesn't move."

I knew exactly what was about to happen. "Yes, ma'am, ready when you are."

She nodded her head. "On three then. One. Two. Three."

On three, she stood straight up and pulled the right leg with all of her strength. Simultaneously, the hip produced a clunk, and the ankle produced a softer snap as they popped back into alignment. The three major bones in the leg, the femur, tibia, and fibula, stretched out, and the overlapping ends snapped back into place. Each fracture produced a series of cracks as it realigned. The entire process took only a violent second to reverse the damage from the accident. The result was an overlapping series of alarming pops and cracks and a remarkably straight leg.

Kirsten kept tension on the leg as she easily hopped down from the bed. She had her hand on the top of the foot, and a strikingly beautiful smile lit up her face. "Please document that pulses are restored to the right foot at 2:14 pm, not the greatest pulses in Montana, but enough to get us to the OR." She turned to CJ, "Lets get a splint on that leg to hold traction and prep him for the OR. I got a couple of patients in the office I'll clear out and then take him for repair." She turned her heart-gripping smile on me and offered her hand. "Nice job, and thanks for the assist, new guy. I'm sure we'll be seeing each other again."

"You'll be my first call anytime we need some cavewoman shit done down here."

With a quick thank you to everyone, she was out the door. I watched her leave and then turned back toward CJ. She wore a thoughtful expression as she regarded me with a sparkling smirk I hadn't seen yet.

CHAPTER 4

Wednesday, May 4
9:26 a.m.

Back in CJ's office, we discussed the plan for the day.

"How did motorcycle man do last night?" I asked.

"Pretty good. Kirsten got the femur and tib-fib fixed with some plates and screws. He'll need further surgeries to fix the knee, ankle and hip ligaments, and about a year of rehab to learn to walk again, but he kept the leg and will keep most of the function."

"About as good of a result as could be expected given his injuries. Kirsten knows her stuff, doesn't she?"

"She does. And there are a few other things you need to know about her. First of all..."

The door to her office slammed open, and Lois stormed in. "Report of an active shooter at the high school. Multiple injuries already."

CJ paused for about a second, and then gave commands as she stood up and gathered her things. "Call a Code Black for the hospital. I want all non-critical patients out of the ER and twelve beds ready to receive patients. Call the OR and tell them I need three rooms on standby with full surgical teams ready to receive patients. Notify the blood bank and have all the O negative available prepared immediately, and look at setting up a blood donation center. Call all our staff and tell them I want everyone available in here immediately. And tell security to lock down the perimeter. This is gonna turn into a zoo quickly. Doc, you're with me on site for stabilization and triage. My kids are at that school. Let's go."

We rushed through the ER, already a flurry of activity to prepare for multiple gunshot patients. Excess staff from all over the hospital converged in the ER to provide dedicated support for each room. We stopped long enough to grab a trauma pack and rushed out to the parking lot.

I threw my keys at CJ and said, "You're driving, and we're taking my vehicle."

"Why are we taking yours?"

"Because mine has another trauma pack and all of Banshee's equipment. You know how to get to the school, so you're driving. I'm gonna put Banshee's gear on before we get there."

CJ hopped in front, moved the painfully slow seat forward and took off, using all the horsepower available. "What are you doing back there?"

"Getting Banshee ready to do his job." I took off his service vest and replaced it with a tactical Kevlar vest. I added titanium plates to the sides. It added weight, but after his last gunfight, the added protection was worth it. Next came the camera attached around his head with integrated earplugs. The camera would allow me to see whatever Banshee was looking at on my iPad, and the earplugs would allow me to communicate with Banshee remotely. The last thing I attached was a small speaker that would allow me to be heard wherever Banshee was. I finished checking his gear as CJ roared into the school parking lot.

"You gonna be okay in there?" I asked.

CJ turned toward me. "I know most of the kids in that school. We're not losing anyone today. Let's go."

We grabbed our trauma packs and headed for the center of the action. Sheriff Stein was already taking control of the chaotic scene. CJ and I rushed up to him. "What do we know, Sheriff?" CJ asked.

"Not much. Likely one shooter with a handgun, last seen in the cafeteria. Multiple casualties reported. Half the kids are locked down, and half escaped outside already. My men are on the way, and we're going in hard in about six minutes."

I heard occasional gunshots from inside the building. "We don't have six minutes, Sheriff. Let me send in Banshee. He can locate the shooter and possibly neutralize him without more shots fired."

The Sheriff looked at the dog dubiously. "I can't be responsible for the dog going in there."

"No worries, Sheriff, he's trained for this environment." I turned on the camera, earplugs and speaker, and gave the command, "HUNT, Banshee."

Banshee took off like a rocket into the front door of the building as we watched on the iPad. "Which way to the cafeteria?" I asked.

"Down the main hallway and to the left. Big open area," the Sheriff replied.

Banshee approached the end of the hallway, and I gave the command to "SLOW, LOOK LEFT."

Banshee stopped at the corner and peered into the cafeteria. His head swiveled back and forth as he waited for his next command. The scene before us showed at least seven children down and bleeding, some conscious and others still. Blood was everywhere.

In the middle of the cafeteria, a large male turned in circles and randomly fired a pistol. "Damn, that's Tom Heller's boy," the Sheriff said. CJ's anxious eyes scanned the screen, looking for her children.

I turned to CJ. "Get the paramedics lined up. We're moving in thirty seconds after Banshee neutralizes the shooter. Sheriff, have your men ready as soon as Banshee takes him down. Let's move forward." I led a group into the front hallway as the Sheriff organized his men, and CJ organized the paramedics.

I gave the next command to Banshee, "STALK, GUN." Banshee entered the cafeteria and slowly stalked toward the gunman. He moved silently, staying low behind tables, chairs, and bodies. When he closed to within twenty-five feet, I gave the command, "STOP." Banshee lowered to the ground and held still. I waited for the gunman to turn away from Banshee and then gave the next command. "ATTACK GUN."

Banshee immediately rocketed off his back legs and accelerated toward his target. He had eyes only for the arm that held the gun. Eight feet away from the gunman, he launched into the air. The gunman had no time to react before Banshee crashed into his arm and clamped down. The result of a sixty-pound dog hitting his arm at twenty mph and biting down at 200 pounds per square inch was instantaneous. Thrown off balance, the gun flew away from him. He fell to the floor with Banshee clamped onto his arm.

I surged forward with CJ, the Sheriff, four other officers, and a line of paramedics. I commanded Banshee to "GUARD." He immediately let go and positioned himself over the gunman with a low, constant growl. I spoke through the speaker to the gunman. "Do not move, or the dog will attack you. Stay where you are, and keep your hands where we can see them."

The terrified gunman had no desire to be bitten again and froze.

Twenty seconds later, we entered the cafeteria and surveyed the damage. A quick count showed nine casualties. CJ's children were not in the cafeteria. She immediately set her gear down and went to work on a girl who lay unresponsive with a gunshot wound to the chest. I turned toward the paramedics. "I want one team on each patient. Stabilize, but do not move anyone. We are sending the most serious injuries first."

I looked over at Banshee to see that the police had the shooter covered. "Here, boy," I said, and he happily sat next to me. I went to work with the paramedics and evaluated the damage. We had three patients hit in the gut. Serious, but they should survive if we got them in the OR soon. He had shot five patients in extremities, and we controlled the bleeding. They would all make it.

CJ's patient was not looking so good. Intubation complete, CJ placed a chest tube in on the left side. She glanced up at me. "Get me an

OR, now. We are bypassing the ER. I'm riding with her. Let's go people, move it."

I was already on the phone with the ER. "CJ is coming in hot with one critical patient, teenaged female with a single gunshot to the left chest. Chest tube in place with significant bleeding. Patient is crashing. We need to go directly to an OR with a thoracic surgeon."

"Thoracic team is ready in room three. We'll get her straight up. What else you got?"

"Three belly wounds. All stable, but needing exploratory surgery to assess the damage."

"I have two more rooms ready now and will have a third one ready in thirty minutes. We will direct them straight up. What else?" the calm demeanor was refreshing.

"I have five extremity injuries, all stable. Going to need orthopedic care once the other cases clear the ORs, but they should all make it. And the shooter is also coming by with a dog bite to his wrist."

"Say again, a dog bite?"

"I'll explain when I get there. Get to work; we're sending the first patients now." I stayed to organize transport of all the patients to ensure that the sickest arrived first so that the most resources were available. The chest injury went first, followed by the belly injuries, and last, the orthopedic injuries. Within twenty minutes, we had everyone packaged and on their way to the ER, except for the shooter.

I headed to where the three officers watched him. He lay spread-eagled on the floor after the officers searched him for other weapons. I sat down next to him. "Why don't you sit up and let me take a look at that wrist?"

One of the deputies was about to say something, and then looked at Banshee sitting by my side. He nodded and allowed me to look at the wrist, about what I expected after a Banshee attack, a complete mess. Large tears on the anterior and posterior sides exposed muscle and tendon. He had feeling in his fingers and wiggled them, but had limited range of motion at the wrist.

"What's your name?" I asked, as I gently wrapped gauze around his wound.

"Marcus."

"Well, I'm Doc, and this is Banshee. Sorry about the injury to your wrist, but we needed that gun neutralized," I said matter-of-factly. "You're going to need surgery and some IV antibiotics for this injury. And you may have a broken wrist as well. We'll figure it out at the hospital."

He looked up at me for the first time. "Why are you helping me after what I did?"

"Because I'm your doctor, and you're my patient. That means I take care of you no matter what happened before. The police and lawyers will figure all of this other stuff out. I'm only here to take care of your arm. Let's go. I'm gonna ride in the ambulance with you."

One officer stepped forward. "I don't think that's necessary, Doc."

"It's absolutely necessary. CJ took my keys with her, and I need to get back to work. So Banshee and I are riding with Marcus. You fellas are welcome to join us."

Sheriff Stein came over. "I want two officers in the ambulance with him, and I want a car following. Everyone else stays here to clear the rest of the school and process this scene. We have some more officers coming in from various agencies to help out." He turned toward me. "Thank you. I wasn't looking forward to a gunfight in a crowded gym. That dog is welcome to join us anytime."

"Thanks, Sheriff. Looks like we both have a lot of work left to do on this one."

Banshee and I jumped into the ambulance with the two officers, and we took off for the hospital.

"Don't you want to know why I did it?" Marcus asked.

I looked him dead in the eye. "Marcus, I've seen a lot of gunshots throughout my career. I used to ask why and try to understand, but I came to realize there's no good answer to explain this. I'm sure you had a reason that made sense to you, but it won't make sense to me. So let's not worry about the why right now and focus on getting your arm fixed up. These gentlemen probably advised you of your right to remain silent. I would also advise you to hold off talking to anyone except your lawyer. Fair enough?"

"Sounds like a plan. Thank you."

"You're welcome, Marcus. You're welcome."

CHAPTER 5

Wednesday, May 4
10:08 a.m.

In CJ's ambulance, a paramedic ventilated the patient with a bag at the head of the bed, while another obtained a second IV to pour more fluids into her. CJ held unrelenting pressure on the wound, willing the ambulance to go faster. She felt the rapid heartbeat under her hand increase speed, but weakening, as the heart fought to pump more blood to compensate for so much loss.

"How long to the hospital?" CJ asked.

"About seven minutes," a medic responded.

CJ quickly calculated that the girl did not have seven minutes. "Prepare for a thoracotomy, and get the epinephrine ready. We're about to lose pulses."

One medic prepared epinephrine for injection, while another retrieved the thoracotomy kit. CJ noted the loss of pulses under her hand as the monitor screamed in asystole. "Give the first dose of epinephrine, and hand me that scalpel."

CJ felt for her landmarks, finding the fourth and fifth ribs. She located the fifth rib, directly below the breast on the left, and made a five-inch incision along the top of the rib. She had to make three passes with the scalpel to cut through the muscle, tendons, and ligaments of the chest wall.

The area between the ribs was far too narrow to allow her hand to pass through, and rib spreaders were unavailable in the ambulance. CJ calmly instructed the medic to grab one rib with each hand to spread them apart. The medic, an athletic man in his twenties, strained to pull the ribs away from each other. A horrible crack accompanied the snapping bones, prompting him to release pressure, but CJ encouraged him to keep pulling until she reached her hand into the chest cavity.

She felt the heart, and it seemed intact, although ominously still. She reached deeper and felt the aorta, tracking it as it branched off the left ventricle and travelled downward. About three inches below the heart, she felt a disruption of the aorta. Further exploration with her fingers confirmed the bullet had passed through the aorta below the heart.

"Give me that clamp. We got a chance," CJ guided the large clamp into the chest with her left hand while her right hand guided it to the aorta. When she had it positioned above the injured area, she closed the clamp tightly on the aorta.

"Begin compressions and give another round of epinephrine." The medic began compressions as CJ stabilized the clamp. Blood leaving the heart out of the aorta would no longer leak out of the wounded area. CJ had effectively cut off any blood from flowing to the lower half of the body, but blood still returned to the heart from the lower body, and if enough blood was in the system, the heart would start beating again.

"Two minutes to the door," the driver called out. CJ evaluated the surrounding team. A medic performed vigorous compressions at a hundred beats per minute. Another ventilated her, and a third pushed fluids through the IV. CJ continued to hold the crucial clamp in place.

"Hold compressions, check for pulses," CJ called out. The medic stopped compressions and felt for a pulse on the neck. CJ placed her free hand on the girl's chest and concentrated. She felt a pulse, weak, but persistent. The medic felt her neck and smiled at CJ, "I have weak pulses in the neck."

Everyone collectively sighed, and CJ announced, "Note time for the return of spontaneous circulation. How long were we pulseless?"

The medic controlling the airway had been watching the time. "Total pulseless time was three minutes and forty seconds, but she had compressions for over two minutes of that time."

CJ forced a small smile. "Great job, everyone. She still has a chance. Let's get her to the OR, quickly, but carefully. This clamp is keeping her alive."

The ambulance arrived at the hospital, where a team escorted them to the OR. CJ held onto the clamp all the way up in the elevator and into the OR. The thoracic surgeon waited with his team as CJ gave her report. "Injury to the aorta about three inches below the heart. Clamp in place above, and total pulseless time was under four minutes.

The surgeon took control of the clamp from CJ. "Strong work. We got it from here."

CJ left to check on the ER.

. . .

We arrived at the hospital to see a scene of frenzied activity. The authorities had established a perimeter to keep the crowd and media back, but the number of onlookers swelled. We took Marcus inside to an exam room. I ordered an X-ray and then checked on the other patients.

Three of the four needing surgery were already in the OR, and the fourth was being prepped. The other patients had initial exams, X-rays, and pain meds. Families of the injured students anxiously waited to see their loved ones. I will never get over seeing them walk into the ER, overwhelmed with fear and anxiety, only to turn to pure joy at seeing their children alive. The ER is an emotional roller coaster.

I asked Lois where CJ was. "Still up in the OR. She had to do a thoracotomy in the ambulance after the girl lost pulses."

That was terrible news. The fact that she was still up there offered hope. The patient was still fighting.

"Let me know when she gets down here. Thanks."

I found my X-ray, which noted that Banshee had indeed broken Marcus' wrist. The radius had a torsion fracture from rapidly twisting it, which required surgery to repair and to clean out the wounds. Dog bites notoriously cause infections. Banshee was fastidious, but not big on dental care. I wrote orders for IV antibiotics and pain meds and arranged with orthopedics to take him to the operating room when one became available. In the meantime, he remained handcuffed to the bed by his good wrist.

I told him the plan and found his father at his bedside. I introduced myself and explained his need for surgery and IV antibiotics. Marcus already dozed from the morphine.

"Is this the dog that bit my son?" the dad asked.

"Yes, sir. This is Banshee," I said cautiously.

"Well, I want to thank him for saving my boy's life. I know if the police went in there, they would have had to shoot him. So, thank you, Banshee."

I held down two fingers, which was the signal for Banshee to smile, which caused a flicker of a smile from Marcus' dad, probably the last he would have for a while.

I walked out to find CJ walking down the hall with blood spattered on her blouse but with relief on her face. "And what have you been doing?" I inquired.

"Holding a clamp on her aorta until the surgeons patched it and restored circulation. Total pulseless time was only about four minutes, and she had compressions for the majority of that time. Once the aorta was clamped, we were able to restore circulation immediately. Touch and go, but the major bleeding is under control. Lots of small bleeders to fix, but those should not be a problem. She is probably gonna make it. How did the others do?"

"The three bellies are in the OR now. The extremity injuries will all be going up soon. They should all make it. Looks like the only casualty is that blouse," I said, pointing at her ruined top.

"I'm more worried about the shoes. I love these shoes," she said, despairingly looking at the blood covered leopard print heals.

"I guess you'll have to head home and change before talking to the media."

CJ laughed. "You don't know me very well. I have three more outfits ready in my office closet at all times. A girl needs to be prepared for anything."

"Well, you were certainly ready today. A thoracotomy and aorta clamp in the back of a moving ambulance, huh? You may be the best dressed BAFERD in America.

Sheriff Stein walked up. "What the hell is a BAFERD?"

"Bad Ass Fucking ER Doctor," we said in unison.

"You were both BAFERDS today, that's for sure. And that dog is a BAFERD as well. He saved our asses in there. Get cleaned up. We gotta talk to the media after I speak with Marcus. Then I got about fifty hours of paperwork to do."

"Don't forget, the poop bandit is still out there as well," I joked.

The Sheriff shook his head and briefly smiled. "He's probably got another couple of days of freedom with this mess."

He walked away as CJ looked at me questioningly. "Poop bandit?"

CHAPTER 6

Wednesday, May 4
12:27 a.m.

CJ strode out of her office ready for the press conference with perfect hair and makeup, along with a new outfit and equally fabulous platform shoes. She had a few moments to check on the patients remaining in the ER, speak with their parents, and thank the staff for their incredible work. She was a masterclass in leadership.

I caught up with her in a quiet hallway. "You doing okay?" I asked.

"Yeah, fine. Why are you asking?"

"Your kids were in that school. You never once tried to call them or even mentioned them."

She paused for a moment as she relived the experience. "I was too afraid to call. What if they didn't answer? I would assume something awful had happened. I just wanted to get there and get inside. If they were among the injured, then I would know I gave them the best chance of survival. If they were not among the injured, then I knew they were safe. To tell the truth, I feel horribly guilty that I was relieved someone else's kids were on the floor and not mine. Does that make me a bad person?"

"No, it makes you human. I couldn't imagine having to go in there, not knowing if my kid was one of the injured or dead."

"Well, hopefully, it's the last time for me. I can't believe all those kids made it. Amazing. The girl shot in the chest is named Hailey and plays soccer with my daughter. I never want to do that again to anyone, let alone to someone I know."

"It is amazing. We did good today. Although I have to admit, I am a little mad at you."

CJ looked offended. "Mad? Why are you mad at me?"

"You told me this place was calm all the time, and it's more exciting than a big city ER," I said, shaking my head.

She smiled. "I guess that was a bit misleading. Come on, time for the media circus."

. . .

They set the press conference up in the lobby, the only area large enough to hold it. The local politicians jockeyed for camera time. CJ pointed out the Mayor, Fire Chief, various city council members, the CEO of the hospital, the Superintendent of Schools and school board members. It seemed like several more people were joining by the minute. Finally, Sheriff Stein called for some order. I stood in the back with Banshee.

Sheriff Stein summarized. "At 9:21 this morning, we received our first call of an active shooter at the high school. This is a scenario we have unfortunately had to train for extensively. A general call went out for all available units to converge on the school. EMS and the hospital were alerted as well and initiated their own emergency responses. The school made an announcement for all students and staff to shelter in place.

"When the first units arrived on site, information from some students who had escaped indicated a single student with a handgun had shot multiple students in the cafeteria. We heard occasional gunshots continuing in the building.

"When the hospital team arrived on site, they had with them a former police dog that had retired because of previous injuries. That dog had audio visual gear that allowed him to enter the building and provide images of what was happening. As officers were still arriving, we sent the dog inside. Images showed multiple injured students and a single shooter in the cafeteria firing occasional shots. The dog disarmed the shooter, allowing medical personnel to enter the area and treat the victims, while officers restrained the shooter and secured the area. At this time, we believe the shooter acted alone, and there is no further threat to the school. I would like to take a moment to recognize the hero that prevented more injuries today. Can you please bring Banshee up here?"

I wasn't aware we were going to be part of the press conference, but nudged our way through dozens of people to the podium.

Sheriff Stein continued, "Ladies and gentlemen, I would like to introduce you to our newest honorary member, Officer Banshee."

I had Banshee step up and put his paws on the podium to receive his loud round of applause. I whispered in his ear, "SMILE" and Banshee hammed it up for the crowd, who responded with increased applause, and even some laughter. The picture of Banshee smiling at the podium made the national news later in the day.

"Before I take questions, Dr. Johnson will give a brief update on the patients."

"Thank you, Sheriff Stein. When we received the call, our hospital immediately initiated our protocols to address this kind of emergency. Dr. Docker, Banshee, and I headed to the scene to supervise stabilization and transport of the patients. Once the scene was secure, we entered to find multiple injured people in the cafeteria. All were students at the high school. The injuries included one gunshot to the chest, three gunshots to the abdomen, five to the extremities, and one student with a dog bite to the wrist. We have admitted all the patients to the hospital, and most of them will receive surgery this evening for their injuries. The patient with the shot to the chest is in critical condition, all the others are serious but stable. We are hopeful that all patients will survive."

She looked up from her papers and stared directly at the camera. "This epidemic of gun violence in schools has to stop. My children attend that school, and I didn't know when I went into the cafeteria if I would see my son, my daughter, or one of their friends lying on the floor in a pool of blood. Thankfully, they weren't, but other sons and daughters were lying there, scared they were going to die. I don't have all the answers, but we need to come together and figure out a way to make this stop. Our children are too precious to be slaughtered in a school shooting. Thank you. I need to get back to work, and then go hug my children."

CJ gracefully left the podium and headed for the ER.

"C'mon, Banshee. We got work to do ourselves."

CHAPTER 7

Thursday, May 5
7:43 a.m.

CJ greeted me the next morning in the ER. "Surprised you came back. Thought you would be halfway back to Texas after yesterday."

"And miss all of this excitement? No way. Besides, Banshee is a local celebrity and loves the attention. Don't you, boy?" Banshee smiled appreciatively. "What's on the agenda?"

"Today, you're running the ER, and I'm catching up on paperwork and media interviews. Due to give an update on the patients in about an hour."

"How is everyone doing?"

"Rough night for Hailey, but she pulled through. If nothing unexpected happens, she should make it. Everyone else got through surgery and is recovering. Minor miracle no one died yesterday."

"Definitely beat the odds on that one. Let's hope the good luck continues."

"Let's hope we don't need any luck today."

I left CJ to her paperwork and headed to the ER. After the chaos of the previous day, the quiet ER was back to normal, with only two patients waiting for lab results.

CJ stopped by after lunch and pulled me and Lois aside. "Heads up, VIP patient is on the way."

Lois sighed and shook her head. "I'm going out on a limb and guessing it's Carol."

"Good guess," CJ confirmed. "Apparently, she had another fall and has a wrist injury and a scalp laceration."

"Shocking. I'll go get a bed ready and see if I can find a red carpet to roll out," Lois muttered as she left.

"Frequent flyer?" I asked.

"The frequentest of flyers. Carol Felton is married to the guy whose name is on the front of this building. She has a ton of money and spends most of it on alcohol and pills. If they ever needed a picture of a drunken, privileged drama queen for the dictionary, Carol would be the model. Oh, and she and Lois can't stand each other."

"Well, at least I'll have something in common with her. Lois doesn't like me either."

CJ waved off her hand. "Lois doesn't really like anybody. She has a list of folks she tolerates. Anyway, good luck. And be careful. Mrs. Felton is a bit of a predator around men when she's been drinking."

Ten minutes later, I got to meet Mrs. Felton. As soon as the door opened, we heard her yelling in her slurred speech. "Took you long enough to get here. Did we drive across the whole fucking valley on a sight seeing tour? I must have missed it, because you dipshits locked me in the back of that steel cage. A bunch of jackasses is what you are. Get me off this damn thing and into a room."

I waited while they got her situated in the room. The paramedics came out all smiles. "Good luck. She's your problem now," the first one said.

"You're lucky. She's in a good mood today. Some days she's really nasty." They both laughed as they left the building. I had half a mind to jump in their ambulance and escape with them.

I steeled myself and entered the room with Banshee at my side. The patient sat up in bed and looked a mess, with a tangled mass of blond hair tinted with blood from a cut on her scalp. The blood oozing down her forehead competed with the makeup streaking down her face to fill in the cracks from a lifetime of sun damage. The 54 years she had spent on this planet had been tough ones on her. "Good afternoon, Mrs. Felton. I am Dr. Docker, but you can call me Doc. How can I help you today?"

"Lookee here. I can think of all sorts of ways a fine looking young man like yourself could help me. What did you have in mind?" She asked in what I am sure sounded to her like a sexy voice. In reality, it was a garbled muttering, difficult to understand.

"Well, for starters, I think we're going to get that nasty laceration on your head cleaned and repaired. And I think we'll get a CT scan of the head to make sure there is no injury to the brain. I understand you also hurt your wrist." She held up a swollen arm that the paramedics had already splinted. "Let's get an X-ray of that as well. Sound like a plan?"

"It's the beginning of a plan. But I have more in mind."

"I'm sure you do, ma'am. Let me do a quick exam." She had a nasty little two-inch laceration on the scalp, and her wrist was definitely broken, but there didn't appear to be any other injuries.

"I assume you're going to get me something for the pain, Doc?" she inquired.

"I think you are pretty well medicated, but we'll keep an eye on that pain level."

"And I will keep an eye on you, Doc. Do you need me to undress and get into a gown? My arm is hurt, so I may need your help."

"The nurses will help you with that while I get some orders started."

As I left the room, I heard her talking to the nurses. "Playing hard to get. He definitely likes me."

The CT scan of the head came back negative, but the x-ray of her wrist showed a non-displaced fracture of the radius. I asked the nurse to call orthopedics for me while I repaired the laceration on her scalp. Serenaded by a litany of suggestions from her that would make a drill sergeant blush, I paused a few times as my hands shook with laughter.

Kirsten walked into the room as I finished. "Hello again, Mrs. Felton. Another fall I presume?"

Mrs. Felton took a moment to focus her eyes on the new intruder. "For fuck's sake, not the dyke doctor again."

Unfazed, Kirsten examined the injured wrist while Mrs. Felton turned towards me. "All those big hunks of men bone doctors and I always get injured when this little thing is covering the ER. She likes bones but doesn't like to bone, if you know what I mean." Her cleverness set her off into a fit of laughter.

Kirsten looked over at me with a hint of a smile on her face as she gently examined the injured wrist.

"Owwww, you fucking bitch. That hurts."

"Sorry, part of the exam. That's where the break is. I'll get you in a cast, but no surgery this time. Any questions?"

"Nah. You scoot that scrawny little ass out of here and leave me some alone time with this man."

I took the opportunity to escape. "I am gonna scoot my ass out of here as well. Good day, Mrs. Felton."

Kirsten and I headed back to the nurses' station. She looked me in the eye. "That's pretty uncool, dumping her on me."

"I'm sorry. I thought you were on call for the ER today."

"I am, but that's still not nice."

"I really am sorry."

She paused for a moment. "When is your shift over?"

"Six o'clock."

"Okay. Meet me at Tito's at seven. You can buy me dinner and continue your apology. I'm getting out of here before the old man shows up. He's as bad as she is." She turned on her heel and left.

I looked down at Banshee. "Montanan women differ from Texan women." Banshee panted agreeably.

As I completed my paperwork, Mr. Felton and his son arrived to pick up the patient. Tom Felton was every bit a stereotypical Montana rancher. Only five feet eight inches and 160 pounds, he was all muscle. He had a slight limp from a busted hip in a rodeo accident years ago, but had a determined gait that ignored discomfort. Every item of clothing from his hat to his boots was high quality, bought locally, well-weathered, and covered in dust. He walked with confidence, like a man who owned the town, which he did.

His son contrasted with that image. Connor was twenty-one and in shape like his dad, but his movements were tentative. His eyes furtively scanned the room constantly. His clothes were disheveled and dirty, not dusty. On his belt, he wore two currently empty holsters that his hands subconsciously sought until he remembered he was not carrying any guns.

Tom spoke in a commanding voice. "Where is she? How is she, and when can we get out of here?" He asked the room.

"Mr. Felton, please call me Doc. I'm taking care of your wife. She's in room six. She has a cut on the scalp, which we repaired, and a broken wrist that is casted. CT of the head is normal."

Tom gave a nod of his head to his son. "Connor, go get her ready." Connor darted off to room six.

Tom eyed me professionally. "I can only imagine what she said to you. Apologies for her behavior. The drink brings out the worst in her."

"No worries. We got her all fixed up."

"Thank you for that. And thank you for your work yesterday. I heard you and your dog were a big part of saving those kids."

"It was a team effort, sir. We only did our part to help out. Glad it didn't turn out worse."

"Damn straight. Kids shooting up schools. What is this world coming to?"

"I couldn't agree more." I went over the discharge instructions with him. "Any questions, and do you think you need any pain meds for her?"

Tom laughed for the first time. "You may have noticed, Doc, that the missus is into self-medication. The last thing she needs is more pain pills. I'm sure she'll get by with what we have at the ranch."

I didn't want to ask what she had at the ranch, but I assumed if it was strong enough to sedate a horse, it would probably work on her. At least for a little while. "Okay, remember, return in five days to get those staples out."

Tom thought for a moment. "I got a better idea. She don't always travel real well. How about you come out to the ranch in five days and take them out at home? I would love to show you the place. What do you say, Doc?"

I normally wouldn't even consider such a thing, but I was curious about the ranch. It seemed more of an order than an invitation, anyway. "Sure thing. I'll stop by and take care of it."

Tom gave me a number to call to arrange the visit as Connor came out of the room pushing his mom in a wheelchair.

"Hey babe, you doing okay?" Tom asked.

"I'm fine. Not as fine as that doctor over there. But I'm fine."

"You take care, Mrs. Felton. I'm going to stop by the ranch in five days to remove those staples."

"I'll be ready for you," she said suggestively.

Connor spoke for the first time. "And so will I." He was staring at me with a strange intensity. His eyes shone with a level of animosity inappropriate for the situation, and every time his eyes flicked toward Banshee, his hands reached for his empty holsters.

. . .

CJ stopped by as soon as they left. "Well, how did it go? Did your patient make any inappropriate remarks?"

"I'm pretty sure all of her remarks were inappropriately suggestive."

"Don't be too flattered. She's like that with everyone. If there are no men around, she picks a woman. I'm proud to say that she has made offers to me that I have not heard since my college days."

"Weird family. What's the deal with them? Especially that creepy kid."

"You got that right. The Feltons are third generation ranchers. They own the Felton Forty Ranch to the east of here. Actually, to the east and south of here. It's about 40,000 acres with God knows how many head of cattle. They also own about a third of the land in town and are landlords to many of the businesses and homes.

"Old man Felton is a mean and nasty son of a bitch who comes from a long line of mean and nasty sons of bitches. He's been running the ranch and this town for a few decades now. His lovely wife has her first drink when she wakes up and stops when she passes out each night. I suppose it is the only way for her to deal with him, but she is on the fast train to an early grave. No way that liver lasts another two years."

"And the boy?" I asked.

CJ visibly shivered. "Excuse my language, but that kid is fucking nuts. He set fires and hurt animals in grade school. Graduated to drugs, fights and theft in his teen years. And don't even get me started how he acts around ladies. He's a sociopath and a walking felony waiting to happen."

"Surprised he's not in jail."

"He's been there multiple times. And each time Daddy makes some big donation to the city, and evidence is miraculously lost and witnesses forget. His old man has probably spent twenty percent of his assets keeping that kid out of jail. Rumor has it the donation that made this hospital possible was to settle a rape charge. The building is beautiful, but the money behind it is dirty."

"Seems like the old man might run out of money or patience with his son someday soon."

"You would think, but he seems to have an infinite supply of both. Family is important to him and leaving the ranch for the next generation is all he talks about. But if he wants to do that, he better adopt soon. Connor was messed up from the moment he was born to a drunk mom and an abusive dad. Kid never had a chance in life."

"So, is it safe for me to go out there in five days to remove the staples?"

CJ laughed. "She talked you into a house call, huh? It's safe. I wouldn't want to be alone in a room with the wife or son, but it's safe. And it's gorgeous. Some say it's the most beautiful ranch in Montana.

You should definitely see it. Will help you understand how this town is funded. I'm headed to some meetings. Enjoy the rest of the shift."

"Will do," I said as she walked away. I wondered how much money a ranch made. I vowed to do some research before my visit out there.

CHAPTER 8

Thursday, May 5
6:45 p.m.

As I dressed to meet Kirsten for dinner, I hesitated to call it a date, but I suppose it was. I chose jeans, a button-down shirt, and black cowboy boots. Based on how other people dressed in this town, that would work. I passed on the belt buckle and cowboy hat, as those seemed to be something you had to earn the right to wear, and I didn't own either, anyway.

I had planned to leave Banshee at home, but the town hero looked at me so pathetically that I changed my mind. "Okay pal, you can go. But you have to wear the service dog vest and a leash."

Banshee jumped up and down with excitement. A trip out meant unfamiliar smells and a plate that needed cleaning.

We drove to Tito's and arrived on time. Apprehensive of a Mexican restaurant in Montana, my initial impression turned favorable. Clean, brightly colored and well lit, the appetite-inducing aroma of fresh salsa greeted me warmly. A mariachi sound track bounced off the neon paint surrounding thirty tables, which were over half full. Every seat in the bar held patrons intermittently gazing at a small television mounted in the corner.

I scanned the room for Kirsten and almost missed her at the bar. She looked absolutely stunning in a short black dress and tan cowboy boots. The snug dress showed off a well-balanced figure that her scrubs hid at work. Hair and makeup were done and a cute little cowboy hat sat on her head at an angle. This was definitely a date.

She broke into a huge smile when she saw Banshee. "I didn't know you were bringing Banshee. Can I pet him?"

"Of course." I turned to Banshee and gave the command "FRIEND," and he walked right up to her for ear scratches. "Be careful. You give him that much attention, and he'll follow you home."

"Wouldn't be such a bad thing," she said playfully.

"This is a pretty nice place," I observed, as a teenaged hostess led us to a table.

"Yeah. Not quite Tex-Mex, but I call it West-Mex. The beef, pork and chicken are top notch, as you might expect, but seasoning is not exactly their forte."

I looked at the menu. "Really, $5.99 for chips and salsa? A real Texan never pays for chips and salsa. They're supposed to bring it out in large baskets and refill it endlessly for free. Makes everyone thirsty, so they order more drinks."

"I'll suggest it to the owners."

"You know everyone in town?"

She laughed. "Not everyone, but I know a lot of folks. I was born here, and except for school, I've lived here all of my life."

"I was curious about how you ended up here."

"This place is like a black hole you can't escape. In high school, I was pretty good at gymnastics and earned a scholarship to Oregon. I was good enough for college, but that was the end of the line for gymnastics. I got interested in medicine and ended up down at UCLA medical school."

"That part is understandable, but how the hell did you end up in ortho? I don't mean to be insensitive, but you don't exactly fit the stereotype of an orthopedic resident."

She smiled. "You mean because I'm a foot shorter and 120 pounds lighter than the average ortho resident? Or is it because I'm a woman in a man's field?"

I smiled back. "Actually, both. Most ortho classes are filled with a herd of alpha male Neanderthals."

"That certainly is an apt description for our class as well. A few of the guys were pretty primitive, but I love it because of all the injuries I saw growing up in gymnastics. Broken arms and legs were fairly common, and I became interested in fixing those. One thing led to another, and here I am back in town doing orthopedics."

"The vortex pulled you back to town after graduation?"

"Immediately. There was a need, and after twelve years away, I missed the mountains and clean air and open skies. It was a simple choice to come back."

The server came by, and Kirsten went with chicken fajitas, and I chose the steak fajitas for two.

"Are you sure you want that for two? It's an awful lot of steak for one person."

"Please bring an extra plate, and I'm sure my assistant will help me." Banshee was already salivating.

"Do you take him everywhere?" Kirsten asked.

"Pretty much. He's well behaved, and we've been through a lot together. Banshee took a bullet for me."

Kirsten raised an eyebrow. "That sounds like an interesting story."

"It's definitely interesting." I was telling the story of how Banshee and I tracked down a Ukrainian gang when Kirsten visibly stiffened, as she focused on something over my shoulder. I turned to find Connor Felton approaching with a drink in his hand.

"Well, hello there, pretty doctor lady. You look nice tonight."

Connor practically drooled on Kirsten, who never broke eye contact and didn't respond to him.

"I see I left you speechless. Why don't you leave this limp dick loser and come over to my table for some drinks?'

Kirsten finally spoke. "Connor, I told you before to stay away. Walk away now, before things get ugly."

"I like it rough. And don't worry about numb nuts over here. He doesn't have the balls to act like a real man." Next he looked at Banshee, once again with his hand straying to his waist. "And this pussy ass dog ain't no hero. About the only use I see for that dog is making a nice soft rug on my bedroom floor, where I can lay you down and fuck you proper."

I had no problem with the numb nuts and limp dick comments, but nobody was speaking to Kirsten like that in front of me, and nobody was turning Banshee into a rug.

I leaned over towards Banshee and quietly said, "FACE."

Before I got the last sound out, Banshee launched straight into the air until his back feet were at the height of Connor's chest. He lunged at his face and let out a growl worthy of a horror film.

Connor must have agreed as he turned ghost white and back pedaled. His feet got caught on a chair, and he landed flat on his back with his margarita spilled all over him. A passing server lost control of her tray loaded with chips and salsa. That landed on him, too.

The restaurant turned quiet, with everyone staring at Connor. His gaze burned into me with an intense hatred I had unfortunately seen before. He stood up and looked a comical mess covered in margarita and salsa, with the occasional chip fragment stuck to him. He stormed back to our table with obvious fury.

"GUARD."

Banshee immediately stood between Connor and me, tensed his body, and lowered his back legs, ready to launch forward. He bared his teeth and growled from deep inside, which would stop any sane man. Apparently, Connor was sane after all, as he froze and looked from me to Banshee and back again.

"He won't bother you unless you approach me. Please walk away and let us enjoy our dinner."

Connor continued to weigh his options, correctly concluding that he had only one. "Fuck you and your little whore friend. I swear to God

I'm gonna kill that dog and make a rug out of him." His hand reached where his holster would be as he walked out of the restaurant.

"RELAX."

Banshee immediately transformed from a killer to a lovable pet as he laid down on the floor.

"Well, that was interesting. Sorry about that," Kirsten said.

"No apologies necessary. I'm sorry I made a scene."

Kirsten smiled with a musical, infectious laugh. "That is the kind of scene this town needs. By morning, 90% of the town will have heard about this, and 100% of those will be happy about it."

"Connor is not real popular around here, I take it."

"Understatement of the year. Bad genetics, a drunk mom, abusive dad, money, privilege. That boy is the poster child for sociopaths. What you saw tonight, he pulls that shit with lots of women in this town. Thank you for doing that. Watching Banshee jump up like that and scare the shit out of Connor really made my day."

"And the night is still young. Only one problem. The server spilled my chips and salsa on Connor. That's $5.99 down the drain."

That musical laugh made my heart dance. "I wouldn't be surprised if you ate free here for a month. They hate Connor, but seriously, be careful. He's violent and crazy."

"Don't worry. Banshee and I have been through worse."

We enjoyed the dinner and conversation, and Banshee approved of his steak. The owner even stopped by and brought us some extra fajitas to go for Banshee, who definitely approved of extra portions.

"It has been a lovely evening, with one minor exception," I noted.

"Definitely memorable. Care to stop by my place for some dessert? I have some day-old cake sitting at home."

"I was just thinking I needed some day-old cake."

"All right. Follow me. It's not far."

• • •

We arrived at her home eight minutes later. In a neighborhood of twenty-year-old houses with large trees towering over them, Kirsten's ranch-style house rested on a bend in the road, allowing for an oversized back yard of almost two acres. Freshly painted with a well-maintained yard, the house had a beautiful view of the mountains and forest in the distance.

Banshee and I jumped out of the G wagon and headed to the front door.

"Is Banshee gonna be ok running around out back?" Kirsten asked.

"He'll be fine." I opened the back door, commanded EXPLORE, and Banshee took off to mark his fresh territory.

Kirsten grabbed a couple of plates of cake and a blanket and walked outside. "Let's join him. You city boys never get to see a real night sky. Sorry again about this evening. The Feltons have been tormenting this town for three generations."

"So they're not very well liked?"

"Try hated. The problem is they own half the retail and a third of the land in town, so everybody has to pretend to like them. That was a neat trick with Banshee. Serves the little prick right."

Kirsten walked to the edge of her property, far from all the light sources. She spread the blanket and then laid down with the cake between us.

I looked up at the night sky with its millions of bright stars. "Quite the view out here at night."

"It's my favorite time to be out here. Sometimes, I lie on my back and stare at the sky. The wind whistling through the trees is the only sound. You should try it sometime, especially after a stressful day."

I laid on my back and stared at the stars. I had never seen so many clear, bright stars at once. Their infinite expanse brought perspective to daily troubles, definitely inducing relaxation.

I turned to Kirsten to kiss her and noticed a small piece of frosting clinging to her lip. Apparently, she noticed my interest. "What are you looking at?" She asked defensively.

I moved closer. "There is a small bit of frosting on your upper lip, and I am dying to taste it."

She leaned forward, offering her lips, and soon we were locked in a passionate embrace. After a few moments, she broke off the kiss and snuggled her head on my chest. We lay there quietly for a few moments before she stood up and walked away.

Confused, I asked her, "Everything okay?"

She stopped and looked over her shoulder. "Everything is fine. I need to get a shower after today." We headed back inside and put the dishes in the sink.

"Okay, let me round up Banshee, and I'll get going."

She replied with a smile. "That's a shame. I was hoping you might want to join me." She unzipped her dress, slid out of it, and turned toward the bedroom.

Her body was firm and limber from her years as a gymnast, which made the shower an active event. The first time is always about passion and energy, and she delivered, leaving us satisfied and out of breath on the shower floor. We helped each other wash up and rinse off, taking our time.

By the time we got out of the shower, a slower round two led to multiple climaxes before we shared one together.

We looked over to see Banshee snuggled up on the couch and followed his lead for a night of dreamless sleep.

CHAPTER 9

Friday, May 6
7:46 a.m.

I woke the next morning to find Kirsten still asleep, adorably snoring. I didn't want to wake her, so I quietly dressed and slid into the driver's seat of my dew covered car.

"What do you say, buddy? Should we stop somewhere and get something to eat?" Banshee gave a short bark, which I interpreted as an affirmative. I hadn't been to Manny's Diner, but had heard good things about it from the ER staff.

Banshee and I arrived at the door as Travis Foster, the attorney we had met on the first day, approached as well.

"After you, Counselor," I said as I opened the door for him.

He grabbed the door. "Doctors and celebrities before attorneys. After you."

We walked into a moderately busy diner that looked like every other decent diner. A few older folks read newspapers with others absorbed by their phones, as they sipped coffee and ate their eggs. Servers bustled among tables carrying up to eight plates at a time without trays. Banshee definitely approved, as his sniffer worked overtime to categorize the greasy smells of fresh breakfast.

"Care to join me, Doc?" Travis asked, as he made his way toward an open booth.

"Happy for the company." I sat down and looked through the unremarkable menu. I didn't need to read past the Belgian waffle for me and some sausage links for Banshee. Travis went with two eggs over easy with bacon and toast, and of course, a mimosa, likely not his first drink of the day.

"You've made quite the first impression in town this week," Travis observed.

"It's definitely been a little more excitement than I anticipated."

"Good job with that school shooting. Amazing no one died. And I want to thank you for your kindness to Marcus. Lot of people would not have been so compassionate in that situation."

"Are you representing him?"

"Yes, sir. Known the family for a long time. Off the record, he suffers from schizophrenia, and their insurance company has been denying payment for his meds. He's a good kid on his meds, but struggles off them."

"Sounds like you should bring a suit against his insurance company."

"You read my mind. Already gathering info."

"What's gonna happen to him?"

"Hard to say. He'll definitely have to serve some time. Hopefully, we can get a minimum security setting where he can get the therapy he needs. Helps that no one died. But we'll have to wait and see. Depends which judge we get."

"Good luck. I hate to see mental illness punished instead of treated."

"I will most certainly drink to that." I had a feeling he would drink to almost anything. "So, I heard you had some excitement last night."

I was surprised by the comment. "What excitement are you referring to?"

"Little altercation at Tito's," he smirked. "A little birdie told me you and your furry companion put Connor on his ass in the middle of the restaurant."

"Actually, a chair leg and poor balance put him on his ass. Banshee encouraged him to move backward. Rapidly."

Travis chuckled. "I would have paid to see that. That boy is a bully and a disgrace. Good to see him receive more than he gives."

"What's the deal with that family? I understand if you cannot talk about them because they're your clients."

Travis pondered the question for a moment. "No, definitely not my clients. They use some big city lawyers from Bozeman. I actually end up litigating against them most of the time. Seems like every lawsuit in this town involves them somehow. Rent disputes. Lease disputes. Land disputes. They're always suing someone or getting sued. They're awful people, but it's certainly good for business."

"They don't seem too popular around here."

"True, but they do supply a lot of jobs and a lot of money to the town. If the money ever stops flowing, they would be run out of town the next day."

"Where do they get all that money? I was under the impression ranches were not all that profitable."

"That, my friend, is the million dollar question. Ranches do all right, and the big ones can make some money, but usually not that kind of money. I've tried to subpoena his financial records, but he has big money attorneys and judges in his back pocket. Any records we get are too convoluted to make sense. The guy has more companies and subsidiaries under his ranch than a major corporation."

"Is that normal for a ranch?"

"It's not normal for a small country. Probably just eccentric and his top dollar lawyers convince him to do all this to drum up more billing revenue for themselves. Believe it or not, not all attorneys are ethical."

"No argument there. Are they dangerous?"

Travis surveyed the room as he pondered the question. "The boy is definitely not wired correctly. He's been involved in some fights and beatings over the years, but so have a lot of other ranch hands. There are rumors of worse. Much worse, but nothing has ever been proven. I do know he likes guns, especially those twin Colts he keeps on his belt most of the time. And he knows how to hold a grudge. I would say he's dangerous."

"Good advice. I think I should pay for breakfast in exchange for that advice."

"You are correct, but if word gets out I made you pay for breakfast, there'll be hell to pay, and as you know, word will get out."

"Thank you, Counselor, and have a good day."

"You, too, Doc."

"C'mon boy. Time to head home."

We drove home for a much needed shower and change of clothes. I unlocked the front door and Banshee jumped inside, but immediately sat down and looked at me. Not good. Banshee's sitting like that inside the door meant he smelled someone new in the house.

"Hold up, Banshee. I forgot my phone in the car," I called out for whomever might still be there. I went back to the car and reached into the center console for my Glock 17 handgun. It was a trusty weapon with seventeen 9 mm rounds in the clip. I press checked to confirm one was in the chamber.

I hurried back and leaned down close to Banshee. "SEARCH." Banshee took off and methodically sniffed through the house, and I followed until only the kitchen and back door remained. Banshee entered the kitchen and immediately growled. I brought my weapon up and entered behind him, but I found him growling at his food dish. Someone had killed a squirrel, cut off its head, and put it in Banshee's food dish, along with a single bullet on top of the head.

A smarter man would have called the police, but I knew word would be all over town within a few minutes, so I called Travis.

"Travis Foster, esquire, at your service. How can I help this morning?"

"Travis, this is Doc, and I wanted to hire you for something."

"What sort of trouble have you found in the last few minutes that requires a lawyer?"

"Actually, trouble found me this time." I explained how we had come home and found the squirrel's head and bullet in Banshee's dish. Travis hesitated before speaking.

"And what exactly would you like to hire me for? This sounds like a police matter."

"Let's say I don't exactly trust the police to be impartial, and I don't want this news all over town."

"You're correct on both accounts. Tell you what, my official advice, which I know you will ignore, is to call the police. Now that is out of the way. Here is what we're gonna do. Make a video of everything exactly as you found it, and then video putting that bullet in a plastic bag without touching it. Tape the bag shut, and sign and date the bag across the tape. Email me the video and drop the bag off at my office next time you're around. It's not perfect, but best we can do."

"What about the squirrel's head?"

"That's yours to deal with. I'll hold everything, and we can use it later if needed. I'm charging you one dollar for the moment as a retainer, so we have attorney client privilege, but if anything else needs to be done, my regular rate is $300 an hour."

"Thanks, Travis. I'll get this over to you today."

I filmed everything and got the bullet sealed in a bag. The squirrel's head went over the fence into an empty field where it would make a nice snack for some creature.

With that completed, I called Kirsten, who answered on the third ring.

"Good morning. I didn't take you for the love 'em and leave 'em type."

"Sorry about that. I was up early and didn't want to disturb you. And I was hungry, so I decided to sneak out, get some breakfast, and let you sleep."

"Good judgement. I needed the sleep after this last week." She paused. "I had an enjoyable time last night."

"Me, too. I would love to get together again."

She thought for a moment. "Pick me up tomorrow morning at ten and wear comfortable shoes and hiking gear."

"Sounds like a plan. How far we hiking?"

"Not far. I'll pack lunch."

"See you tomorrow."

. . .

I headed to the hospital for the afternoon shift. "Ready to check out?" I asked CJ as she left an exam room.

"Sure. I only have one patient to hand over to you, a fifty-year-old lady with abdominal pain. Exam is unremarkable, and labs are pending. She can probably go home if labs look okay."

"That's it?" Checkout in a busy ER involved ten or more patients and took a half hour.

"Only the one patient. There are some advantages to working in a smaller town."

"How are the school kids doing?" I asked.

"Great. Three of them should be going home today. Hailey is still in the ICU, but getting stronger each day. They should be able to extubate her later today. Everyone else is already on the floor. I hear you had quite the night last night," she said with a glint in her eyes.

"So there is no confusion. What are you referring to?"

"Rumor has it you were getting an orthopedic consult at Tito's last night."

"Are there any secrets in this town?"

"Not many. If the rumor mill is true, sounds like Banshee and Connor got to spend quality time together as well."

"You should have seen the look on his face."

"Actually, I have. Someone got a video of the whole thing and is sharing it on social media. Most of the town has seen it by now."

"Hooray, my first viral video in Montana."

"Honestly, Banshee stole the show. The way he jumps straight up in the air and barks in Connor's face is cinematic genius. And Connor's face as he falls and gets covered in margarita, chips and salsa–Oscar worthy. He deserved it for that kind of language. Glad it ended without violence, although Connor did look blood soaked covered in salsa like that."

I was thinking it might come to a blood covered Connor eventually, but held my thought.

"So, how was the dinner with Kirsten besides the Connor excitement?" CJ probed.

"She's good company. Not your typical orthopedist."

"Probably a good thing. Can't imagine you hanging out at dinner with a guy named Biff telling you he can still bench press as much as he did in college when he won a rowing championship."

"Truer words were never spoken. The other day, you were about to tell me something about Kirsten when we got interrupted by the whole school shooting thing."

"There is one thing you should definitely know about her. She is…."

Screams erupted from the waiting room. We rushed out to find a ten-year-old girl with blood covering her scalp and face. Carried by her father, she cried softly and mom screamed something unintelligible. We brought them straight back to a room.

CJ calmed the parents while I looked at the patient. "Good morning, young lady. What's your name?"

She stammered out a response through the tears. "Brooke, but everybody calls me Squirrel."

"All right, Squirrel, I'm sure there's a story there which we will get back to, but why don't you tell me what happened first?" I explored her scalp for the source of bleeding as she spoke.

"I was doing some flips with my friends and fell back and hit my head on something."

"You certainly did. Are you good at flips?"

Squirrel told me all about flips as I explored her scalp. Distraction is the best medicine for kids. By the time she finished telling me about her flips, I had found the laceration, actually only about an inch long, but scalp wounds are notorious for aggressive bleeding. Even a minor cut can look like a fatal wound with all the blood. I applied pressure and the bleeding immediately eased. I turned to the parents.

"Good news. I know it looks like a lot of blood, but the cut is only about one inch long and is only through the skin. The bone underneath is fine. We can have her fixed up and home in no time.

The parents smiled, but Squirrel cried. "What's wrong, Squirrel?"

"I hate needles. I don't want any needles."

"Squirrel, I hate needles, too, so I'll make you a deal. No needles, okay? I'm going to fix this using your hair and some glue, but no needles. Do you like dogs?"

She brightened up at that. "I love dogs. Is your dog friendly?"

"Squirrel, I would like you to meet Banshee." I motioned for him to hop up on the bed and Squirrel scratched his ears. Banshee was on his back immediately looking for a tummy rub.

I nodded at CJ that everything was fine and she could head home while I fixed the laceration. I soaked the gauze in some lidocaine with epinephrine and placed it on the cut. The epinephrine stopped the bleeding completely in a few minutes.

"Squirrel, let's get that blood cleaned up." We headed over to a sink and I washed the blood out of her hair and off her face. She looked like a normal little girl again. With the wound clean and the bleeding stopped, the cut did not look that impressive, but it still needed to be closed.

"All right, Squirrel, while I fix this with no needles, tell me how you got that nickname."

Banshee laid his head on her lap as Squirrel explained. When she was two, she collected all the acorns that fell in her neighborhood, eventually ending up with a five-gallon bucket of them. From then on, she was known as squirrel. That's the short version, but Squirrel was telling the extended version, describing all the best places to find acorns.

I sterilized the wound and cleared the hair away, separating a thin strip of hair from each side of the wound. I took a few strands of hair from each side, gently pulled the opposing edges together, and tied it in a knot above the wound. The hair effectively closed the wound. I applied a little skin glue on the exposed edges to seal it. I finished at about the same time Squirrel finished her story.

"Squirrel, we're all done, and the best part is that you don't need to come back. Just leave it alone for five days. After that, you can untie the hair and wash it like normal."

Squirrel beamed at me. "That was fun. Thank you, Doctor, and thank you, Banshee." She gave him one last hug before he jumped off the bed.

"Thanks for being so brave. Let's get you out of here." I finished her paperwork and looked for CJ. I wanted to finish our conversation about Kirsten, but she had already left for the day. I would catch up with her on the next shift.

CHAPTER 10

Saturday, May 7
9:55 a.m.

Banshee and I picked up Kirsten right on time. She wore leggings, a sleeveless athletic shirt, and sturdy hiking boots. Her ponytail hung out the back of a baseball cap with a logo of broken bones on the front. She threw her Osprey backpack in the back seat and hopped into the G wagon. A quick kiss on the cheek for me and a snuggle for Banshee, and we were on our way.

"You gonna finally tell me where we're headed, or should I guess?" I asked, as I pulled out onto the road.

"Head west, and I'll tell you where to turn."

"Sounds good. How long is this hike today?"

"It's a baby hike, only about seven miles, with 2400 feet of elevation change. Should take about three hours, plus stops for lunch and any recreation along the way."

"Sounds exciting. I haven't had a chance to get up into the mountains since I arrived. I'm especially intrigued by the opportunity for outdoor recreation along the way."

Kirsten leaned back in her seat and smiled.

We rapidly approached a massive stone structure arching over a double lane road on the right. "Whoa, that's quite the entrance. Someone is compensating for something," I noted. The arch had to be thirty feet high and at least fifty feet across. Two steel gates lay open, and "Felton Forty" and the "F40" brand emblazoned the top of the arch in huge gold lettering.

"That's the entrance to the Felton ranch. They started with forty acres, and now they're closer to 40,000 acres. They own everything you can see to the north of here, right up to the national park," Kirsten explained.

"The Felton Forty Ranch. Not the worst name ever for a ranch."

"A running joke is Felton 40 describes the average IQ out there. Those people are nuts."

"Well, I'm supposed to head out there in a couple of days to remove the staples from Carol's scalp."

Kirsten burst into laughter. "You better watch yourself out there. Carol will pounce on you if she gets half a chance. She's like a dog in heat humping any leg she can find."

"You're not getting jealous, are you?" I teased.

She laughed harder. "You couldn't afford to cover her alcohol costs."

"I'll try to escape with my virtue intact."

"Any escape from that place is an achievement."

We pulled up to the trailhead parking area, a small gravel lot with only one other truck. We slung our backpacks over our shoulders and set out on the trail.

"Banshee gonna make it the full seven miles?" Kirsten asked.

"Don't worry about him. He'll probably do closer to twenty miles on this hike with all of his side excursions."

"You're not worried about him being off leash? There are wild animals out there."

"Banshee can out fight almost anything we run into, and he can outrun the rest."

Large shady fir trees with a mixture of spruce, cottonwood, and aspen trees cooled the trail as we settled into a relaxed pace.

Kirsten stopped and pointed toward a large spruce tree. "Look about halfway up."

My eyes searched the branches to fall upon an enormous set of dark eyes staring back at me. "Is that a bald eagle?" The bird leapt from the tree and soared out over the forest, his large wings gracefully riding the air currents. "That is the biggest damn bird I have ever seen."

"They get much bigger than that. Lots of animals out here. We have elk, mule deer, bison, bighorn sheep, and black bears."

"Do we need to be worried about bears?"

They're not too active this time of year, and black bears are pretty shy. You wave your arms and make a lot of noise, and they'll go away. Usually."

"Usually? I feel like I should have received some more bear training for this hike."

"I have some bear spray in my pack if we need it. Besides, we have Banshee on our side."

"I don't think he knows the 'fight bear' command."

Kirsten laughed. "Relax and enjoy the walk. I'll protect you."

Banshee loped ahead of us on the trail, cataloguing new smells, and suddenly went still. I approached cautiously to see what spooked him and found a mother deer and fawn on the trail ahead of us. The mother backed away, and her fawn tried to follow, but gave a little cry and held her back leg off the ground.

"Poor thing is injured," Kirsten whispered to me.

"Something's wrong with that leg. What do we do?"

"Stay here and let me see if I can get close to her."

I motioned for Banshee to remain still and silent as Kirsten slowly approached the fawn, murmuring soothing words as she walked. The fawn made another attempt to back up but couldn't because of the injured leg. The mama deer lowered her head and looked like she was ready to charge, but Kirsten continued her slow approach and soothing words. Eventually, she knelt down next to the fawn and reached out a hand to the scared animal. She slowly stroked the animal's fur under the watchful eyes of the mother.

The baby calmed as Kirsten pulled her in tighter for a hug. Slowly, she explored the animal's injured leg while continuing to pet her with the other hand. She started at the hip and eased down the leg with no signs of discomfort from the animal until only the hoof remained. She gently lifted the leg, and a smile formed on her face. She squeezed the fawn tight with one hand, and with the other, quickly removed a large splinter from the hoof. The fawn gave a small cry, but Kirsten held her tight and continued to whisper to the fawn. Kirsten ignored the mother deer, who stared with growing concern.

Kirsten held the fawn until she calmed down, then let her go and moved back a couple of steps. The fawn tentatively put the leg on the ground and added more weight when she felt no pain. A cautious first step led to more confident steps, and the fawn ran to her mother and hopped around her, overjoyed.

Kirsten called out with her arms open, and the mother and fawn seemed to nod their thanks before running off into the woods.

"Do orthopedists get veterinary training as well?" I asked as I caught up with her.

"Got lucky it was just a splinter. An ER doctor might even have been able to handle it."

"I'm not sure that momma deer would let me get that close. She looked ready for a fight."

"All moms are protective of their young, but they know who to trust."

"You certainly made their day. Ready to see what else awaits us on the trail?"

"Lead on, Banshee." Kirsten grabbed my hand as we continued our walk.

We stopped for lunch beside a small waterfall about two thirds of the way up the trail. Kirsten had packed sandwiches, fruit and chips, and I had brought some dog food and turkey slices for Banshee. After eating, we laid back on the blanket with sunlight streaming through the trees and the waterfall babbling behind us. Kirsten leaned over to kiss me.

"You know, if we weren't on a public trail, this might get real interesting," she observed.

"Afraid of a little risk? There was only one other car in the lot."

"It's a small town, and I would hate to have some of my patients round the corner and catch us naked out here."

"Then I have some great news for you." I looked over at Banshee. "BARK, NEAR," and pointed down the trail. Banshee stood up and ran down the trail, disappearing from sight.

Kirsten looked at me with suspicion. "You really trust that dog to warn us if someone approaches?"

I reached over and removed her shirt. "Right now, a Navy Seal couldn't get within 100 feet of us without Banshee barking. So lay back and enjoy the moment." Kirsten enjoyed every minute.

Twenty minutes later, we were dressed again. "That was more exhausting than the hike," she observed.

"My favorite type of exercise. Shall we continue on with our adventure?" We cleaned up our area, packed our supplies, and I gave a quick whistle. A moment later, Banshee strode silently out of the woods.

"It's kind of terrifying how quiet he is. Glad he's not hunting me."

"If he were hunting you in these woods, you wouldn't know until he found you. Let's go."

We trekked to the top of the trail and stopped to snap pictures together before ambling down the backside of the forested hill. Walking along a tree-lined mountain trail with a gorgeous, intelligent woman by my side under clear cerulean skies made a perfectly relaxing day.

Banshee brought me a smooth gray stick that I threw into the forest, and he bounded after it to return for another throw.

"Does he ever get tired?" Kirsten asked.

"Eventually, but not before my shoulder gives out. I gave the stick a mighty throw off to the right side of the trail, and Banshee disappeared after it. We heard him rooting around in the woods, but he suddenly stilled and gave a single sharp bark.

Kirsten looked at me inquisitively, and I shrugged. "Come here, boy," I called. Banshee once again gave a single bark.

"RETURN!" I commanded, and we heard padding through the brush on his way back to us. He arrived with a different stick in his mouth and sat obediently in front of me. "GIVE," I ordered.

Banshee dropped a human hand at my feet.

CHAPTER 11

Saturday, May 7
12:48 p.m.

A normal couple would have run away screaming, but an ER doctor and an orthopedist stood oddly intrigued, evaluating the hand. Kirsten leaned over to inspect it. "Looks like an adult female. Growth plates are fused. No evidence of arthritis, too small to be a man. I think we're looking at a young female hand."

It had definitely been in the ground for a while. Some soft tissue still clung to the bones, but something had been feasting on it.

Kirsten stood up and looked at me. "Any suggestions on next steps?"

"We could bag it up and bring it into town with us, or we can call the cops and have them come out here. I wouldn't go in the woods to find the rest of the body. We'd likely mess up any evidence, and finding the rest of her body right now wouldn't help anyone. I say we call and have them meet us here."

Kirsten gave a resigned nod. "Agreed. I'll call."

"Will 911 work out here?"

"She held out her phone and showed it had a signal. "I have a faster way." She thumbed in a number and put her phone on speaker.

After two rings, a male voice answered. "Sheriff Stein, how can I help you?"

"Daddy, it's Kirsten. I've got a problem out here at the Granite Peak hiking trail."

Kirsten chuckled at my incredulity evident all over my face. I had no clue that Sheriff Stein was her father.

"What sort of problem?"

"I'm out hiking with a friend, and his dog found a human hand in the woods off of the trail."

There was a moment of silence. "Did you say a dog found a human hand out there?"

"Yes, sir. A human hand, likely a young female, been in the ground awhile."

"What about the rest of the body?"

"We presume it's off the trail as well, but we haven't gone near it."

The Sheriff regained his composure. "Okay, where exactly are you?"

She pulled up her text messages with "Daddy" and sent him our current location.

"Okay, stay right there, and don't touch anything or go off trail. I need to get my crime scene team together, and it'll take us about forty minutes to get there. Hang tight."

"Yes, sir." She ended the call and looked back at me, amused. "So, anyway, my dad is the Sheriff here."

"Your dad is Sheriff Stein? Why didn't I know that?"

"Why would you know that? We're hardly at the stage of meeting each other's parents."

I shook my head. "I thought small towns weren't supposed to have any secrets. What's with the different name?"

Kirsten sat in the dirt and relaxed against a rock, and I perched beside her. "My dad and I have a complicated relationship. When he divorced my mom, she took her maiden name of Jenkins, and I changed my name to Jenkins as well. When I moved back here after school, he asked me to change my name back, but I never did. We don't really see much of each other anymore. We live separate lives.

We laid down on the trail and got comfortable, enjoying the peaceful symphony of singing birds accompanied by a breeze rustling through the leaves, as we tried hard to ignore the hand lying ten feet away. After nearly an hour, four wheelers motored toward us. Banshee had his hackles up, but I calmed him, as Sheriff Stein and three other officers approached on their all-terrain vehicles loaded with equipment. He greeted Kirsten with a polite nod and me with a stern gaze. He looked back and forth between us briefly and then turned to make introductions.

Larry, the crime scene expert tasked with collecting evidence, was in his fifties and had a frail build and a receding hairline. His thick glasses magnified the surroundings and made his own eyes look huge and insectile. He efficiently and purposefully unloaded his gear.

"From the beginning, for everyone, tell us what happened," Sheriff Stein requested.

I explained how I had been throwing the stick as we walked and Banshee had been chasing it into the trees. On the last throw, he had stopped and barked, which was abnormal for him. "And when I told him to return, he dropped that hand at our feet."

The whole group slowly approached the hand on the trail and surrounded it. Larry took pictures from all angles before picking it up with his gloved hands and bringing it close to his face. His eyes widened behind the thick lenses as he observed it on all sides and then sealed it in an evidence bag. "So where did the dog find this?" he asked in a nasal voice.

I pointed in the general direction. "Banshee should be able to take us directly to the site," I offered.

Larry thought about it a moment. "Okay. You, me and Banshee are going back there first after we gown up to minimize contamination of the scene." Larry opened another bag and handed me a one-piece gown, booties and a hairnet. When we were both ready, I asked him to give me the bag that contained the hand. I held it up to Banshee. "FIND, SLOW" I ordered.

Banshee put his nose in the air and walked slowly and confidently into the trees with me by his side and with Larry following. Banshee sniffed constantly, making minor course adjustments as he walked. About thirty feet into the treeline, we passed twin oaks and emerged into a small clearing. The center was mostly bare dirt with only a light growth of weeds. The dirt appeared disturbed where some animals had apparently been digging. Pieces of clothing and bones were clearly visible, some of which had been scattered around the area. I commanded Banshee to sit and turned to Larry, whose professional eye scanned the clearing. "If I am not mistaken, there are at least two bodies in this grave."

Larry called out for his other two officers, and together, they photographed the site and processed the evidence, grisly and tedious work that would take the rest of the day. Each bone and piece of debris had to be photographed and then sealed and labeled in a collection bag. A computer program kept a detailed account of the location of each piece of evidence.

Kirsten and her dad ignored each other, until finally, he had to collect detailed statements from us. We explained the day's timeline as he jotted down his notes. When he told us we could go, Kirsten reached for her backpack, but I held up my hand to stop her.

"Sheriff, what if this is not the only grave site out here?" I asked.

Kirsten and the Sheriff stopped and stared at me. "What leads you to believe there might be more bodies out here?" the Sheriff asked cautiously.

"Look at this location. It's only about a half mile from the trailhead parking lot. A fit person could haul a body out this far, and the odds of anyone ever finding it are almost zero. It was dumb luck that Banshee was back in the woods. So if it's a good place to hide a body, it's a good place to hide more than one body. While we're here, want to let Banshee sniff around? If there are more bodies out there, he can find them."

The Sheriff took only a second to decide. "Can't hurt. Let him go hunt, but don't disturb anything if he does find something."

"We're on it. I need to borrow this for a moment," as I grabbed the hand in the evidence bag. I led Banshee north of the current work area and held out the bag for him to sniff. "FIND," I ordered. Banshee leapt into the woods, and we listened to him root around in the underbrush, interrupted by a single bark only two minutes later. The Sheriff raised his eyebrows as I shrugged.

"STAY," I ordered into the woods. The Sheriff pointed for me to lead the way. "BARK." Banshee immediately answered. As I followed the sound of two more barks about fifty feet from the original grave site and about forty feet off the trail, Banshee appeared, sitting still at the edge of another small clearing. The ground was intact, but had clearly been disturbed in the recent past.

The Sheriff stood with his hands on his hips and glared at the dirt. "Sweet Mary and Joseph, what the hell is going on here?" He took off his hat and wiped sweat off his brow. "We need to lock this whole area down. Can Banshee keep searching?"

"As long as he has water, he can do this all day. This is a fun game for him."

"Glad someone is enjoying himself today. Have him keep searching. I need to make some calls and get some more resources out here. I need to let the feds know about this, as we are technically on federal park land. This is about to turn into a major circus. Get to work, please, and thanks for your help."

Over the next hour, Banshee found three more probable grave sites for a total of five, one of which had at least two bodies in it.

We returned to the trail to find a small command center. The State Police had arrived with a second evidence team. Forest service personnel had a team of dogs to take over a formal search of the surrounding areas. Hungry for the emerging story, the media harassed local officers who worked hard to keep them away from the sites.

I found Kirsten lying against her pack and scrolling through her phone. I collapsed down next to her. "Nothing like a quiet, relaxing walk through the woods," I commented.

She shook her head. "I can't believe this is happening. I've hiked this trail for years and now feel lucky to have survived. I hope they can identify these victims quickly and bring some peace to their families. I hear Banshee has been busy." He rolled over on his back at the mention of his name and she rewarded him with a good belly scratch.

"We're up to five total sites. State police have a dog team taking over, so Banshee is officially retired again."

"What do you say we get out of here?"

"That's the best idea you've had since our lunch break. Let me see if I can get an update from Larry before we leave."

Kirsten raised an eyebrow at me. "Really?"

"I'm the curious type. It'll only take a minute."

I found the Sheriff who already looked ten years older than he did earlier in the day. "You hanging in there, Sheriff?"

He shook his head. "This is the clusterfuck of all clusterfucks. We're up to seven different jurisdictions involved, and it's gonna take us two days at least to process all this evidence. The paperwork will take months."

"Not to mention the poop bandit is still on the loose."

"Damn straight. He's definitely not Waterford's most wanted anymore."

"Don't forget the media," I suggested helpfully.

"Fuck them. Don't tell them I said that. I'm up for election next year, but they can wait. I don't know anything yet, anyway. God damn serial killer running around, and we didn't even know."

"Hang in there. You'll catch him. You mind if I check in with Larry before we go? I'm curious about what he found."

The Sheriff waved his arm in that direction. "Fine. Don't cross the barrier and not a word to anyone. Not that we have a chance of keeping this quiet."

I stopped at the yellow tape barrier as directed. Larry and his team had excavated a hole about three feet deep and four feet wide. I waited for him to finish talking to another technician and waved him over.

"Sorry to ruin your weekend," I offered.

"No worries. Don't tell anyone, but this is actually pretty damn exciting. We never get interesting cases with pristine crime scenes like this."

I shook my head. Amazing how one person's horror show turned into a career defining moment for another. "What have you uncovered so far?"

Larry shifted back into professional mode. "First grave contains two bodies, male and female, both in their twenties. Early guess is that they have been there for three to four weeks, but we'll get more accurate data from the lab. Both shot in the back of the head at close range with a large caliber round."

"Did it happen here or elsewhere?"

"Definitely here. Bone fragments, brain matter and blood are on the floor of the grave."

"That is some cold-blooded shit."

"You ain't lying. Best guess is he had them kneel in the grave and then popped them at close range. Doesn't get much colder than that. We're gonna be looking for a seriously fucked up individual."

"All right, Larry. I'll let you go. Glad you're here to help catch the monster who did this."

As I walked back to Kirsten, I noticed the Sheriff talking with Connor. "Good afternoon, Connor," I said with my best smile and a nod of my head. Connor focused on me with his dead eyes. Eventually, his eyes twitched to face Banshee beside me, and a sneer deformed his face. Once again, his hands reached toward his holster, which currently contained two Colt pistols.

The Sheriff noticed and immediately intervened. "Connor stopped by to offer his help. The ranch property line is about a hundred feet over that way, and he offered us access across their land if we need it. We are good on access and resources at the moment."

Connor stared through me with his death glare. "Must be kind of scary knowing there is a killer this close to your property," I probed.

Connor smiled mirthlessly, more terrifying than his blank stare. He spat on the ground at my feet before he spoke. "Feltons ain't scared of a little violence. Maybe he'll cross the fence, and we can have some target practice. Anything on Felton land is fair game."

I looked around. "Six bodies seem like more than a little violence."

He shrugged, and his dead eye stare returned.

A buzzing sound overhead interrupted us. "Dammit! Someone find out who owns that drone, and get rid of it. I don't want this footage on the national news," the Sheriff shouted.

An explosion startled me as Connor fired his Colt at the drone, blasting it from the sky. All eyes turned to Connor. He holstered his pistol and calmly turned his attention to the Sheriff, who fought to control his anger.

"Connor, if you ever pull any shit like that around me again, I swear to God I'll lock you up. Understood?"

Connor nodded with a malicious smile.

"Get the hell out of here. We got work to do."

Connor sneered at Banshee and silently disappeared into the woods toward the Felton Forty. "That is one seriously deranged young man," I noted, as he walked away.

The Sheriff shook his head as he watched Connor disappear. "He does the best he can with cards he's been dealt." He looked like he wanted to say more, but abruptly snapped out of his brief trance and turned back to me and held out his hand. "Thanks again, Doc. Now get out of here and go home."

Kirsten and I grabbed our packs and followed the trail back toward the G wagon. Along the way, I told Kirsten what Larry had found, but she remained quiet and distant.

The parking lot had turned into a five ring circus since that morning. With the police, forensics, media, and onlookers, over 200 vehicles jammed the small area. When some reporters saw us, they immediately surged and shouted questions. I stepped forward and held up a hand to silence them. "We don't know anything. We came out for a quiet walk this morning and came upon the police on the trail. We have no idea what they are doing, and they asked us to keep moving, get in our car and leave."

It took two police officers twenty minutes to help us maneuver our car out of the lot, and we finally broke free. Kirsten remained silently pensive, and I left her alone with her unshared thoughts.

CHAPTER 12

Sunday, May 8
7:56 a.m.

Back in the ER, as an incredibly energetic CJ checked out to me after a quiet night shift, I contemplated how she could look so refreshed and perky after an all-nighter, while I felt drained after getting some sleep, though restless. "I heard about all that excitement you had yesterday. You should've taken my shift. It was much more relaxing than a quiet walk in the woods," she said with a wink.

"You ain't kidding. Old Banshee here keeps stirring up trouble with that nose of his. Any new info come out last night?" I figured CJ was wired into the gossip chain, and I wasn't disappointed.

"A little bit. State police found one more site a little further out from where you were searching, so that's a total of six sites with seven bodies."

"Any IDs on them yet?"

She leaned closer. "This is where it gets interesting. The first grave you found was a man and woman, and preliminarily, it looks like a couple that went missing three weeks ago. The families thought they were hiking around here, but their car was found at a trailhead about a hundred miles north of here, so no one looked for them around here."

"Pretty smart, moving the car north. Without Banshee and a little luck, folks would have been looking in the wrong place forever."

"He's smart, and he must have had help. Someone had to drive him back after dropping the car off up there. It's not the kind of place you can find an Uber."

Most serial killers are loners. The idea of a serial killing team terrified me even more. "What about the rest of the bodies?"

"Also interesting. All of them were young males, and at least three of them Hispanic. That's rare around here. Montana is a pretty homogenous state."

If I remembered correctly, Hispanics were only about three percent of the state's population. "That's odd. Why would someone target a young white couple and Hispanic males? Serial killers usually stick to one particular type of victim. No one reported these guys missing?"

"Nope. They're checking missing persons' reports in the surrounding states as well, but so far no hits. Nobody reported them missing, so no one looked for them."

"Were they all shot?"

"Yes, sir. Each one with a single large caliber shot to the back of the head at close range."

"You seem to have excellent sources."

She gave that winning smile. "Don't forget I'm in charge of hospital communications, and those bodies are all downstairs awaiting autopsy. I'll be giving a press conference with the Sheriff in a couple hours."

"Is that why you're all cleaned up this morning?"

She looked down at her outfit in confusion. "This? I've been working in this outfit all night. Soon as I'm done here, I need to go change and get cleaned up."

"Someday you'll need to explain to me how you can do an overnight shift and not have a single wrinkle on your outfit in the morning. Speaking of Sheriff Stein, I figured out that little tidbit about Kirsten you tried to share with me."

"Ah yes, the whole Sheriff is her daddy thing." CJ suddenly looked a lot more subdued and uncomfortable.

"Out with it. Let's have the entire story."

CJ sighed and sat back in her chair. "It's not really a secret, so I don't mind sharing. Kirsten grew up in a seemingly perfect family. Dad was Sheriff, and mom was principal of the elementary school. Kirsten was an A student and a champion gymnast. Then one day it came out that her dad was sleeping around on mom. And you'll never guess who he was sleeping with."

She paused with raised brows, and I threw up my hands and shook my head. "No idea. I don't even know anyone in this town."

"Well, you know her. Carol Felton of drunken rancher's wife fame."

"Seriously? He hooked up with her?"

"Yep. In his defense, she was much more attractive in those days before the years of alcohol ravaged her, and she aggressively pursued powerful men, something that hasn't diminished with age," she said with a pointed glance.

"Warning understood. Continue."

"Not much more to say. The divorce was public and ugly. Carol took every opportunity to keep it at the forefront of the rumor mill. Kirsten went to live with her mom, and they both dropped Stein's name. The next year, Kirsten went off to college, and her mom was diagnosed with colon cancer. She died angry and alone, and Kirsten never forgave her dad. They pretty much don't ever speak now, unless it's professional."

I shook my head, as my heart ached for Kirsten, and I tried to process it. "So what's the deal with the Sheriff and John Felton? They seem to get along better than one might expect, given that he slept with his wife."

"That's a mystery even I can't solve. Carol has certainly had her share of affairs over the years, and John seems to have tolerated them pretty well. Some suggest that he gets off on watching her with other men, but who knows. John and the Sheriff seem tight and an odd pairing. Except for intimate time with Carol, they don't seem to have anything else in common. It's some of that strange alpha male bonding that us rational females have difficulty comprehending. Welcome to small town Montana politics."

"Of which Kirsten has been collateral damage, which means Stein will guess I know all about it."

"Don't worry. Everybody knows all about it. Good luck on the shift today. I need to go get cleaned up for the press."

"How are the school kids doing?"

"Two more going home today. The three belly injuries are doing well, but will be here most of the week for antibiotics. Hailey was extubated, is talking, and doesn't appear to have lost any neurological function, which is miraculous."

"Great news on all fronts. Good luck with the press. I'll be sitting here trying to figure out small town politics between patients."

• • •

Deep in his third hour of sleep, Sheriff Stein was startled when the ringing phone dragged him to abrupt wakefulness. He had left strict instructions not to be bothered unless absolutely necessary. He rolled over to answer the phone, dreading the news. When he saw who was calling, his dread intensified. "Morning, John."

"Good morning, Sheriff. Hope I didn't wake you." John Felton sounded like he had been up for hours.

"As a matter of fact, you did, but I'm up now, so how can I help you?"

"I was looking for an update on the investigation into those bodies."

Sheriff Stein attempted to contain his exasperation. "John, we're still processing the damn scene. We haven't even removed all the bodies yet, let alone started to investigate."

"All right, settle down. Those bodies are close to my property line, and I don't want anyone assuming the ranch had anything to do with them."

"John, nobody has even mentioned the ranch. Relax."

John raised his voice. "Don't tell me to relax. You know what's at stake."

Sheriff Stein let the threat linger before responding. "Be very careful what you say next, John."

"Shit, I'm sorry. Damn stressful situation out here. My men have been spreading a rumor that the killer might be a fellow out in Seven Springs. I strongly advise you to focus your investigation there. If I hear anything else, I'll let you know. And if you need anything, you let me know. We need to close this case quickly."

"All right, John. I'll take a look out there. Don't talk to anyone but me, and you need to keep Connor quiet and out of sight. I don't need him fucking things up."

"I'll take care of my end. You go find a killer in Seven Springs." John hung up before the Sheriff responded.

Sheriff Stein rolled over in bed and thought about his options. John was right that he needed to solve this case fast. Too many agencies were poking around town already, and the longer they poked, the more likely they would find something.

Seven Springs, a small community about ten miles east of town comprised almost entirely of Hispanic families, seemed like a logical place to start the investigation, given that most of the victims were Hispanic. Only about four hundred people lived there, and they rarely caused problems. Most of the adults worked in town to support their families. Seven Springs hosted a fair number of illegals. No one paid any attention unless they broke the law, and they generally stayed out of trouble.

John sighed again, resigned that sleep would elude him for the rest of the day. Time to get cleaned up and head to Seven Springs.

CHAPTER 13

Sunday, May 8
10:22 a.m.

"What's the plan when we get there?" Deputy White asked.

"We're going to see Mamacita. She knows everyone, and if something's going on, she knows about it. Whether she'll tell us is another story."

"Is she as mean as the rumors say?"

"First time, eh. You're in for a treat. Mamacita yells a lot, and she can be scary as hell, but she's never violent. Good thing, too. She could kick both our asses."

They reached the outskirts of Seven Springs, greeted by depressing ramshackle houses mixed in with trailers that had seen their best days thirty years before. Old trucks and debris littered the landscape.

A collection of buildings dating back to the 1960s spanned two blocks of Main Street. Half of the shops were abandoned or boarded up. The people of Seven Springs directly contrasted with the buildings. Families ambled along the sidewalks dressed in bright clothing. Smiling people exchanged greetings. Children played hide and seek or kicked cans with each other. Happiness thrived in a depressing setting.

The most brightly painted structure dominated one end of town, Mamacita's Restaurant. She encouraged local artists to use her building as a canvas and even chipped in extra money for paint. The resulting collection of contrasting styles somehow worked together to express both sorrow and hope.

The Sheriff and deputy parked nearest to the front entrance and walked the broken concrete path to the neon yellow door. Three families eating at tables stopped all conversation as they entered. All eyes looked from the Sheriff back to the kitchen until finally, the kitchen door banged open and Mamacita stormed toward them.

Big-boned and full-figured failed to describe Mamacita's bulk. Over six feet tall in her sandals that strained to contain her spreading feet, she had to be pushing 300 pounds. Her colorful muumuu shook as she approached the officers. She stopped before them and, without breaking her piercing stare, bellowed at the crowd to return to their breakfasts. The diners immediately looked down at their plates and focused on ignoring Mamacita and the cops.

"Why are you here, Sheriff?" Her voice rumbled much lower than expected.

"Got a few questions for you. Do you have a moment to talk?"

Mamacita's head remained perfectly still as her eyes darted from the Sheriff to Deputy White. "Who is this man?"

"This is Deputy White. He's working with me."

"Does he understand the rules?"

Mamacita turned on him in a moment of amazing agility for her size. "First rule, do not interrupt me. Ever. Second rule, do not speak bad about me. Ever. Final rule, do not piss me off. If you break the rules, Mamacita stops talking. Comprende?"

Deputy White nodded, as he nervously gulped, and the Sheriff suppressed his smirk. Mamacita turned on her heel to lead them to a table in the back corner with chairs on three sides and a small bench on the other side that accommodated her mass. She settled onto her bench as the two men sat across from her.

"I'm sure you've heard about the bodies found outside town. Almost all the victims were Hispanic men. We're looking for any information about them, no matter how minor, that might lead us to their killer," Sheriff Stein explained.

Mamacita made the sign of the cross while murmuring a brief prayer in Spanish. "Dios mio. This is much evil. A bad man is out there, but not possible that these men lived in Seven Springs. No men are missing from here."

"No men have been reported missing..." The Sheriff let the suggestion hang in the air.

"Give me a day, and I will call you. I must talk to some of my people." She scooted her bench back to push off the table to rise, but the Sheriff gestured for her to wait.

"One other thing, off the record. Who in this town could be capable of killing five men so quietly?"

"This is a dangerous question."

"It's a dangerous situation. If I had to look here, who should I start with?"

She again made the sign of the cross. "Forgive me. I know everyone in this community, and only two names come to mind. Diego Herrera and Alejandro Ramirez. Only these men could do this thing." She leaned in closer. "And if I hear you mention my name about this, they will not find your body. Ever. Understood?"

Both men solemnly nodded.

Mamacita smiled for the first time. "Good. Now get the hell out of here. You're scaring my customers."

"How good of a source is she?" asked Deputy White after they closed their car doors.

"Not much happens in this town without her knowledge. I'm actually surprised she didn't know the victims. Let's see what she comes up with. In the meantime, let's quietly find out everything we can about Diego and Alejandro."

. . .

I called Kirsten into the ER later that afternoon for a construction worker who had snapped his forearm and presented with it bent at about 30 degrees. He had climbed a ladder on an uneven surface, so he put two bricks under one leg to level the ladder and destabilized it. Fifteen feet later, he writhed on the ground with a bent forearm. Gravity caused a lot of ER visits.

Kirsten arrived, looking like her old self in a pair of fresh scrubs. She greeted me with a warm smile, but kept it professional in front of the staff, even though everyone in town seemed to know everyone else's business, including mine. After stabilizing the patient and preparing him for the OR, we had a quiet moment to talk in an empty exam room.

"You get any sleep last night?" I asked.

"I slept like a log, after a half a bottle of wine."

"Yeah, stressful day."

"Not quite the relaxing nature walk I had planned for us."

"The first two thirds was relaxing and enjoyable."

She smiled at the memory. "True, but the whole mass grave thing kind of ruined the mood. I can't believe there's a serial killer around here and no one noticed."

"Gonna be interesting to see the IDs on all the bodies and figure out where they're coming from. They have to have something in common. The cops will figure it out."

"Listen, about that. I'm sorry that I didn't mention that the Sheriff is my dad earlier. Our relationship is… complicated."

I held up my hands. "No apology necessary. If you want to talk about it, I'm here to listen. No judgment."

"Thanks. Yesterday was the longest I've been around him since I moved back to town. It's weird, like he's my dad and a stranger at the same time." She paused, as if she didn't want to discuss it anymore.

"To me, he's only the Sheriff. Do you think he's up to solving these murders?"

She thought for a moment before answering. "I don't know. He's a good man and will do his best, but this is the biggest case we've ever seen around here. We've had a few murders, crimes of passion, where the guilty party was obvious. So I don't know how this one is going to turn out."

I listened silently, but racing thoughts of the defenseless victims seared through my mind, and I felt some level of responsibility to find justice for those folks who must have had families suffering somewhere from their absence. Heartlessly dumped in shallow graves in the middle of a forest, they deserved better. Banshee's dropping that hand at my feet seemed as if the dead woman reached out to me for help. I resolved to stay informed on the investigation to make sure the murders stopped.

CHAPTER 14

Monday, May 9
8:02 a.m.

Sheriff Stein called the meeting to order. "All right everyone, let's grab a seat and begin." Muttering, everyone topped off their coffee mugs and settled into their seats.

The meeting took place in the school cafeteria, since the crowd of thirty-four people, too large for any room at the police station, was the largest law enforcement gathering in the city's history. Members of the local police force, forestry service, state police, and even an FBI agent from Bozeman huddled at lunch tables and watched the Sheriff expectantly.

"Thank you for taking the time to come here today. It's been a long weekend processing the crime scene, and I appreciate all of your work. Larry Watson is in charge of processing the scene and will give us the first update. Larry?"

Larry approached the front of the room dressed in khakis and a white button-down shirt, complete with a pocket full of pens.

"Good morning, everyone. We completed our initial processing of the scene last night, and all of the evidence has been transferred to the appropriate labs. We uncovered a total of seven bodies in six graves.

The couple in the first grave has been preliminarily identified as Tom Hunt and Laurie Vaughn, based on belongings found in the grave and the ages of the bodies. They were reported missing three weeks ago. Final confirmation from DNA is pending, but for the moment, we are confident in the ID of these two bodies."

"I don't want anyone leaking to the press until we have DNA confirmation, understood?" the Sheriff interrupted. He got a sea of nodding heads in response. "Sorry, Larry. Continue."

"We have no preliminary identification on the other five bodies. All of them are young, healthy males, likely between twenty and thirty-five years of age. The dark skin and dentition suggest that at least three of them are likely Hispanic males. All the bodies were buried sometime in the last year. Autopsies will be performed later today."

"Preliminary cause of death for all seven is a single, large caliber round to the back of the head at close range. All of the victims were shot in the grave, based on the presence of blood and bone fragments. In each case, it was a through and through shot that exited the face. There is not much hope of getting a decent likeness from the victims, but we recovered all seven bullets. They were mangled after passing through the skull so we will not have any ballistics or fingerprints to match, but they are all similar composition and weight to indicate a .45 caliber round."

"Were any of the shells found at the scene?" one of the state police officers inquired.

"Unfortunately, no. An extensive search failed to uncover the shell casings. This implies the killer either picked up the brass himself or used a revolver."

"The rest of the evidence consists of personal belongings of the victims and is being processed as we speak. So far, we haven't discovered any trace evidence that can be tied to the killer. We may get lucky, but at this time we don't expect to find any DNA on the remaining evidence."

Sheriff Stein returned to the front of the room. "Thank you, Larry. I don't need to tell everyone how important it is we solve this thing quickly. There're a lot of scared people in town and it's up to us to find the killer. We've received tips from local citizens, most of which are useless, but an anonymous caller stated he knew for a fact there were some men who had gone missing from the Seven Springs area in the last year that were never reported."

The FBI agent interrupted. "Excuse me, Sheriff. What is the Seven Springs area?"

"Apologies. I forget some of you aren't local. Seven Springs is about twelve miles east of here. It's a small community of about four hundred folks, mostly Hispanic. Not much more than a gas station, grocery store, and one bar and restaurant out there. Good folks who work in the local communities. Never have any trouble with them."

"Wouldn't five missing men in a year be obvious in such a small community?" the FBI agent persisted.

"You'd definitely think so. Folks move in and out of the community pretty regularly, but I would expect that many disappearing would be obvious. We also received a tip that the killer might live in Seven Springs."

The existence of a lead set off general discussion among those gathered, and the Sheriff quieted the room. "The tip came from a confidential informant that we judge to be trustworthy. That informant will remain confidential for his own protection. Based on the information, Deputy White and myself drove to Seven Springs yesterday. Speaking with some of the locals, we came up with two names: Diego Herrera and Alejandro Ramirez. I would like to stress that neither of these men are suspects at this time, but they are persons of interest. Deputy White will share what we've learned so far.

Deputy White took two folders to the podium. "Diego Herrera is twenty-seven years old and an intermittent resident of Seven Springs. He does odd jobs around town and stays with friends. He has no permanent address on file. Early indication is that he suffers from mental illness and has unpredictable violent tendencies. He's been arrested a couple of times for drunk and disorderly and misdemeanor assaults, but nothing beyond that. He has no guns registered to his name, but did have a 9 mm handgun on him at one of his arrests that he claims was bought at a gun show for cash. He's never been known to carry a .45 caliber handgun."

"Alejandro Ramirez is a little more interesting. He's thirty-one and has never been arrested. He lives in a trailer on the east edge of town and is known to own multiple weapons. He has an unofficial firing range set up on his property and frequently fires his weapons. He is considered anti-social by the few people we've spoken to and is considered a loner. He is proficient at operating heavy machinery and trucks and does odd jobs around town.

Sheriff Stein turned his attention back to the larger crowd. "Thank you, Deputy. We've broken this investigation into five working groups, and each of you has been assigned a group. Groups one and two will focus on our two persons of interest. By tonight, I want to know everything about them. Group three is focused on identifying the victims. Group four will follow up on all the evidence, and group five will look for other suspects. Seven Springs is a good lead, but we need to be open to other suspects."

"All information will be centrally documented and available for everyone to see. I cannot stress this enough. We're not gonna solve this working independently. We work as a team, and the only goal is to identify and arrest this killer. Now, split into your groups, and let's get to work. We'll reconvene at five to exchange information."

Each group spent the next sixty minutes reviewing their area of responsibility and forming a plan. Finally, everyone dispersed and went to work.

. . .

I had the day off, and Banshee and I brought burgers, fries, onion rings and salad to Kirsten's office for her and her coworkers. After I produced cupcakes for dessert, I was part of the family.

Kirsten and I had a moment to talk after lunch, and I asked if she had heard anything further about the investigation.

"Not a word. Dear old dad and I are back to normal, silently ignoring each other."

"He's probably busy."

Kirsten smirked. "Nothing new there. He's been too busy for the last thirty years."

"Well, at least he's consistent."

Kirsten laughed. "You got me there. The man has many faults, but unpredictability is not one of them. Got any plans this evening?"

"Nothing at the moment."

"Why don't you come by around six? I'm pretty sure it's a pizza and Netflix type of evening."

"Best offer I've had all day."

"Now, get out of here. Some of us have work to do."

Banshee and I arrived in the lobby in time for a media update from CJ, decked out in a new outfit. Today she went with a light blue blouse with a dark blue blazer, contrasting with her bright red high heeled boots. Her brief statement offered little, but the journalists scribbled furiously, anyway. The autopsy results were expected today, but no identifying information would be released until families were notified. The press shouted questions, and she coolly parried them all. Impressive to watch, CJ thoughtfully responded quickly, as if she'd had infinite time to prepare. She finished by noting that four of the high school shooting victims remained hospitalized.

She finally dodged the crowd to scratch Banshee's neck as he happily soaked up her attention. I walked with her back to the ER.

"Anything new in the investigation?" I inquired.

"Not really. Usually I hold stuff back from the media, but in this case, there's nothing to hold back. We don't know who the five guys are, and the autopsies haven't come up with anything. Hopefully, the sheriff is having more luck."

"Please, let me know if anything interesting pops up."

She stopped to look at me directly. "What exactly is your interest in this?"

I shrugged my shoulders. "I don't know. It's crazy, but I feel some sort of responsibility for these folks since I found them. I want to know that their families get some closure, and I want to help in any way I can."

CJ nodded. "Fair enough. See you tomorrow, my friend."

. . .

Sheriff Stein called after lunch. "John, this is Sheriff Stein and Deputy White calling with some questions for you. Do you have a moment?"

"Of course, Sheriff." John's caution hid behind the lighthearted tone. Deputy White was not involved in their work.

"Thank you. As usual, this needs to remain confidential. We're looking to see if a man named Alejandro Ramirez ever worked on your ranch."

"Do you think he had something to do with the murders?"

"We're only collecting information right now."

"The name sounds familiar, but I'll be honest, I don't interact with a lot of the men regularly. How about I have Rogelio call you in a couple of minutes? He would know."

"Thank you, John. We'll be waiting for his call."

John disconnected and tried to figure out what the Sheriff was up to. Rogelio, the supervisor for the ranch, took care of all day-to-day operations. John called him to the house, and while he waited, received another call from the Sheriff.

"Sheriff, Rogelio is not up here yet."

"I only have a minute. When Rogelio gets on, he needs to implicate Alejandro as a strange guy who likes to fire a .45 at your range. Don't fuck this up."

Sheriff Stein disconnected before John replied. Rogelio arrived, and they conferred before they called the Sheriff back on speaker.

"Hello, Sheriff. I have Rogelio here if you want to ask your questions."

"Thank you. Rogelio, what do you know about an Alejandro Ramirez?"

"He has worked here some over the last couple of years. He's a good driver and can operate most of the heavy machinery. We use him during the busy seasons or if someone gets hurt. He works hard."

"All right. Did he ever cause any trouble out there?"

"No, not trouble, but he is a little strange. Kind of a loner who doesn't really get along with others."

"Not a team player?"

"Definitely not. Like I said, he works hard, but he has a bit of a temper, especially on the shooting range."

Sheriff looked at Deputy White with a raised eyebrow. "Can you be more specific?"

"Well, you know the men like to have competitions out on the range. Alejandro was always shooting out there. I think the only reason he worked for us was to use our range. He was an excellent shot, but would get furious if he lost to someone."

"Did he ever get violent?"

"No, but we have strict rules about violence on the ranch, especially on the range. Zero tolerance."

"Sounds like a good rule. What did he shoot out there?"

"He would shoot anything, but mostly his .45 Glock."

"You sure it was a .45?"

"Oh, yeah. The damn thing makes a noise like a cannon. Few of the men fire large caliber out there because of ammo costs, but Alejandro didn't seem to care. He would fire boxes of the stuff."

"Thanks, Rogelio. This has been helpful. I need to remind you to keep this quiet, please. This is an ongoing investigation."

"No problem, Sheriff."

Rogelio hung up and looked at John, who smiled for the first time in days. "Good job, Rogelio. That should keep their attention focused on him for a while."

. . .

The task force reconvened at five o'clock to share their findings. No progress had been made on the identification of the bodies, but the team asked for missing persons in Mexico. Hampered by the number of missing young men in Mexico and by the lack of a centralized reporting system, the team didn't expect immediate answers.

The evidence failed to reveal any DNA or other clues to identify the killer, and the autopsies yielded nothing.

The background on Diego Garcia disclosed limited intelligence and likely some mental illness, with no indication that he could kill seven people without leaving a clue.

In contrast, a concerning picture of Alejandro Ramirez emerged. Multiple interviews confirmed he was a loner who lived at the edge of society. His temper had led to bar fights, but nothing extraordinary. Sheriff Stein's information about his frequent use of the gun at the ranch piqued the interest of the other officers.

"Folks, Alejandro is now our number one person of interest. I want a search of every gun store within a hundred miles over the last three years. Get a list of everyone who bought a .45 during that time."

"That's gonna be a lot of names, Sheriff," came a voice from the crowd.

"True, but we're looking for only one name in particular."

. . .

I arrived at Kirsten's house around five, and Banshee took off out the back door. We ordered a pizza, half cheese for me and half pepperoni with jalapeños for her, and settled on the couch to wait for it.

"How're you liking Montana so far?'

I thought for a moment. "A lot more exciting than I expected. I figured it would be a nice little three month vacation, but I'm still seeing shootings and bodies at the same rate as in the big city."

"Do you miss the big city?"

"Not really. It was great for training with the high volumes and acuity, but eventually, I had enough, and it was time to move on, definitely time for me to move on."

"Is it lonely being a traveling doctor? A new town, new hospital, new staff every three months?"

"But the same Banshee. I look at it like a new adventure every three months. Plus, sometimes I get to meet interesting and beautiful new orthopedic doctors."

She laid her head down on my lap and looked up at me. "Tell me about your childhood."

She must have felt me tense up as she laid a calming hand on my leg. "I don't like to talk about my childhood that much. Grew up in the Midwest, went to college, and left for good."

"Do you ever go back?"

"Nah, I'm more of a look to the future than live in the past kind of guy."

"Family?"

"Only child. Dad died when I was fourteen of a heart attack at work. Mom was already too fond of the bottle, and her drinking worsened after dad died. She passed from liver failure during my senior year in high school. Since then, I've been on my own."

She traced circles on my chest as she spoke. "So, are you looking for something or running away from something?"

That question stumped me. "Maybe a little of both. Why do you ask?"

"You're an ER doc, which means you spend about ten to fifteen minutes with the average patient and never see them again. You're almost forty and single. You're traveling the country to be in a new place every three months. Sounds like a guy afraid to put down roots."

"In my defense, I've never had a good reason to settle down."

She took my hand and placed it under her shirt. "Do you suppose you could ever settle down?"

"You're making an awfully strong case. Do we have enough time before the pizza arrives?"

She sat up and straddled me as I helped her out of her shirt. "I don't know, but let's give it a try."

The action was fast and furious, but we finished moments before the doorbell rang. Kirsten curled up in the blanket. "You get the door. I'm gonna lay here naked, choose a movie, and wait for you to bring me pizza."

I could definitely see myself settling down in Montana.

. . .

Mamacita called the sheriff that evening. "I hear your people are taking a closer look at Alejandro."

"Where did you hear that?" the sheriff asked, as he wondered who was leaking information to her.

"Sheriff, if your people ask questions about my people, I hear about it, but I've done some more digging, and I don't think he had anything to do with it."

The Sheriff pretended exasperation. "You're the one gave us his name in the first place!"

"Don't raise your voice at me, Sheriff. You asked for the people who could do such a thing, and Alejandro could do this thing, but now the question is whether Alejandro actually did, and I am sure he did not."

The Sheriff stayed silent for a moment. "My investigation will continue."

"Continue your investigation, but if you try to blame an innocent man for this, you will answer to Mamacita." She hung up.

The Sheriff wondered whether Mamacita was more dangerous than the Feltons. This mess would not end well.

CHAPTER 15

Tuesday, May 10
8:11 a.m.

I awoke to clear skies and warm weather and felt intrigued by my pending appointment at the Felton Forty Ranch to remove Mrs. Felton's staples. I had asked to come by around ten, before she hit the bottle too hard and increased the likelihood of complications.

I chose jeans, a golf shirt, and my new cowboy boots, but I did not feel like I had earned the right to wear a cowboy hat yet. I put Banshee in his full tactical Kevlar vest, partly to make him look like a bad ass and mostly to protect him. I still didn't trust Connor and his itchy trigger fingers around Banshee.

At 9:45, I passed through the oversized gate to the ranch. The wide driveway wound throughout the property for over a mile to reach the main house. Along the way, I passed three semi trucks headed out of the ranch, and I gained an appreciation for the size of the ranch and the amount of work that took place there. Forty thousand acres is over sixty square miles of land. Men on horseback herded cattle around open fields, barns, and miles of fencing.

As I came around the last bend, an impressively gorgeous house lay atop a small rise. At least 20,000 square feet and constructed of timber and stone with multiple porches and balconies, its weathered look somehow made it seem a timelessly permanent part of the land. Hundred-year-old oak trees towered over the home, providing shade and privacy.

A friendly Hispanic lady in her mid thirties waited for me as I parked the car and jumped out. With a few extra pounds on her frame, she wore black pants and a black button down shirt with the ranch logo on it and moved with unexpected grace and athleticism. "Hello, Señor Doctor, welcome to the Felton Forty Ranch. I'm Luna, and I can take you to see Mrs. Felton." Her eyes lit up as Banshee jumped out of the car behind me. "Dios mio, what a gorgeous dog! May I pet him?"

"Por segura, Señora. El es amigable," I replied.

She reached down to pet Banshee. "Not many of our guests speak Spanish."

"Not many of your guests spent twelve years in a Houston emergency room, either. Shall we go take care of Mrs. Felton?"

Luna sighed as she stood up. "This way, please. She is resting in the sunroom."

She led me down a hallway at least eight feet wide and twelve feet tall. The floors, ceilings, walls, and doors were made of solid, aged wood. Large beams crisscrossed above to support the rest of the house. A small forest and an army of wood workers must have constructed the entrance hall.

"How's Mrs. Felton doing?" I asked, as I admired the wood work.

Luna shrugged as she walked. "Some days she is well, and some days she has problems. Today she is well."

"Does she have problems frequently?"

Luna turned to look me in the eye. "There are many problems on this ranch." She opened the door to the sunroom and led me inside. "Señora, the doctor is here."

Appropriately named, the sun room featured floor to ceiling windows that lined one entire wall to capture the sunrise over the mountains. The view looked more like a spectacular painting than reality. Rolling green hills led to the base of the mountains, and open fields competed with forests for space. Cowboys on horseback moved cattle in the distance, while in other fields, the cattle aimlessly grazed.

Seated on a large, warm brown leather couch facing toward me with her back to the windows, it struck me that Mrs. Felton chose this room, but opted to look away from the ranch. It probably said something about her feelings for the place, but I didn't have time to contemplate the thought as she rose to greet me.

"Doc, thank you so much for coming out here today. You brought your cute little dog friend! Come here, Banjo." She set her drink down on a rustic table that looked like petrified wood and leaned down to pet Banshee's head. Her silk robe fell open, exposing a pair of robust, and presumably expensive, breasts.

Luna shook her head and rolled her eyes at me, as she stepped forward to assist. "Señora, let's get you seated, so he can look at your head." Luna rearranged her robe, but the thin material left little to the imagination.

Mrs. Felton grabbed her drink and sat down in one of the matching leather chairs. Her eyes flashed. "Okay, Doc, I'm all yours. What do you want me to do?" She crossed her legs, allowing the robe to open dangerously high on her thighs, but prepared, Luna spread a blanket on her lap.

"Thank you, Luna, that will be all. We'll call if we need anything else."

Luna looked at me with raised brows, and I smiled back. "Thank you, Luna. I'm sure we'll be fine, and this won't take long."

Luna sighed as she left, and I set my bag down to get my supplies ready and gloves on. "Any pain or bleeding from the wound?"

"No. I mostly forgot about the head injury, but this damn cast is driving me crazy," holding up her injured wrist. "Itches all the time, and I'm sure that bitch Doctor put it on too tight on purpose."

I let the comment slide as I looked at the scalp wound, healing nicely with no evidence of wound breakdown or infection. "This scalp is looking good. I'm going to pull out these staples. You may feel a little tug, but it shouldn't hurt."

She laughed and took another long sip of her drink. “No worries. I stay pretty well medicated for pain. Makes the days tolerable.” She took another long drink from her glass and giggled. “Little tug, huh? I may have to return the favor.”

I gritted my teeth and pulled out the staples as efficiently as possible, planning to get out of this room as quickly as possible.

As I pulled the last staple, the door abruptly opened and a smiling Mr. Felton appeared, dressed like a traditional rancher in jeans, a long white sleeved shirt, leather belt, cowboy boots and hat.

“Impeccable timing. Did you come to watch?” Carol taunted.

John ignored her and slapped me on the shoulder. “Thanks for coming out, Doc. How’s it looking?”

“Looks fantastic. I removed the staples, so unless it gets infected, she’s healed.”

“Great news. If you’re all done, I would love to show you the ranch.”

Even without my curiosity about the ranch, I would have accepted an offer to clean out horse stalls to escape Carol. “It would be an honor to see the ranch. Thank you. I’ve never had the opportunity to see something like this.”

“Gather your stuff and let’s go.”

I packed my supplies while Carol pouted. “I was so looking forward to thanking the Doctor personally for coming out here today.”

John’s eyes narrowed as he glared at Carol. “That’s enough.”

Carol laughed, threw off the blanket, and stood up. She must have untied the robe, and it fell completely open.

“Oops,” she said, as she slowly re-wrapped her robe and sauntered back to her original nest in the couch’s corner.

John turned to me. “Lets go.” I couldn’t agree more. Carol’s laughter faded into the background as I hurried after Felton. “Apologies, Carol has trouble with alcohol, and it makes her inappropriate at times,” John offered.

“No explanation or apologies necessary.”

John sighed with thanks and led me to a dark green Bronco bearing the Felton Forty logo on the side. "I guess we're not gonna see the ranch on horseback," I observed.

"You know how to ride?" John challenged with a raised eyebrow.

"I can ride fairly well."

"Hmmph. Fairly well riding would take a couple of days to see everything out here. The ranch is over 40,000 acres, which is about 65 square miles. If we had straight boundary lines it would be about an eight mile by eight mile square. But since we acquired it piecemeal over the years, the actual boundary is highly irregular. It runs about thirteen miles north to south and six miles east to west." John shifted the truck into gear and set off away from the entrance.

"That's a hell of a piece of property to take care of."

"You ain't lying. Seems like we spend half our time putting up fences, taking down fences, moving fences and repairing fences. Sometimes I think our main product out here is fencing."

"What are your main products?"

"How much do you know about ranches, son?"

"Not much. I've never been to one."

"Our main product is beef cattle. We raise over 15,000 head of cattle at a time. It takes a small army to keep them fed and healthy, but we make over a five percent profit margin."

I whistled in appreciation. "That's quite the profit margin."

"It's certainly a nice margin, but this place costs a small fortune to run. Lots of labor and transportation costs, medicine and food for the animals, and fences. Always another fence to work on. That's why we opened other revenue sources over the last ten years."

We approached dozens of large greenhouses. "This area over here is one of the recent additions."

"Greenhouses?"

"Yes, sir. We have a problem with low productivity in the winter. We need to feed and take care of the animals, but that's not enough to keep all the employees busy, so we always let some of the men go and have to hire again in the spring. That's inefficient. Plus, we don't have any money coming in over the winter, so we started growing plants."

"How in the hell did you settle on growing plants out here?"

"I would like to claim I'm a genius, but it was actually a bit of luck. We were delivering cattle to one of our customers, and he complained that he wished he could get plants as easily as he could get cattle. Turns out, it's difficult to get plants in this part of the country, because all the growers are down south. With transport costs, everything is too expensive. He mentioned that a local grower would make a fortune. So I did some homework, made some phone calls, and decided to grow what I knew I could sell to customers I already have."

"So you're running a nursery?"

John laughed. "Hell, no! We work with a distributor that works with area nurseries. They place orders for quantity and type of plants, and then we grow them. Best part, they pay half when they order and half on delivery. If they don't take delivery, we keep the deposit and sell to someone else. It's turned out to be a great business for us."

"Is that what all these trucks are doing going back and forth?"

"They move plants and mulch. We collect the dead wood on the property and over there it's shredded into mulch. We used to spread it out in empty fields until I figured out if I bag it, someone will buy it. Another nice little revenue stream for the ranch."

"It's certainly a busy place," I noted as I watched all the activity.

"That's the downside of this business. Lots of traffic to move supplies in and product out. Kind of ruins the peaceful nature of the ranch, but the money is good, and I can keep people employed year round. C'mon and let me show you how it works."

John parked the Bronco and led me to the nearest greenhouse, explaining as he went. "Each greenhouse is 30 feet wide by 96 feet long with full environmental control. The containers range from one gallon to fifteen gallons in size. Depending on the pot size, we can fit up to about 20,000 plants in each greenhouse, and we have 46."

That was a total of almost 125,000 square feet of greenhouse space and well over a million plants at a time. We walked inside and found a neat layout, with a central aisle and rows of plants lining the length of the greenhouse. A central hose fed smaller black tubes that branched off to every individual pot.

"Quite the irrigation system," I observed.

"It's a pain in the ass to set up, but worth it. It's computer controlled and regulates the amount of water each plant receives down to the last drop. Since we installed it, we have less than one in 400 plants die in here, and mostly that's because of a broken water hose. The irrigation system allows the workers to focus on planting and pruning."

Seven workers scattered throughout the greenhouse replanted from smaller pots to larger pots, pruned bushes, and loaded finished plants onto pallets for delivery.

"Are all the greenhouses this impressively efficient?"

"They're all pretty similar. This one's a little busier at the moment, because they're getting ready to ship out. Some of them are growing at the moment and are almost fully automated. A couple of greenhouses in the back contain supplies and tools. Seems like something always needs repair around here."

A man approached John. "Excuse me, sir. Can I borrow you for a moment?"

"Of course. Rogelio, this is Doc, the new ER doctor in town who has been doing great work for the community. Doc, this is Rogelio. He's in charge of all my operations."

"Nice to meet you, sir," Rogelio held out his hand. Of average size and dressed like all the other ranch hands in jeans, boots, and a hat, his strong, calloused handshake indicated a well-muscled body used to hard work.

"Nice to meet you as well, Rogelio. Impressive operation you're running here."

"Thank you, sir."

"Doc, excuse us for one moment, please. Just a quick bit of business," John assured me.

I waved him off and turned to watch the loading process. John and Rogelio stepped away and held a hurried and hushed, animated conversation in Spanish. I silently translated most of it over the noise.

Rogelio: "We got a problem with the next delivery. We're gonna be short some product."

John: "How the hell did that happen?"

Rogelio: "One of the irrigation pipes got clogged, and no one noticed. We lost about five percent of the plants."

John: "We cannot afford fucking mistakes like that. Not now."

Rogelio: "I know, boss. We can still get the order out tomorrow night. We can load after dark and get on the road by 2 a.m. It'll still arrive on time."

John: "Okay, let me know the final weight, so I can give them a heads up on the shortage, and no more mistakes. We need to meet our quota. You know what happens when we're short. Get moving, and smile for Doc before you go."

John tapped me on the shoulder as I continued to watch the greenhouse activity with feigned interest. "Sorry about that, Doc. Have a problem with one of our trucks."

Rogelio waved. "Sorry for the interruption and nice to meet you."

"How about some lunch?" John offered.

"Thank you, but that's not necessary."

"Of course it's necessary. I need to show you the best part of the ranch."

As I followed him to the Bronco, I looked at my phone and dropped a pin on our current location.

CHAPTER 16

Tuesday, May10
11:47 a.m.

After only five minutes on a dusty gravel road overseen by majestic, lush green mountains, we arrived at a small log cabin surrounded by thick pines. Eight work trucks rested in the shade, while ranchers ate lunch at tables scattered around the cabin. Smoke flowed from the chimney and carried the most enticing aroma of barbecue. A hand carved wood sign hung above the door to identify this location as "The Retreat."

The Retreat's interior combined the rough settler's log cabin décor with a modern barbecue restaurant, complete with a bar nestled into a corner. Across the back, the stainless steel kitchen produced the appetizing aroma of spices that permeated the room. Two cooks busily attended a grill, stoves, and ovens, handing out a steady flow of food to a buffet, where ranch hands plated their lunches. A smattering of tables, a worn pool table, and a vintage jukebox currently playing a George Strait song filled the rest of the cabin. A bearskin rug covered the floor in front of a large, stone fireplace across from the bar. Animal heads and vintage rifles decorated the remaining wall space. A large, wall-mounted flat screen television, the only concession to the modern world besides the well-appointed kitchen, featured rodeo highlights.

John proudly smirked as he patiently waited for me to appreciate the full effect of the ultimate cowboy man cave.

"This is an impressive surprise," I finally noted as my voice returned.

"Thank you. Most folks have the same response when they first see it. My grandfather built this cabin in 1911 as a guest house. After several decades, it became too old and tired to house guests comfortably. About fifteen years ago, we decided on a makeover to turn it into a feeding station for the ranch hands, since it is centrally located. Suggestions kept piling in until it evolved into this. We serve breakfast and lunch daily, and every evening the bar gets lively. Better to have them drink here than have them driving and causing problems. Grab a plate."

John received quiet hellos and tipped hats as we approached the buffet. The barbecue spread would have made a cardiologist cringe. A variety of smoked meats, hamburgers, corn on the cob, onion rings, beans, cornbread and potatoes lined the bar. Fruit and salad were noticeably underrepresented.

I fixed a burger for myself and quietly asked John, "Will I offend the cooks if I give a burger to Banshee?"

John laughed and waved his hand at the buffet. "The food is for everyone, even Banshee. Help yourself."

We loaded our plates and headed for an open table. Banshee sat patiently as I cut up his burger and placed it on the floor next to a bowl of water. He waited until I gave a subtle command with my hand before eating.

"Quite the well-behaved dog," John observed.

"Definitely well trained. He was a police dog before he got injured saving me from getting shot. He had to retire from the force, and I adopted him. He's a great companion and goes pretty much everywhere I do."

"I heard what he did at the school. Brave dog. We don't see violence like that around here."

"That's what I hear, but what do you make of all those bodies found the other day? That's not too far from here."

John stopped eating and fixed me with a hard stare before answering. "Those bodies have nothing to do with this ranch. They were found on federal land, and everybody knows not to come around here uninvited. We are gracious hosts to invited guests, but don't tolerate strangers wandering around here."

"Zero tolerance for trespassers?"

"Our fence line is sacred. A trespasser is target practice up here." He motioned to my food. "Eat up before it gets cold."

I took a bite of the burger, well-seasoned with a smoky flavor and the freshest meat I had ever tasted. I hungrily took another bite.

John noted my reaction. "If you want the best meat, you have to grow it yourself. And another secret," he said as he leaned forward. "I stole that cook from Bozeman and pay him a fortune. Worth every damn penny."

"You must have some of the happiest ranch hands in the state."

"We got the happiest ranch hands in the country. Men fighting to get a job here."

I looked around the room. The workers seemed about eighty percent male, and about half were Hispanic. "Where do you find new hires? I noticed a lot of Hispanic folks, and we are quite a ways from the border."

John leaned back in his chair. "That we are. There is a Hispanic community about fifteen miles east of here, formed a long time ago. Nobody is quite sure when they got there, or why they settled so far north, but they're hard working folks and a lot of them come to work on the ranch. We enjoy having them on the team, but they do have some bad characters out there, just like everywhere else."

I chewed thoughtfully. "Do you think all those bodies found last weekend are from that community?"

John shrugged. "Who knows? I heard they were all Hispanic males, so I assume they came from that community. There's a lot of gossip out here that someone from that town is a killer. I passed the rumors to the

Sheriff, and I'm sure he's out there right now rousting the usual troublemakers."

"So you think the killer is from that town?"

"Bet my ranch the killer is out there, but that's the Sheriff's problem, not mine."

I decided to see where this would go. "Sheriff seems like a good man."

John nodded enthusiastically. "Sheriff Stein is a man of honor and serves this community well. I've known him my whole life. He does a good job protecting this community. He'll catch the killer."

I savored the last few bites of my burger and decided that now was not the time to bring up past indiscretions between the Sheriff and his wife. I sat back contented. John smiled. "You're thinking about a second burger, aren't you? Go ahead and help yourself, and then I have one more thing to show you."

I happily grabbed a second burger for myself and another for Banshee.

. . .

John led me outside and around the building. Banshee tensed as the sound of gunfire cracked through the trees.

"Don't worry. There's a shooting range out back. That's what I wanted to show you."

I gave Banshee the sign to relax, and he immediately lowered his hackles and settled down. John looked from Banshee back to me. "I need me a dog like that. C'mon."

We rounded the corner to find ten shooting platforms facing a wide open meadow. The clearing gently sloped down before a small rise about two thousand yards away, which provided a natural backstop. Targets stood at multiple distances throughout the meadow.

"One advantage of having a lot of land is room for your own gun range. The boys like to come out here and wager on their shooting. I bet a million dollars has changed hands out here over the years."

"You should take a commission on each bet."

"Not a bad idea, but there's danger in taking money from men shooting guns. That set of targets is for close-in work. They can set paper targets or cans anywhere from ten to fifty yards out. The rifle targets are over there. They begin at 200 yards and go out to 2000 yards. Those are all metal, so you can hear if you hit them. Nobody wants to walk that far to check for a hit."

"Two thousand yards is over a mile. You don't have anyone that can hit a target that far out, do you?"

John laughed. "Every man here claims they hit the damn thing, just not when anyone else was looking. Half their rifles can't even shoot that far. We got one sniper rifle that could reach that far, but the rounds cost five dollars each, so it doesn't get much use. Care to take a few shots?"

We approached the lone shooter on the range, and he took off his ear protection to greet us. "Doc, you remember my son, Connor, from the ER, don't you?"

I remembered him more from Tito's than from the ER, but apparently, his dad had either not heard that story or had forgotten about it. One thing was sure; Connor remembered. He glared at me and then at Banshee as he nervously tapped his pistol.

"Connor is one of the best shots out here. Of course, he spends a lot of time on the range, and he has some pretty nice guns. Connor, show Doc that revolver."

Connor handed the gun to me with the barrel pointed right at my chest and an evil smile on his face. He silently mouthed the word "Bang," as he thrust the pistol at me.

I grabbed the pistol, flipped open the cylinder, dumped the empty rounds into my hand, spun the cylinder closed and then pointed it down range as I laid it on the table. "Proper gun safety says never point a gun at anything you're not ready to shoot."

Connor blankly stared back at me with a smirk.

John ignored the drama. "I custom ordered those pistols about twenty years ago. A senior gunsmith at Colt spent six months getting them just right. I expect them to stay in our family for generations.

I looked over the pistol as he spoke. I admired the absolutely beautiful workmanship with outstanding balance and a smooth trigger pull. I had held a few guns, but nothing of this quality.

"Why don't you give it a try?" John offered.

I stepped into an empty stall and donned some ear and eye protection from a hook. John placed a box of ammo in front of me, and I carefully loaded six rounds into the chamber and spun it to make sure it was clear. The gun was longer and heavier than what I normally shot, but the added mass provided additional stability.

In a two-handed stance, I focused the front site on a set of target cans at fifteen yards. I let a deep breath out, and then steadily pulled the trigger. At five pounds of pressure, the gun fired a round down range to strike the first can in the center, sending it flying. Because of the weight, there was limited recoil, even with the high caliber rounds. I brought the sight picture to the second can and again pulled the trigger. I settled into a steady rhythm and got all six shots off in about eight seconds, then looked at the results.

"You rushed the fifth shot and were too high. Other than that, it was damn fine shooting," John observed.

I opened the weapon to confirm it was empty and placed it on the shelf pointed down range. "That's a beautiful pistol. Smooth pull and perfectly balanced," I commented.

Connor smirked and, without saying a word, pulled his matching revolver from his holster with blinding speed and fired all six shots in under six seconds. Six cans at twenty yards went down, all of them hit dead center. By the time I looked back at Connor, he already had his weapon holstered with a ready sneer. "A real shooter knows how to draw his weapon and doesn't miss."

We stared at each other for a few seconds, and then, without warning, I pulled my Glock out of my back holster and fired a series of double taps at the cans. The first shot lifted the 25-yard can in the air, and the second shot hit the can in mid-flight. Twelve shots later, all six cans had been hit twice, and I holstered my weapon.

John laughed uproariously. "That's a neat trick. You could make some money off my guys shooting like that." Connor's expression smoldered into deeper fury.

"It's a little shooting game we practice in Texas. Shooting at stationary paper targets gets old. Let me clean up my brass," I said as I bent down to pick up the empty shells.

"Not necessary at all," John argued, but I persisted in picking up the empty shells. No way I was leaving shells from the gun I had been using out here, and I picked up one of the empty shells from Connor's revolver to go along with the bullet I had already palmed when reloading the gun.

I stood and pocketed the shells. "Thanks for letting me shoot out here. This place really is incredible"

"You're welcome to come out anytime you want. Now let's get back to the house. I'm sure both of us have work to do." He leaned over to give Connor a hug goodbye, who wrapped his arm around his dad in a fake hug and made a gun out of his fingers, pointing it at me and pretending to shoot me. His cruel smile distorted his face.

"See you, Dad, and I'm sure I'll see you around again sometime, Doc."

"Looking forward to it. Have a good day."

Before we drove out of sight, I looked back, and Connor still stared at us, tapping his revolver.

• • •

"John, I can't thank you enough for your hospitality," I said as we arrived back at the main house.

"You're welcome, and thank you for your service to the community, and thank you for taking the time to come out here to care for Carol. I apologize again for her behavior. The alcohol..."

I held up my hands to stop him. "I understand."

"And I hope when you tell folks about your visit, you focus on the good parts of the ranch," he said.

"Folks will hear nothing but good things about the ranch, and any interactions with Carol are covered under doctor–patient confidentiality. You have my word."

John nodded. "Be careful driving home. Those truckers tend to speed."

I had a lot to think about as Banshee and I made our way home in the G wagon.

CHAPTER 17

Tuesday, May 10
2:41 p.m.

At home, I pulled Connor's bullet and shell casing from my pocket and studied it under the bright light in the kitchen. It appeared similar to the bullet left in Banshee's dish, but I would need to visit Travis' office to verify a match.

I pulled out my phone and looked at the pin I had dropped on the greenhouse's location. In the northwest quadrant of the ranch, the nearest access road snaked through the trees three miles away. A quick check of Google Earth revealed relatively flat terrain, and no streams. A simple hike, even at night, solidified my plans to visit the greenhouse the following night to see what was so special about the plants loading at midnight. Banshee thumped his tail when I told him.

. . .

Late afternoon muted sunlight cast shadows across town by Travis' office. Fortunately, he sat with an afternoon drink in his office before his usual trip to the local watering hole for his evening round of drinks. I found him reclined in his well worn and well-padded leather office chair with his iced drink sweating in his hand.

"Good afternoon, Travis."

"Wishing you well this afternoon, Doc and Banshee. What brings you to my humble place of business?"

I held up the bullet I had lifted from the ranch. "Wanted to get a look at that bullet I left you and see if it matches up with this one."

Travis squinted as he swirled the glass in his hand. "Am I to understand you had another visitor to your home?"

"No, just something I picked up earlier today out at the Felton Forty Ranch."

Travis momentarily forgot his cocktail on the desk and sat up straight. "Well now, that is a most interesting piece of information. I am intrigued by the possibilities." He spun in his chair and reached down to a small safe in the cabinet behind him. His fingerprint unlocked it with a click, and he turned back with the bullet I had left him earlier, still in the original bag. He tossed it casually on the desk.

I lifted the bag to eye level to compare the markings on both bullets. They appeared identical. I silently placed them back on the desk.

Travis picked them both up and studied them as well before trading them for the remains of his glass. "Doc, you definitely know how to create excitement in a small town. Those are definitely a match, but I'm not sure it will prove what you think it does."

"Why not?"

Travis held up the bullet from the ranch today. "This here is a .45 caliber bullet made by Federal. It's probably the number one selling round in both gun stores in town. My best guess is at least twenty percent of the local population has similar rounds lying around their homes."

"Well, shit."

"Shit is right. It doesn't mean the two aren't related. It would be impossible to prove in court, but I am sure they're related. What were you doing out there, anyway?"

"I had to take the staples out of Mrs. Felton's head."

Travis laughed and dribbled some of the whiskey onto his shirt. "Let me guess. She wore a thin little robe that kept falling open every time she moved."

I looked at him, dumbfounded, but he waved me off. "I'm not psychic. Carol has been playing that game for the last twenty years. Every man and half the women in town who have been out there have gotten the loose robe treatment. It's pathetic, and the poor woman needs help, but refuses all offers of aid. She sits out there drinking herself to death." I couldn't tell if he recognized his own alcohol abuse as Travis finished his current drink and poured himself another from the bottle on the corner of his desk. "As your attorney, I advise you to stay away from that place. Bad things happen out there."

"You think the ranch has anything to do with those bodies?"

He pondered a moment. "It wouldn't surprise me if they were involved, but I don't think they are. They've had questionable business practices over the years, and they're not afraid of a good fight, but murder is not a part of their playbook. Rumor has it the Sheriff has some leads out in Seven Springs. We'll see how it plays out."

"By the way, how's Marcus doing?"

"Good and bad. The psychiatrist found out that he had been hallucinating and had some sort of breakdown over the last few weeks. They got him on some meds, and his mind is clearing up. The bad news is that he's now aware of what he did and feels horrible. Gonna take a long time for him to get over this, if he ever does."

"So what's gonna happen to him?"

"Yours truly will work my magic, and he'll end up in monitored psychiatric care. Since everyone is recovering, the prosecutor is not as eager to throw the kid in jail for life, and Judge Morestrand is reasonable. He'll get the care he needs. In a few years, he might even have a chance at a normal life."

"Good to hear. Big city prosecutors would try to lock him up for life."

"Us small town folks know how to do some things well."

"Thanks for the info. Have a good day."

. . .

The task force reconvened late in the afternoon, and for the first time, excited energy permeated the room. Sheriff Stein called the meeting to order. "Everybody, settle down and find a seat. Deputy, you have the floor."

Deputy White moved to the front of the room. "Thank you, Sheriff. We've had a number of developments today. First, we found records that Mr. Ramirez has purchased at least four guns legally in the last three years. One of those is a .45 caliber Glock that is consistent with the murder weapon. In addition, he has multiple purchases of ammunition similar to those used in the killings."

The audience stirred, but the Sheriff silenced everyone. "Settle down, people. Glocks and .45 caliber Federal ammunition are not exactly uncommon around here. What else do we have?"

Another member of the task force stood. "It's almost impossible to confirm his movements. He has no credit cards and buys everything with cash he gets from working odd jobs. He drives an old pickup around town and to work. He is known to spend a lot of time in the woods, presumably hunting his own food. Although we can't place him near the murder sites, we can confirm he is very familiar with the trails in the surrounding area."

Sheriff Stein pondered the findings for a moment. "Let's summarize means, opportunity, and motive. Mr. Ramirez certainly has the means to commit the murders with his gun and ammo consistent with that used in the crime. He frequents the trails around here. He also has had the opportunity to commit the murders, but they were a long time ago, and we can't even account for his movements last week. So means and opportunity are covered, but what's the motive?"

A team member spoke up. "Motive is hard to determine when we don't know the identities of the victims or what they have in common."

Another member spoke up. "It's not robbery or financial gain. All the victims had some money or jewelry on them at the time of death, and the couple had some high end gear and a car that were ignored."

"Maybe it was a lover's quarrel," someone joked from the back.

Sheriff Stein held up his hand to silence the laughter. "Do we know if Mr. Ramirez is gay?" He was met with silence and shrugged shoulders. "Make that a priority to discover. If we rule out love and money, we're left with revenge or silencing people. Big question. Do we have enough to bring him in?"

Eventually, they decided to arrest him in the morning. They would have 48 hours to hold him before he had to be formally charged. A search of his belongings and a forensic study of his gun needed to produce only one shred of evidence to tie everything together. Mr. Ramirez might also confess when questioned. The Sheriff closed the meeting with another warning not to speak about the case. They didn't want Mr. Ramirez to disappear overnight.

• • •

The phone rang as Travis sauntered out his office door. He considered ignoring it, but duty won, and he relented. "This is Travis."

"This is Mamacita."

"Long time no talk. How can I be of service?"

"A bad thing is about to happen. I believe the police are about to arrest an innocent man." She explained how she had provided Alejandro's name to the Sheriff.

"I see. And what makes you think they are about to arrest him?"

"Too many questions, and too many police are in town."

Travis thought for a moment. "How confident are you that Alejandro is innocent?"

"One hundred percent. I have talked to many people in town, and no one lies to me. He did not do these things. Will you help if he is arrested?"

"Of course."

"He is not able to pay your fees."

"Then he'll be like half of my other clients. You have my word. Let me know if anything happens, and I'll defend him. If he's innocent, I'll keep him out of jail."

"You are a good man, Travis."

"Thank you. Good night, Mamacita." Travis hung up, worried that he may have made a promise he couldn't keep.

• • •

I laid on the blanket with Kirsten snuggled on my chest and Banshee curled up at our feet. The clear sky twinkled with millions of bright stars defying the darkness. I savored the moment to remember it forever.

"What patient hurt the most to lose?" Kirsten's question broke ten minutes of silence.

"Is that what you've been thinking about?"

Kirsten propped herself on an elbow and looked at me. "We all have that one patient whose loss hurts more than most. Who is it for you?"

I paused before replying. "During my pediatric rotations, I spent a month on the oncology floor. A little five-year-old kid, Billy, had leukemia and had been through three years of therapy, including multiple rounds of chemo, two bone marrow transplants, and even an experimental protocol. Nothing worked.

"Billy was famous for his great attitude, always smiling and kind, even when he wasn't feeling well. He was a perfect patient, and he loved to play video games. He challenged the staff when they had time to play, and won almost every time. One night I was on call, saw he was in the hospital, and stopped by his room. His mom had run home for a bit, and Billy was playing his games. I walked in, and he pointed to the other controller. I grabbed a seat, and he reset the racing game. Billy immediately started beating me. Normally, he would be talking trash while he played, but he was quiet that night.

"Eventually, I asked him how he was doing and got a shrug for an answer, which was atypical. We kept playing, and I asked again if he was okay. After a pause, he said, 'I'm sorry,' and never took his eyes off the TV. I wasn't sure what he was sorry about and asked him to clarify. He waited a moment, then said he was sorry he wasn't getting better. He knew all the doctors were working hard to make him well, but he was getting worse, and he was sorry about that.

"We kept playing, and I assured him he had nothing to apologize for. He was a great patient and sometimes medicine didn't work. He paused the game and looked at me. 'So no one is mad at me?' I assured him no one was mad at him and that everyone loved him. He smiled for the first time that night, and we went back to playing the game, only now Billy was back to his normal self, talking trash and beating the hell out of me. Eventually, I had to go back to work. Billy stood up to say goodbye, gave me a hug and told me 'Thank you.'

"What happened to Billy?" Kirsten asked.

"He died peacefully three days later with his family at his side, and I never saw him again after that night. I still can't imagine the grace it takes for anyone, let alone a five-year-old, to be worried about others as they're dying."

Kirsten curled back up on my chest. "You did a good thing, Doc. Billy died with a clear conscience. Sometimes words are the best therapy. Thanks for sharing." She gave me a peck on the cheek and curled back up on my chest.

"Thanks for listening." We laid there in silence, watching the stars blink.

CHAPTER 18

Wednesday, May 11
5:32 a.m.

Sheriff Stein addressed the team. "Listen up. I don't want any mistakes out there today. We wait until he leaves his house and get him before he gets in his truck. He has weapons, and I don't want a standoff. Let's go over your responsibilities one more time, so we don't have any friendly fire. The plan is to take him alive with no shots fired."

Five groups for the arrest included a surveillance team already watching the house. Team two would sneak up behind his truck to make the actual arrest. Teams three, four, and five would cover the remaining three sides of his house to prevent escape.

In place before sunrise, the teams waited patiently for Mr. Ramirez to start his day. At seven o'clock, lights came on inside the trailer. Thirty minutes later, the front door opened, and Alejandro stepped toward his Dodge pickup. Four officers sprung from behind the truck with weapons raised and advanced on him. Too surprised to put up a fight, Alejandro calmly lowered himself to the ground with his arms outstretched. In seconds, he was safely cuffed, and officers moved inside to clear the rest of the house.

With the scene secure, Sheriff Stein informed him of his rights. "Do you understand these rights?"

"What am I being charged with?"

"Murder."

Alejandro shook his head at the assembled officers. "You got the wrong guy."

"That's what everyone says. Get him downtown and get the evidence team in here."

The officers led him toward a squad car, but Mamacita blocked their path. "Ma'am, I'm gonna need you to step aside."

Mamacita lumbered forward to tower over the officer. "I will move when I want, where I want. Understand?" The officer nervously backed up. She spoke rapidly to Alejandro in Spanish. "Don't say a word to these motherfuckers besides lawyer. I will get one to meet you at the jail, and you can talk to him. Understand?"

Alejandro nodded gratefully, and Mamacita stepped aside to let them pass. A relieved officer put Alejandro in the back of a patrol car as Sheriff Stein approached.

"What was that all about?" he asked Mamacita.

"I need to make sure my people get a fair hearing."

"You're the one who gave us his name in the first place."

"I know, Sheriff, but I'm not gonna throw him to the wolves. If he's guilty, he can serve his sentence, but until then, he is innocent and gets a lawyer. No funny stuff in this investigation, or you'll answer to me." Mamacita turned her considerable bulk away and left the Sheriff in silence.

Sheriff Stein turned back to Larry Watson, waiting to collect evidence. "Good morning, Larry. No mistakes on this one. I want everything in that house documented and processed. Priority is to identify any .45 caliber handguns. I want those processed first."

Larry pulled on his coveralls, booties, and hairnet and entered the trailer. The room was neater than expected, sparsely furnished with second-hand leftovers. Washed breakfast dishes dried in the sink. A quick look in the back bedroom revealed a twin bed, neatly made, and a few items of clothing hung neatly in the closet or folded in drawers. Alejandro had little, but he took care of what he had.

Larry hit the jackpot immediately in the top drawer of the nightstand, which held a well used .45 caliber Glock. After photographing it in place, he placed it in an evidence bag, sealed it, and signed his name across the seal, before bringing it outside to show the Sheriff.

"That was fast."

"It was in the top drawer of the nightstand. Definitely not trying to hide it."

"All right. Tear the rest of the place apart and see if anything else shows up. I'll take this to the lab right now."

Larry hesitated before handing over the bag with the gun in it. "I would prefer this stays with all the other evidence, and we can bring it all at once. Separating it would be a bit unusual."

"I know, but we have a time crunch, and you may be out here all day. We need to get this processed. We'll fill out a chain of custody form and keep it legal."

Larry reluctantly let him go, understanding the need to process the gun as quickly as possible. The form filled out, the Sheriff placed the gun in his bag and drove off. After about five minutes, he pulled his car behind a long abandoned gas station, out of sight from the road.

He sat there for a full minute, appalled at what he was about to do, but he felt he had only one logical choice. Mind made up, he moved efficiently.

He put on some latex gloves and pulled the evidence bag with the gun out of his bag. He dragged it along the buckle to rip it enough to access the gun. He removed a syringe of blood from Laurie Vaughn that he had removed from the lab's freezer. He had drawn it out of one of the extra tubes used for DNA typing, and the two milliliters of blood would not be missed. He squirted a small amount of the blood onto a cotton swab, then gently reached into the torn evidence bag and wiped it on two spots on the barrel of the gun. He packed up his syringe and swab into a separate bag, as the blood dried, now invisible, but it would shine like neon in the lab. He carefully removed his gloves and drove to the lab.

Bill O'Neal was on duty and expected the Sheriff. New to the job, he looked younger than his twenty-six years and had awaited the Sheriff to arrive with the most important piece of evidence he had processed in his nine months on the job. "Good morning, Sheriff. Larry told me to expect you with a gun to process."

"Good morning, Bill. That's correct. Let me get it signed over to you." In a move he had practiced last night, Sheriff Stein lifted the evidence bag out with one hand while holding his bag in the other hand. As he raised the weapon, he dropped his work bag and yelled, "Damnit!"

Bill hurried around the desk to find the Sheriff holding a torn evidence bag, with his worn tan canvas shoulder bag heaped on the floor. Bill looked on in horror. A ripped evidence bag was a nightmare. The Sheriff looked into his stunned face. "Damn clumsy of me. Get Larry on the phone, and let's make sure I don't fuck this up any worse."

Bill called Larry and put him on speaker. After explaining what had happened, Larry took charge. "So the rip occurred in front of both of you, and the weapon never fell out of the bag?"

"Yes, sir." They answered in unison.

"Okay, we can salvage this. Have another tech bring a fresh evidence bag. I want you to place the ripped bag inside the fresh one, seal it, and all three of you sign it. I need two sets of eyes on that bag until it's sealed again. Understood?"

Bill nodded and called another tech to the front with a fresh bag. The Sheriff carefully slid the ripped bag wrapped around the gun into the new evidence bag under the watchful eyes of two witnesses. All three signed the newly sealed bag. Larry was still on the phone. "I'll need an affidavit of exactly what happened, but we should be fine. This happens sometimes, and the chain of custody is intact, which is the important thing."

"Sorry, Larry. I guess I'm out of the transport business."

"No worries, Sheriff. I need to get back to processing this scene, and Bill needs to get to work on that gun."

"Thanks for all your help. I have a suspect to interview."

. . .

A tech carefully checked the seal on the evidence bag containing the gun, then entered the information into his log. With sterile gloved hands, he laid the gun on a sterile cloth. He removed the clip and emptied the round sitting in the chamber, double checking to make sure the weapon was empty and safe to handle.

His first test checked the weapon for blood under a black light. Two areas of the barrel immediately lit up, and he carefully collected samples from each site and packed those swabs for DNA analysis with an expected turnaround time of 48 hours.

. . .

The Sheriff arrived at the jail, as Travis Foster approached the front door. The Sheriff held the door open for him. "Good morning, counselor. Not surprised to see you here."

"Good morning, Sheriff. One does not ignore calls from Mamacita. I assume my client is being processed."

"They should be about done. I haven't even had a chance to talk to him yet."

They walked inside together and learned that Alejandro already sat in a holding cell.

"Has my client been read his rights?"

"He was informed of his rights at the time of his arrest in front of three witnesses, all captured on body cam."

"Good. I'll need a copy of that video. Has he said anything?"

The officers who had transported and processed him shook their heads. "Not a word."

"That's the best type of client. Please bring him to a room where we can speak privately."

The Sheriff motioned to move the prisoner. He had wanted to interrogate the prisoner before he spoke to a lawyer, but now that Travis was here, he would not get that chance.

The officers led Alejandro to the interrogation room, uncuffed him, and left. "I'm Travis Foster, and I'll be representing you on these charges."

"I can't afford a lawyer."

"Don't worry about money at this time. Mamacita and I have an arrangement."

"I don't need a lawyer. I didn't do anything."

"That's exactly why you need a lawyer. You're going to be charged with multiple murders, which carry the death penalty in this state. You said you were innocent. For me to be effective, I need the truth from you. Did you know any of those people? Did you kill any of those people?"

"No, sir."

"All right. Let's get to work."

Two hours and a legal pad full of notes later, Travis advised Alejandro. "Remember what I told you. No one in here is your friend. You don't say anything about the case to anybody except me. I'll be by a couple times a day, and you let me know if you have any questions or concerns. Anything else before I leave?"

"Why are you doing all this work for me, Mr. Foster?"

Travis paused a moment to gather his thoughts. "I've been a lawyer for over thirty years in this town, and I've seen some things. I don't believe anyone innocent should have to spend time in jail, and I definitely don't think anyone innocent should be tried for murder. If you're innocent, then I'll work hard to prove it. You have my word."

"Thank you, Mr. Foster."

"Get some rest, and remember to eat and exercise. Most importantly, don't talk to anyone."

Travis knocked on the door. The Sheriff had been waiting for Travis. "I don't suppose he's ready to confess," he addressed Travis, as Alejandro, head down, shuffled back to his cell.

"My client is innocent, and we will proceed accordingly. Please call me if you have any questions for him. He has been instructed to say nothing, and any attempts to interrogate him without me present will be inadmissible"

"I know the law, Counselor."

"I know you do. It's a polite reminder to make sure everyone follows the rules. I assume the arraignment will be on Friday in front of Judge Morestrand?"

"That's what the prosecutor said."

"Then I have work to do. Good day, Sheriff."

"Good day, Travis."

Travis muttered to himself as he left the building, pondering how he would keep his promise to prove his client's innocence.

. . .

The District Attorney met with Sheriff Stein late in the afternoon to review evidence. Don Anderson had been a local prosecutor for eight years, the last three as the District Attorney. An ordinary looking man of average height and weight in his late forties, he always dressed in a conservative suit and tie with glasses perched halfway down his nose and files clutched in one hand. A competent District Attorney, he looked forward to this challenge, easily the biggest case of his career.

"What do we have, Sheriff?"

"They found a .45 Glock and ammo consistent with the crime scene at his home with his fingerprints on the weapon."

"Half the homes in town have a .45 and ammo at home. What else do you have?"

"There's a trace of blood on the gun barrel."

The DA raised his eyebrows and pushed his glasses back into place. "That's more interesting. Animal or human blood?"

"Unknown, and it's gonna take 48 hours to see if it matches any of our victims."

"That's cutting it close on the arraignment. Anything else that can tie him to the victims?"

"Not yet. Still processing all the evidence, but no obvious trophies from the victims."

Mr. Anderson scowled at this. "The blood can tie him to the murders, if it matches. Without that, we don't have enough to charge him."

"Let's see what the blood shows. If it matches a victim, we have him."

"Sheriff, if it matches, he'll get the needle, I promise. Keep me updated." The DA left, and the Sheriff contemplated the unstoppable system he had set in motion. The blood would match, and Alejandro would be convicted and likely executed. The Sheriff decided it was probably time for him to retire while he still had a bit of his soul left.

CHAPTER 19

Wednesday, May 11
10:24 p.m.

Darkness shrouded the town. I scanned the assembled gear on my table as Banshee watched expectantly, sensing a forthcoming adventure.

"If we do this, boy, you need to watch my back. Promise me?"

Banshee tilted his head, puzzled. None of those words made sense to him, but he thumped his tail energetically.

"Okay, let's do this." Banshee jumped up and down as I reached for his tactical vest. He settled enough for me to get him latched in, and then I made one last check of my equipment. This was going to be a reconnaissance mission, and while I didn't expect trouble, I was prepared in case problems arose.

Since the visit to the ranch yesterday, I couldn't stop thinking about the conversation I had overheard between John and Rogelio. Something was happening with a truck tonight, and I was curious to see what it was.

Banshee and I hopped into the G wagon and headed toward the ranch. With the pin I had dropped on the greenhouse yesterday, Google maps, and Google earth, I had a good idea about where to park and how to access the area. I drove past the ostentatious entrance of the ranch and found the correct dirt road past the fence line. I followed it about a half mile until I found a hidden area to park off the road. It was unlikely anyone else would come this way at night, but the last thing I needed was someone investigating my vehicle.

I fitted Banshee with his earphone so he could hear my whispered commands. I checked my microphone, hefted my backpack onto my shoulders, and began our hike. The four foot high fence line, meant to keep cattle in, not humans out, posed no impediment. I carefully climbed over while Banshee effortlessly jumped.

I chose the night vision goggles to avoid use of a flashlight. With those and the ambient light of the moon, visibility was fine. Dressed in dark clothing with dark shoes, I would be all but invisible in the fields.

I occasionally glanced at my dimmed phone to make sure of my direction, and the walk proceeded without incident. I took a moment to appreciate the night sky. With no electrical light source within a mile, the immensity of the Milky Way spread above me like an infinite sparkling dome. Stars normally obscured by artificial light dazzled proudly. I laid on my back and Banshee rested his head on my chest. I scratched his ears as I lie there admiring the night sky. Banshee's slow, steady breathing and the winds rustling through the trees relaxed me. I vowed to myself to spend more time outside at night, more time with Kirsten, and more time in Montana.

After ten minutes and a quick drink, we stepped back into the grass. My map showed only a mile before we reached the location. I gave Banshee a command to move quietly, and he instantly became a black hole next to me.

Lights and noise intruded on the peacefulness of the night as we approached the greenhouses, and I removed the night vision goggles and stuffed them into my backpack. We moved forward silently until we topped a small rise and had an elevated view of the greenhouse area. I sat down quietly and pulled out my binoculars.

Although almost midnight, a fair amount of activity bustled around the greenhouses. Rogelio supervised a team of seven men moving in and out of the greenhouses, as forklifts carried pallets to the road in front of the greenhouses.

Banshee and I crept to within about fifty feet of them, hiding within thick, tall grass beside a cluster of mossy boulders. With the workers in the bright light and us in the darkness, I thought it was impossible for them to see us. A semi-truck rattled down the road and expertly backed up to the stack of pallets. Connor climbed down from the passenger side and walked up to Rogelio, who pointed around the yard as he explained.

The workers opened the back doors to the truck, and forklifts loaded the pallets. The efficient activity seemed well-rehearsed, as if routine. I needed to get closer to see what they were loading.

I switched on Banshee's microphone, camera, and ear piece and commanded him to stay silent and approach.

Controlling Banshee meant whispering commands as I watched a screen from behind the rocks. I sent him the long way around the activity, so he approached from the back of the greenhouses. I directed him up to one pallet that still waited in darkness to be loaded. It was filled with plastic bags stacked neatly to seven feet high with at least two hundred bags on each stack. Unfortunately, wrapped in plastic under poor lighting made identification difficult, but eventually the camera captured an image of writing on each bag, "Felton Forty Mulch."

I ordered Banshee to return silently, staying in the shadows, and I turned my attention back to the loading process. About a third of the truck was already full, and many more pallets of mulch were lined for loading.

Activity paused for a moment, and one forklift moved to the back of the work area and went into one of the back greenhouses. Its driver returned shortly with another pallet that looked similar to all the others, but they treated this one differently. He brought it to a scale next to the truck, placed the pallet on the scale and backed away. Rogelio and Connor checked the reading on the scale, and then ordered the driver to lift the pallet. They reset the scale to zero, and the driver set the same pallet down again. After double checking the weight, he loaded the pallet onto the truck. He brought one more pallet from the last warehouse, meticulously weighed it twice, and loaded it onto the truck among the mulch.

While all of the attention focused on the special pallets, I slowly crawled through the shadows to the front of the truck. I attached a magnetic GPS tracker I had bought from Amazon to the underside of the trailer, and then silently scampered back to my observation post. The tracker had a three-day battery life. As long as the tracker was within range of a cell tower, I could see where the truck went.

After the two special pallets were loaded with more mulch to fill the rest of the truck, Rogelio and Connor spoke briefly to the driver before he departed.

Rogelio ordered the men to finish up, and the workers expertly put the scale and forklifts into the greenhouses within a few minutes. I planned to get in that greenhouse, but my plans changed when one man grabbed an AR-15 from his truck and settled into a chair near the last row of greenhouses. The rest of the men made some jokes about him having a pleasant night as they climbed into their individual pickup trucks. Soon, only the solitary guard lounged in front of the greenhouses.

I watched him closely for fifteen minutes. He got up and wandered around, more to stay awake than to follow any sort of organized patrol. Clearly bored and not expecting trouble, he shut down some lights, leaving only enough to see, but reducing the harshness of the glare.

In the dimmer light, I noticed a tiny blinking red light from a corner of one greenhouse. I quietly unpacked my binoculars and focused them on it to discover a small camera. I scanned right and found another camera on the opposite corner. I scanned all three greenhouses in the back row, and every corner was covered by a camera.

I packed up my gear, turned off Banshee's microphone and camera, and placed them in the backpack, and we slid quietly into the night. We made our way back across the fields toward my hidden G Wagon, stopping once again in a deserted meadow to appreciate the night sky. I pondered everything I had seen, as I stretched on my back, enjoying the spectacular sight.

CHAPTER 20

Thursday, May 12
2:49 a.m.

Hector made the trip every two weeks, weather permitting. The strict rules for the drive were non-negotiable. He couldn't stop; he couldn't speed; and under no circumstances could he get in a wreck. His location and speed were monitored for the entire trip, and any deviation from the route would have severe consequences.

A professional truck driver, the monotony of the long drive soothed him. He packed a cooler with sandwiches, snacks, and energy drinks. A separate bottle lay on the floor of the passenger seat for when the inevitable need to urinate arose. Extra padding on the seat and satellite radio made the five hour trip comfortable. With a full tank of diesel, the rigid rules seemed reasonable.

He entered the outskirts of Salt Lake City and felt the adrenaline surge that accompanied the end of a long trip, arriving right on time.

Tim's Garden Spot, a nursery based in Salt Lake City, had seven locations scattered around the city and sold flowers, shrubs, trees, and mulch. Hector expertly backed his truck to the loading area and thankfully shut off the engine. He climbed down from the cab, stretching his back and leg muscles that had tightened during the trip.

A crew immediately unloaded the truck. A forklift raised the first pallet of mulch and placed it in the yard. The full truck would yield twenty-six pallets.

In the seventh row back, the forklift driver came upon the first pallet with the plastic lining ripped and taped back together in the upper left corner. He backed the forklift out of the truck with this pallet and moved it toward the other pallets, but instead of laying it next to them, he drove to a garage behind them. All but invisible from the road, he pulled into the garage. They had moved a broken truck out of a corner, exposing a platform. He set the pallet on the platform and drove the forklift back to the truck. In the eighth row, he found another pallet with ripped plastic taped on the corner. This also went into the garage onto the platform. The forklift driver turned to unload the remaining pallets as the platform lowered.

The underground room was nothing like the junky, dirty garage upstairs. A team of four rolled the pallets off the platform and unloaded the bags into two piles. Regular bags of mulch were placed on a pallet to be raised back upstairs. Bags with yellow strips visible under black light were efficiently placed on an industrial scale, resulting in 45 bags placed on the scale weighing 1803.4 pounds. Short of the 2000 pound quota, the men grimly murmured among themselves.

They rechecked the regular bags of mulch one by one, scanning them on both sides and making minor cuts in each bag to confirm only mulch. Finding no additional product, they sent the mulch bags back up the lift for legitimate sale.

A different fate awaited the 45 bags of product, carefully cut open, and the outer layer of plastic removed and discarded. Inside each bag lay another layer of plastic, tightly wound and immaculately clean. They carefully stacked each of the forty-pound packets onto a clean metal cart, recounted them, and pushed them through a door into another room.

Bright LED lights shined down on pristine metal tables. The stark white walls and floor were immaculately clean. Four workers waited to receive the product, each of them in a white full body suit, booties, hair nets and gloves. They unloaded the packets slowly, inspecting each one for tears or defects, and loaded them onto another scale for a second weighing. The men in the outer room observed the process from windows on their side of the door. The final weight of 1801.7 pounds, the difference accounted for by the discarded outer plastic, authorized the men in the outside room to gather up their gear, take the platform upstairs and move the broken truck back on top of it.

Outside, the unloading complete, the men went back to their usual activities at the nursery. Hector waited for the final weight confirmation, as his payment depended on it. As always, he spent the time checking his truck for damage that may have occurred during the trip. A stickler for maintenance, Hector relied on his truck as his only source of income to feed his family.

The walk down the driver's side yielded no evidence of damage, and all the tires looked acceptable. As he made his way up the passenger side, he noticed an unusual shape attached to the underside of the trailer, likely a small piece of debris that flew up from the tires and embedded in the trailer. With a firm push, he dislodged it and it fell to the ground. His heart nearly stopped as he realized its significance.

Hector debated keeping it secret, but he knew the severe penalties if they found out. Maybe the bosses placed the tracker. Hector called over the supervisor to show him the device.

Luis, proud to be the leader for such an important operation, took his duties seriously, and had never had an issue with any delivery. He glanced at the receiver, and immediately, the crushing problem led to swearing and praying to the Virgin Mary for protection. He pulled out his phone and called his boss.

"I hope that everything is well, Luis."

"Boss, Hector found a transmitter on his truck."

Silence reigned for a tense few seconds. "Luis, listen to me carefully, and make no mistakes. Do not touch that transmitter or move that truck. I want all the product loaded and ready to move in the next fifteen minutes. Understood?"

"Yes, Boss." Sweat shined on Luis' brow as he gave orders. They had a plan in place to evacuate the product if needed, but it had never been tested.

Luis called a man downstairs. "We have a problem. Pack up everything and prepare to evacuate."

In this business, such problems could lead to twenty-year prison sentences. The men downstairs immediately packed critical items. Luckily, only two of the packets had been opened. Placed in fresh bags, all of the product was sealed and loaded on a cart. Their equipment was loaded on a second cart, and they called upstairs for the lift.

When they arrived at ground level, the product and equipment were hurriedly loaded into a panel van. More mulch and plants were hastily loaded around it. As they finished, Tomas arrived.

A slight man in height and build, he dressed in anonymous jeans, a blue button down shirt, and plain, black rimmed glasses. Often mistaken for an accountant or insurance agent, Tomas was no white collar employee. As the boss, Tomas knew no boundaries when it came to solving problems.

"Be prepared to leave in three minutes. Luis, show me this object."

They approached the truck, where Hector visibly trembled. Tomas ignored him, bent down, and pulled on some gloves to pick it up and inspect it in the sunlight. "Show me exactly where you found this."

Hector leaned down and shone his phone light on the trailer's underside. "It was attached right here. I thought it was debris, and I brushed it off. I swear I didn't know it was there."

Tomas slowly rotated and viewed the underside of the carriage. "You did well. It's definitely a GPS tracker, but I don't think it's the police. It's a commercial piece of crap anyone can buy on Amazon, and there was no genuine attempt to hide it. Dirt shows it made the ride from the ranch. This place is blown."

Tomas reattached the device in the same location and gave instructions to Hector. "You do everything the same. Your schedule does not change at all. Continue to carry loads here, but none of them will be our special product. If you find other trackers, let me know, but do not touch them. Luis will pay you for this trip, but all future trips are regular rates. Understand?"

Gratefully relieved, Hector nodded, took the envelope from Luis, then jumped in his truck and instantly took off. He would miss the extra money, but he still had his life.

Tomas turned to Luis. "Make sure everything is out of the basement and then fill it with nursery equipment and supplies. I want every surface covered in dirt like we have been using it for twenty years. No more product will ever be delivered here."

Luis nodded. Within an hour, no evidence that the basement had been anything other than a dirty storage area remained. Tomas took one last look at the nursery. He would never return, a shame, as the nursery provided a perfect distribution front. By the time he reached his car, he had outlined his plan to plug the leak.

. . .

Tomas arrived at the warehouse to supervise the setup, making sure that no product disappeared during the move. They had prepared for this possibility, and the room was largely set up. Within an hour, the team had already prepared the product for delivery.

They bought the marijuana in bulk from the ranch for one thousand dollars per pound. Once cut and bagged, they sold it to distributors for $2500 per pound. The distributors could sell it on the street for about four thousand dollars per pound, depending on the market. Tomas' group processed two thousand pounds each week, half of it from the ranch, which meant a three million dollar weekly profit. At that price, they tolerated no disruptions.

A business person at heart, Tomas grew up in a home that valued academics, and he had excelled in school. His professorial father taught mathematics at a university, and his mother spent hours with him on school work each week. His family had little money, but he never lacked for attention.

Tomas earned a full scholarship to UCLA, where he studied business and economics. After his undergraduate years, Stanford Business School fine tuned his education. He excelled in his classes, but bias against his Mexican heritage became obvious in interviews. Companies politely informed him he was "just not right" for them and "were sure he would find a good job with the right firm." Bitterness tormented him as he watched less talented classmates acquire prestigious jobs.

His father introduced him to Javier in the spring of his final year of school. A family friend had mentioned the young, successful business person in Salt Lake City, who had rapidly grown a nursery business and needed professional business advice. Tomas and his father assumed his legitimacy, and Tomas made a small vacation out of his visit.

Tomas and Javier hit it off immediately. An enthusiastic business owner, young Javier had not yet started his eventual dependence on heavy drinking and drugs. He had built three nurseries in the area with plans for two more within the next year. Javier showed him around and discussed his business problems. Tomas listened attentively and quickly determined that he ran his business well and had only a few suggestions to improve efficiency.

On his last night there, Javier pitched his job offer in the nursery's office. "Tomas, I have enjoyed your company these last few days, but I must apologize. I have not been entirely truthful with you. I run another business besides the nurseries. This other business is the reason I have asked you to visit."

"I have enjoyed my time with you as well, but I am disappointed that you have misled me."

Javier nodded. "Yes, it was wrong, but necessary. I had to trust you before I took the next step. Come, I will show you."

Javier led him to a warehouse and unlocked a rusty padlock in the back to open the door of a small storage room. He turned on the lights, displaying scattered shovels, rakes, and storage bins. He opened one bin, full to the brim with cash. Tomas stepped forward to inspect it. Disorganized, the money comprised everything from five dollar to hundred dollar bills.

Javier stood taller. "I now have seven of these bins filled with cash."

Tomas tried to do the math in his head, but couldn't come to an accurate estimate without more information. "There has to be millions in here."

"Yes, eight, maybe ten, million dollars. My problem is I have nowhere to put it."

Tomas stared at the cash. "I assume this money is not from selling plants."

Javier laughed. "The money actually is from selling plants. I have a marijuana distribution network that controls much of the state already. All the states around here have legalized weed, but not Utah, so I fill a niche in the market."

"Javier, it is time for honesty. Do you move any other drugs or just weed?"

"You have my word, only weed."

Tomas replaced the lid on the bin of cash. "I must think about this tonight. I will have an answer for you in the morning."

Tomas reached an agreement with Javier in the morning. He would launder the money, but only for marijuana. He would not be associated with any other drugs. He would need complete control of all the money and operations to launder all the cash effectively. Javier agreed.

He organized procedures for counting and storing the cash and set up new businesses to launder it, investing clean money into legal businesses that generated more clean money. Eventually, Tomas invested in a failing ranch. On the decline for years, the Felton Forty Ranch could grow product as well as launder money. It didn't take long for John Felton to grasp the opportunity to save his legacy. Tomas, now a silent partner, owned half the ranch.

As Tomas became more successful, Javier became more addicted to drugs. His uncontrollable behavior and spending risked Tomas' businesses. Ever practical, Tomas waited for Javier to pass out from drinking and heroin use and injected him with enough extra heroin to kill ten men. Javier passed in his sleep, and Tomas took control of all aspects of the business.

Over the last eleven years, Tomas had successfully laundered close to a billion dollars, and now everything was in jeopardy because of a single GPS tracker on a truck. He would find the owner of the tracker and eliminate the problem.

. . .

I logged into my tracker account to check the truck's progress. The app mapped its journey to Salt Lake City, showing a single hour long stop. Now the truck was back on the road. I pulled up the coordinates of the stop on Google maps and found Tim's Garden Spot, which made perfect sense. The truck delivered the mulch to a nursery in Salt Lake City. I had some research to do before my trip.

. . .

After assuring operations were in order, Tomas called John. "John, we had a problem with the delivery today."

"I'm aware we were a little short on weight, but we told you, and I promise we'll make it up next week."

"That's good, but that's not the problem I am calling to discuss. We found a GPS tracker attached to the trailer."

The silence intensified as John processed the information. "I don't see how that could happen. We scan the truck and trailer before each load out. The only tracker signal we found was our own, and the truck didn't stop on the trip there."

"John, the only time that tracker could have been placed was during loading after the scan. One of your men placed it."

"Impossible, and all of them know where the truck goes, anyway. There's no reason for them to place it."

"If not one of your men, then an intruder placed it, which concerns me even more. Review the tapes. I expect answers today."

"Yes, sir." John hung up and found Rogelio. They pulled the video from the previous night and reviewed each image. After almost an hour, one camera revealed a shadow of a man who kept to the edge of the light. Too dark to discern any details, they confirmed that someone had watched them last night. They replayed the video.

"What's that?" John pointed at a shadow near the man.

They magnified the image. "Sir, I think that shadow might be a dog."

John stormed out of the room.

. . .

I tapped a contact on my phone, and as usual, got an immediate answer. "How the fuck are you, Doc? What do you need?" The twenty-year-old hacker known as The BT, whom I had used previously, inhabited his mom's basement in Houston, with enough computer power to hack the Pentagon. Given enough time, he could discover almost any piece of information on the web. Fueled by Adderall and energy drinks, he wasted little of his precious time communicating with other humans, but he loved dogs, especially Banshee.

"I'm looking for some financials on two businesses, a nursery in Salt Lake and a ranch in Montana."

"A thousand bucks. Email me the details. I'll have an answer in a few hours." His keyboard rattled as he pounded away at keys the entire time he spoke.

"Thanks, The BT."

"Doc, you looking to invest or looking for trouble again?" The BT had previously helped me bring down a Ukrainian crime syndicate, so he knew what kind of trouble I was capable of finding.

"It's not an investment."

"Then be careful." The BT hung up.

My stomach rumbled, and a fresh grilled cheese and fries called to me. Marty's Diner, mostly full with the dinner crowd, hosted Travis Foster, who beckoned me to join him. I slid onto the bench across from him.

"Evening, Counselor. Thanks for letting me crash your party."

"Not much of a party, but happy to have you join me."

"I hear you have a new client."

"Damn, even the new guy hears things in this town now. Yes, I've picked up Alejandro's case, and he'll likely be charged with murder tomorrow."

"Awful fast work by the Sheriff."

Travis nodded. "Conveniently fast. Some might even argue impossibly fast."

"They must have something if they're bringing charges."

"I'm sure they have something, but I haven't seen it yet. They don't have to disclose anything until the hearing. Damn shame. Lots of my clients are guilty, but I'm sure Alejandro is getting railroaded for political expediency. Pisses me off when they go after vulnerable folks like him."

"Sorry to hear that. I'd be happy to help, but not sure there's much I can do."

"Unless you have a world class forensic expert in your back pocket that owes you a favor, probably not. I know they don't have any witnesses to the crime, so they must have some forensics to implicate him. If I can trash the evidence, the case falls apart. Unfortunately, my client can't afford an expert, and the pro bono guys are probably not good enough."

He finally looked up from his double old fashioned to meet my satisfied smile. "Travis, you may be in luck. Morquist Levy, a good friend of mine, is one of the top forensic pathologists in the country. I worked with him in Houston. Great guy, and always happy to help a just cause. If you need some evidence reviewed, let me know."

"Mighty kind of you, Doc. I'll be in touch."

. . .

That evening I opened a brief email from The BT. "Be extra careful. Both are dirty." Spreadsheets were attached.

CHAPTER 21

Friday, May 13
9:00 a.m.

Alejandro's arraignment began in the courtroom that had stood for eighty-seven years, most recently upgraded seven years earlier by the Felton Foundation. In an impressive two story room lined entirely with dark stained oak and intricate moldings, the judge would sit on a dais six feet above the floor, allowing him a commanding view of the cavernous space. Today, all twelve rows of seating supported a crowd, and more people stood along the perimeter.

The bailiff made his announcement exactly on time. "All rise. Court is now in session, the Honorable Nick Morestrand presiding."

Judge Morestrand climbed the stairs to his chair, waving for the crowd to be seated. An imposing figure at six foot four, with his gray hair and famously bushy gray eyebrows, he exuded a calm, wise presence. He had easily won re-election for the last twenty-three years as an academic powerhouse known to preside fairly and compassionately.

"Prosecution, the floor is yours."

Don Anderson, dressed in his best pin stripe, dark blue suit with a red tie, made his point succinctly. "Your Honor, the state charges Alejandro Ramirez with seven counts of first degree, premeditated murder in the deaths of Laurie Vaughn, John Hunt, and five John Does over the last year. The state requests that he be held without bail pending trial, as he is both a flight risk and a danger to the community." The District Attorney sat down, and the judge looked to the defense table.

Travis Foster waited a moment and then slowly rose, indicating for Alejandro to stand up next to him. Travis had arranged for a haircut and a conservative blue suit for Alejandro to wear in court, while he himself remained his usual unkempt self with gray hair fighting gravity in all directions and in a fifteen-year-old wrinkled gray suit. "Your Honor, my client pleads innocent to these charges. Furthermore, we ask that these charges be dismissed with prejudice, as the prosecution has failed to produce any evidence of my client's guilt."

A banging gavel silenced the murmuring crowd. "I would like to remind everyone that you are observers, not participants, in these proceedings. Interruptions will not be tolerated." He punctuated his words with a long, slow stare across the entire crowd. "Prosecution?"

"Your Honor, it is an insult to this court and to the people to suggest that the trial will be ended before it has even begun. The state has an abundance of evidence which will tie this man to the murders of those innocent people."

Travis stood up, "Your Honor, I believe the DA is a man of his word, and that he would never claim to have a mountain of evidence unless such mountain actually existed, but we have seen nothing, not one bit of evidence to connect my client to these murders. If he wishes to deny my client bail, he must show at least some reason to do so."

Expecting this, the DA immediately responded. "The state is still processing the evidence, but among other things, we discovered a .45 caliber Glock and ammunition consistent with the type used in the murder in Mr. Ramirez' possession. The gun is legally registered to him and was found in his nightstand. His fingerprints were on the weapon. The state will show, through forensic evidence, that Mr. Ramirez did indeed kill those people."

Travis audibly chuckled. "You have something to add, Counselor?" the judge asked.

"One moment, please." He shuffled through papers before finally holding one up. "Aha, here it is. Your Honor, there are one hundred thirty-seven .45 caliber Glocks legally registered in this city. An additional three hundred and eighty-two .45 caliber weapons of various manufacture are legally registered in this city. Let's see, there have been over 50,000 rounds of Federal ammunition .45 caliber sold in this city in the last year. That means Mr. Ramirez is one of over five hundred people who have a weapon and ammo similar to that used in this crime. Certainly, that is not enough to hold a man without bail?"

The judge raised an eyebrow as his gaze swung back to the DA, now fidgeting a bit. "Do you have something more compelling?"

The DA had hoped to avoid disclosure of the blood on the gun, but he had to proceed with the case. "Your Honor, the gun recovered at Mr. Ramirez' home exhibits traces of human blood."

The crowd required silencing again by the judge. Outwardly calm, Travis smiled inside as he stood up. "Has this blood been matched to any of the victims?"

"The DNA results will not be back until tonight."

The judge folded his hands in front of himself as he looked thoughtfully between the parties. "The Court finds itself in a difficult position. Mr. Ramirez has rights and cannot be held for charges that are not backed up by evidence. On the other hand, the court has a duty to protect the community from a potentially dangerous individual. I think that…"

"Pardon me, Judge." Travis was up and out of his seat, all evidence of his previously lackadaisical behavior gone. "I'm sorry to interrupt, but I believe I have a solution that will be acceptable to all parties."

"It better be one hell of a solution to justify interrupting me in my court."

Unfazed, "I propose we delay these proceedings until Monday to get all the information back from the lab. My client will remain in jail over the weekend, pending continuance of the arraignment on Monday. I ask only that we get immediate access to a sample of the blood found on the gun and a chance to review it over the weekend."

The judge turned back to the DA, who accepted Travis' suggestion.

"Per agreement of the parties, Mr. Ramirez will remain in custody for the weekend, and we will continue this hearing at 9 a.m. on Monday. Mr. Anderson, I expect the defense to have full access to everything they need to evaluate the bloodstain in the next hour. Delays will not be tolerated. Court is adjourned." The judge banged the gavel and swept out of the room.

Travis gathered his papers. Now aware of the basis for their case, all he had to do was poke some giant holes in it over the next two days.

. . .

Tomas arrived at the Felton Forty by noon, and John sat with him on the porch as a fresh pitcher of lemonade glistened on the table between them. Tomas helped himself to a long drink before getting directly to the point.

"This tracker has caused a major disruption to our business. I am not pleased."

"I'm sorry," a nervous John replied. "We've doubled security around here, and we're working hard to track down whoever placed it."

"I understand there was a man and a dog on the security tape."

"Yes, but we only saw shadows, nothing to definitively identify anyone."

Tomas leaned back. "So, you have no leads at all?"

"One possibility we're checking is a new guy in town who always has a dog at his side."

"This man must be brought in for questioning and then made to disappear."

John shifted uncomfortably in his seat. "I'm afraid that's not possible. He's an emergency room doctor here in town, and he's also dating the Sheriff's daughter. With all the other bodies recently found, there's no way we can make him disappear."

"How is our friend the Sheriff doing? He did a good job finding someone responsible for all those murders so quickly."

"He's stressed, but hanging in there."

"He's stressed because you are making too many mistakes. I am also stressed, which is not good for your long term health, my friend. If you continue to create stressful situations, you will no longer be of use."

Well aware of what Tomas was capable of, John had no desire to become an object lesson for others. "The Sheriff has resolved the issue of the dead bodies with Alejandro. I'll confirm who put that tracker on the truck and take care of them."

"See that you do." Tomas stood to leave. "One more thing. Your mistakes have caused a significant disruption to our operations. I expect a free load of product on the next delivery. I hope this is acceptable."

John nodded. His life was worth much more to him than a few million dollars of product. "Thank you, Tomas."

Tomas left without another word. The disruption to his operation was minor, and things like this were expected, but it was still nice to make a few million dollars from the mistake.

• • •

I analyzed the spreadsheet in a soft breeze on the sunlit back porch. Banshee busily chased scents only he detected through the fluttering aspens. The spreadsheets and other documents The BT had sent me last night included bank accounts and tax forms, as well as an analysis by The BT. Part of me really wanted to know how he got his hands on information like this, while the rest of me wanted to make sure never to piss him off.

At surface level, the books for Tim's Garden Spot appeared unremarkable. Yearly reports correlated with amounts shown on tax forms, and they paid all their taxes on time, but Tim's Garden Spot was too profitable, showing almost four million dollars of profit for the year, an awful lot for seven nurseries. More concerning, it showed good cash flow in the winter months. I was willing to bet the average nursery didn't sell too many plants during the winter in Utah.

I turned my attention to the Felton financial documents that showed a complex set of accounts and companies, but fortunately, The BT had provided a summary. In the past ten years, the ranch had been unbelievably profitable, pouring almost $100 million into their Felton Foundation to offset tax obligations. The Foundation had been buying up assets and businesses in town, providing some charitable services, but also making a profit on those businesses, which was reinvested to own more assets.

It actually reflected a brilliant plan to launder money. Excess cash was declared income for the ranch and transferred to the foundation, where some donations were made, but the majority was reinvested into other businesses that produced cash, which was used to buy more businesses. Not only were the Feltons using laundered money to buy up assets, but they were also doing it tax free.

I sat back in my chair and watched the clouds sail across the turquoise sky as I put all the pieces together in my mind. I had to appreciate the intricacy and sophistication of the operation, and I doubted the Feltons could pull it off on their own. The records showed that the increased profitability began about ten years ago. Prior to that, they earned only a modest profit each year. Old man Felton had made a deal ten years ago, and dirty money flowed through the ranch, hidden under the guise of a benevolent charity.

I looked over at Banshee lying beside me with his head on his paws after all of his explorations. "Banshee, how do you feel about visiting a nursery in Salt Lake City?"

Banshee thumped his tail.

. . .

Larry conference-called the Sheriff and the DA late in the afternoon and spoke before anyone even said hello. "We got a match on the blood, Sheriff! We got him!"

The Sheriff had to remember to act surprised, even though he knew exactly what the blood would show. "Slow down and catch your breath and start from the beginning."

"The DNA typing on the blood from the gun was completed about an hour ago, and we compared the results with Mr. Ramirez and all the victims. The blood on the gun matches Laurie Vaughn's. We ran a confirmatory test, which is more sensitive, and it matches perfectly."

"How sure are you that this is a match?" the DA asked.

"The results show there is a one in 5.3 billion chance this blood is not hers. That's the maximum sensitivity for the test."

"Okay, good job, Larry. I need two copies of those results brought over to my office immediately. I'll call Travis and let him know the results, and he can have a copy. Do we have enough blood left for him to have a sample if he wants one?"

"Yes, sir. We can run DNA on microscopic amounts, and there is enough for him to have a sample if he needs it."

"Good job, everyone. Make sure no one says a word to anyone, not even to your wives. This stays quiet until the hearing on Monday."

Everyone hung up and looked forward to celebratory dinners that night.

• • •

Travis stopped by the DA's office a half hour later to pick up his copy of the report. Like the man who occupied the seat, the office personified mediocrity. A few pictures of family hung on beige walls with old law books neatly lined up on the shelves. A single folder in front of him adorned a clean, uncluttered desk. The Montana flag in the corner sported the only concession to color.

"Travis, thanks for coming by so quickly."

Travis lowered himself into a chair and addressed the DA. "I assume from your barely suppressed smile that the DNA results have come back favorably for your case."

Don pushed the file across the desk. "Quite favorable. This is your copy, and the results are a perfect match for the DNA of Ms. Vaughn."

Travis picked up the folder and briefly flipped through the standard report from the state lab with about twenty pages of scientific terms. He turned to the last page to read the summary. "One in 5.3 billion chance it is not her blood." He closed the file and set it back on the desk. "So there's a chance it's not hers."

Don actually laughed at that. "You know better than that. We've got the victim's blood on his gun. A first year law student could get this conviction. Your client has no chance, but I'm willing to make a deal. If he pleads guilty, I won't seek the death penalty. If this goes to trial, we will, and we'll win."

Travis nodded as he stared at the Montana flag for a full thirty seconds, pretending to consider the offer. Abruptly, he stood up and grabbed the file. "Thank you, Don. I'll make sure my client is aware of the offer, and we'll have a response ready on Monday. In the meantime, I would like to review this report. I'll need a sample of the blood for our own studies. Please let Larry know I'll be picking it up this afternoon."

Travis called Doc as he walked back to his office. "It's Travis. What's the name of that smart forensics guy in Houston?"

. . .

I called Kirsten that evening. "Good evening, gorgeous. Got any plans for the weekend?"

"I'm not on call and my calendar is free. Did you have something in mind?"

"Do you like basketball?"

"A bit of an odd question, but yes, it's okay."

"How about joining me for a quick road trip to Salt Lake this weekend to catch a Jazz game? The Lakers are in town for the playoffs and it should be a good game."

Kirsten pretended to think about it. "You'll need to sweeten the offer. Basketball is okay, but not worth a five hour drive each way."

"Okay, how about I add in a five star hotel, a ninety minute massage in their spa, and breakfast in bed?"

"That's more like it. What time are we leaving?"

"I'll pick you up at eight tomorrow morning."

"See you then."

Banshee was looking at me with his head sideways. "Don't worry, boy. I'll find some place that allows service dogs."

CHAPTER 22

Saturday, May 14
8:03 a.m.

I picked Kirsten up on time, and Banshee begrudgingly settled for the back seat with views out the side windows. We headed west until we picked up I-15 for a straight shot south to Salt Lake.

"What's with the last minute plans?" Kirsten curled up in a ball in her seat.

"Had the weekend off and wanted to do something that didn't involve mass graves. I was watching TV, and they mentioned the Jazz - Lakers game on Saturday. Checked availability online and decent seats were still available, so I decided on a road trip."

"It certainly makes it easy to road trip in this thing. This seat is more comfortable than anything I have in my house."

"Mercedes specializes in features you don't need, but definitely want. For example…" I pushed some buttons on the control panel and briefly waited for her response.

"Oh my God, you gotta be fucking kidding me! A seat massager?"

"Yeah, and that's only one of ten programs. You can also add heat to any of them."

"Slow down and take your time driving. I'm gonna check out all these options." Kirsten reclined her seat, closed her eyes and reveled in the massage.

The easy, beautiful drive wound between green hills and mountains on both sides. Signs pointed the way to Yellowstone and Jackson Hole, and I made a mental note to put them on my travel list as well. We stopped for gas and a chance for Banshee to run around Malad City, a small town north of Utah's border before we hopped back in the G wagon to continue south. By one o'clock, we reached northern Salt Lake City, near where the truck had stopped at Tim's Garden Spot. "I'm starving. Let's get some lunch," I suggested.

Kirsten yawned and stretched. "That sounds nice after 250 miles of continuous massage."

I pulled off at the next exit and chose an IHOP.

Kirsten looked at me sideways. "Seriously?"

"I'm feeling a waffle calling my name, with a side of pancakes and onion rings, and maybe a glass of carbohydrates to wash it down."

Kirsten reconsidered. "I wasn't thinking waffle until you said it, but let's do it."

We finished our waffles, and Banshee made quick work of his sausages. Loaded with carbs, we lumbered back to the Mercedes for the rest of the drive. I swung onto the main road back toward the freeway and made an immediate right into a parking lot.

"What are you doing?" Kirsten asked.

I pointed at the sign. "I'm getting a plant. Come on." I opened the door, and Banshee jumped out after me. We walked into Tim's Garden Spot with a puzzled Kirsten following us.

Clean and well organized, a large, open building filled with indoor plants and supplies welcomed wandering customers. The back led directly into greenhouses containing larger outdoor plants. Further back, an open yard showcased trees and bulk supplies, including mulch.

"Is this what you're looking for?" Kirsten was holding up a small pink flower about the size of my pinkie in the world's smallest pot.

I pretended to study it for a moment. "Too manly. I need something daintier."

Kirsten rolled her eyes, as she put it back on the shelf. "Why the sudden interest in plants?"

"I had an incredible yard in Houston. I've been meaning to get some plants for the house, but haven't had time. Call it an impulse buy. Let's look around."

The well-organized nursery harbored no sign of criminal activity. In the yard, I recognized the Felton Ranch mulch right away. I pointed the bag out to Kirsten. "Seems like we can't get away from those guys."

Kirsten scrunched her face up in disgust. "If you buy one bag of that stuff, I'm walking home."

"No worries, mulch is not on my list for today." I leaned down and whispered to Banshee, "DRUGS."

Banshee immediately sniffed all around the area, methodically circling the stacks of mulch bags. He returned to me without indicating the presence of drugs. Disappointed, but not surprised, I scratched his ears and told him to RELAX.

Inside, I chose a fern and a small ficus for my home. I talked Kirsten into a matching fern for her place. All I had learned was that Tim's Garden Spot existed and did a steady business. On the plus side, I had some new plants for my house.

"Any more stops planned?" Kirsten asked.

"Nope, we're heading for the hotel."

"Good. My massage is scheduled for three."

. . .

Back at Tim's Garden Spot, the manager made a call.

"Luis, we had a guy walking around with his dog, checking the place out, like you said might happen."

"What was he driving?"

"A black G Wagon."

"Was he alone?"

"No. He had a pretty lady with him."

"Send me pictures. Did he buy anything?"

"Just a couple of small plants."

"Send me the credit card receipt as well."

Fifteen minutes later, Luis had the pictures passed on to Tomas, who passed them onto the Feltons.

"Do you recognize this man?"

Glancing at the photo, his whole body clenched. "Yeah, that's definitely Doc and his dog. Son of a bitch! What's he doing out there?"

"Following the transmitter you allowed him to place on my truck. Who is the woman?"

"Kirsten Jenkins, an orthopedic doctor here. Rumor has it they're dating. You should also know that she's Sheriff Stein's daughter."

"I have some decisions to make." He hung up before John responded.

. . .

The beautiful hotel assigned us a room that overlooked the mountains. We stood outside on the balcony with our arms around each other, breathing in the fresh air of the perfectly warm spring day.

"It's so relaxing out here. Makes me want to take off my clothes and feel the breeze."

"Don't let me stop you."

"Maybe later. Right now I have to get ready for my massage."

"How do you get ready for a massage?"

She took my hand and led me toward the shower.

"At your service, m'lady."

After an exhilarating shower, Kirsten left me planning my next move in a hotel robe on the balcony with Banshee at my side. I knew the Feltons and Tim's Garden Spot were likely laundering money, but I couldn't prove it.

"What do you think, Banshee? Seems like I'm the one breaking laws to find proof these guys are doing something illegal. Ironic, huh?"

Banshee turned his gaze to me.

"Don't worry. I'm confused, too. What do you want to do next?"

Banshee thumped his tail on the balcony.

"Good idea. Let's go for a walk."

Banshee jumped up and down as he heard his favorite word. I decided to tell Kirsten everything.

• • •

Kirsten returned from her massage, relaxed and glowing with a sleepy countenance. We dressed for dinner, and Kirsten ordered a petite filet mignon with crab cakes, while I went with a burger and fries. We walked ten minutes to the arena. The Jazz pulled off the victory with a last second shot, sending the crowd into a frenzy. Caught up in the excitement, we were still feeling the high as we hiked back to the hotel.

"Thanks for this. I forgot how good it feels to get out," Kirsten snuggled into my arm.

"You have to do the right things with the right people."

"This definitely feels right."

We ambled in silence to our room. Excited to see us, Banshee virtually threw his leash at me. "Okay, let's get you a quick walk."

"Go ahead without me. I'm gonna get ready for bed."

Banshee and I walked around the hotel grounds. I let him off leash to burn some energy. He marked his territory before we headed back to the room.

I found the room empty, and the balcony door open. Kirsten, lying naked on a blanket, gazed into the night sky. "Glad's it's you and not housekeeping. Care to join me?" She patted the blanket next to her. I quickly stripped and laid down next to her.

"The stars are so beautiful tonight," she observed.

"So are you."

She gently climbed on top of me. "Thanks for a memorable day."

CHAPTER 23

Sunday, May 15
8:42 a.m.

We woke in each other's arms with Banshee curled up at the foot of the bed. I wiggled out of her embrace, threw on a robe, and stepped quietly onto the balcony. Another perfect morning with a light breeze, the sun bloomed low in the sky. Fifteen minutes later, Kirsten slid out next to me in her robe.

"Good morning. Did you sleep well?" I asked as I gave her hand a little kiss.

"I was out cold. It's beautiful out here." She turned to me. "I really enjoyed yesterday."

"Me, too. We need to do this more often."

We sat in silence for a few minutes. "Kirsten, I need to tell you something."

She looked at me sideways with a raised eyebrow. "If this is the part where you tell me about your wife and four kids, I'm gonna throw you off this balcony."

"Nah. My wife and I have only two kids." That earned a playful punch in the shoulder. "Seriously, though, I need your opinion. Something's going on with the Feltons."

"Something is always going on with those idiots."

"This is more serious. When I was at the ranch, I overheard them talking about a special delivery from the greenhouses, so I decided to do a little investigating. Banshee and I snuck in at night and watched them load a truck. They gave special attention to two pallets of mulch, and everyone walked around with guns. Something weird was definitely going on."

Kirsten faced me with wide eyes and her jaw hanging open. "That's crazy. You could have been killed. You can get shot for trespassing on any ranch, but especially on that one."

"I was careful and stayed out of the light. I don't think anyone saw us. I put a tracker on the truck, and it traced the delivery to Tim's Garden Spot here in Salt Lake."

"That's why we stopped at that nursery. I have to admit, it seemed weird you were shopping for plants on vacation."

"I actually love plants, but you're right, I wanted to see the nursery."

"Did you see anything weird? All I saw was a nursery."

"Nope. Everything looked normal. I even had Banshee smell for drugs, but he didn't detect anything."

"Drugs? You think the Feltons are dealing drugs?"

"I contacted an acquaintance of mine from Houston. He provided me with tax and bank records from the ranch and the nursery. They demonstrate a lot of extra cash moving through both businesses. The ranch is operating like a money laundering operation."

Kirsten leaned toward me. "Hold on. You're telling me you overheard a conversation, and based on that, trespassed onto their property, tracked their truck, and got some hacker to look into their financial info for you? And you concluded the Feltons are laundering money made from drugs? Did I miss something?"

"That's pretty much everything."

"So that makes you James fucking Bond."

"And that makes you my perfectly beautiful Bond girl."

"That's not good. Bad things always happen to James Bond's beautiful assistants."

"That won't happen. What should we do now? Should I let the Sheriff know what I've found?"

Kirsten laughed out loud. "My first piece of advice is to stay away from the Sheriff. The only proof of criminal activity you have at the moment is your own actions. The Feltons have too much power. If you go after them with this, they'll walk away free and make your life a living hell. No way the Sheriff will pursue it without actual evidence."

She made sense. I was 99% sure I knew what was happening, but I couldn't prove it. "Looks like I'll need to make another trip out there to get some evidence, but first, we need to get breakfast and go home. You want to shower first?"

She grabbed my hand and pulled me after her. "I believe in water conservation. Let's shower together."

. . .

Morquist called Travis at exactly two o'clock. "Good afternoon, Travis. I have completed my review of the materials."

"Thanks for your help. Turn up anything interesting?"

"One anomaly I cannot explain."

Morquist succinctly shared his findings with Travis, who took precise notes. Morquist answered a few questions, and Travis had a plan for his defense of Alejandro.

. . .

We arrived back in town in the late afternoon after a lazy, peaceful drive home. I helped Kirsten unpack and then helped her pick out a place for her new fern.

"Remember, you need to turn it frequently so it grows evenly, and don't over water it."

"Yes, sir!" Kirsten gave a mock salute to me.

"I had a good time this weekend."

"Me, too, Dr. Secret Spyman. Are you sure I can't come with you?"

We had talked about it for the last hundred miles. Kirsten really wanted to go visit the ranch with Banshee and me, but I didn't want her to get into trouble. "It would be embarrassing to have your dad arrest you."

She pouted. "Okay. You and Banshee have all the fun. I'll stay here and safely take care of my plant."

I pulled her into a hug. "It won't be that exciting, and I want you safe. All kidding aside, if they're into money laundering and drugs, this could get dangerous. Don't say a word to anyone about this."

"My lips are sealed. Now get out of here. I got some things to get done before work tomorrow." She gave me a long, passionate kiss before pushing me out the door. "Goodbye, Mr. Bond."

CHAPTER 24

Monday, May 16
9:00 a.m.

The courtroom appeared even more crowded than it had been on Friday. Palpable excitement rippled through the gathering as nine o'clock approached. The DA looked classically sharp in his best-fitting navy suit, white shirt starched to the point of uncomfortableness, and a red striped silk tie. Travis wore the same suit from Friday and looked like he had slept in it over the weekend. The DA bounced with nervous anticipation as Travis stared blankly at the papers scattered across the table in front of him.

Promptly on the hour, the Bailiff announced the judge's arrival. Judge Morestrand swept into the courtroom to take his seat on the bench. He shuffled a few papers before glancing up at the packed courtroom. "This is a continuation of the bond hearing for Mr. Ramirez from last Friday. The prosecution asked for the time to review evidence, and the defense graciously agreed to the extension. Mr. Anderson, are you prepared to present evidence to justify your request for no bail in this case?"

"We are, Your Honor."

"Then please proceed."

"Your Honor, we would like to call Larry Watson to the stand." Larry took his place in the witness seat and was sworn in.

"Mr. Watson, will you please tell the court your qualifications?"

"Yes, sir. I'm a Board Certified pathologist with twenty years of experience in forensic pathology. I'm the Chief Medical Examiner for the county and oversee all of the evidence collection and autopsies for the county."

"In your capacity as Chief Medical Examiner, did you have the opportunity to process evidence collected from the home of the defendant?"

"Yes, sir. We received a .45 caliber Glock pistol, which was recovered at the home of Mr. Ramirez. That evidence was processed per our usual procedures and scanned for fingerprints, blood, and any trace evidence. The results are summarized in this report."

The report was entered into evidence without comment from Travis.

"What did your study of the gun reveal?"

"We detected multiple fingerprints on the gun, all of which belonged to Mr. Ramirez."

"There were no other fingerprints on the gun? Only Mr. Ramirez's?"

"That is correct. We also found two areas of blood smeared on the barrel. The report shows a closeup of the bloodstains."

The DA showed a picture of the bloodstains to the judge and led Larry through a tedious description of the processes used to collect and analyze the blood. A disinterested Travis continued to peruse through the papers on his table. Finally, the DA was through the analysis details. "And there is no doubt in your mind that the blood was collected and analyzed correctly, and the findings summarized in this report?"

"Yes, sir. That report contains the true and accurate findings of the blood collected from the gun found at the Ramirez home."

A suddenly alert Travis abruptly stood up. "Pardon the court for the interruption. As an old man, my hearing is not always the best. Can you please repeat that last statement?"

"Would the court reporter please repeat back the last question and answer for the defense?"

The court reporter dutifully read back the last exchange. "Thank you, Your Honor. Apologies for the interruption."

The judge looked thoughtfully at Travis. He had tried hundreds of cases in this courtroom, and this was the first indication of a hearing problem.

"Mr. Watson, now that we have established the custody of the gun and the collection and analysis of the blood, can you please summarize the results in this report?"

"DNA analysis of the blood revealed a positive match to Laurie Vaughn, a deceased victim found on the tenth of this month."

A firm rap of the gavel and an even firmer stare from the judge silenced the crowd. "If you feel the need to talk, please remove yourself from the courtroom now." A few journalists walked out of the courtroom, hoping to be the first to report the news. "The rest of you will remain seated and quiet for the duration of this hearing." He punctuated his words with a prolonged stare of the crowd that left each person thinking he spoke only to them. "The state may proceed."

"Thank you. Mr. Watson, how sure is the lab that this blood is a match for Ms. Vaughn?"

"The results indicate there is a 1 in 5.3 billion chance this is not actually her blood. That is the most accurate analysis available with current technology."

"In your professional opinion, there is no doubt whatsoever that the blood found on the gun belongs to Ms. Vaughn. Is that correct?"

"I am certain beyond any reasonable doubt that the blood belongs to Ms. Vaughn."

"Thank you, no further questions at this time."

The judge looked over to Travis, still fumbling through papers on his desk. "Defense, do you wish to question the witness?"

"Yes, Your Honor. One moment, please, while I find the correct document." On the witness stand, Mr. Watson prepared himself for cross examination. He had testified against Travis' clients many times over the years, and he knew what a bulldog Travis could be.

Finally, Travis held up a document, stood, and leaned casually against the Defense table as he spoke. "Mr. Watson, I have here a copy of the report that you gave to my office on Friday. Is this a true and accurate copy of the report that was submitted into evidence?"

"I cannot speak to the document in your hand, but the document you received on Friday was an exact duplicate of the document submitted for evidence."

"Fair enough." Travis dropped his copy and picked up the copy that was entered into evidence. "Mr. Watson, have you had a chance to review this report?"

"Yes, sir."

"This is a very detailed report. Nineteen pages with all sorts of scientific words and graphs and tables. Did you skim this report, or did you read every word?"

"I read every word of that report, and I stand by my statement as to its accuracy."

"Very impressive. Not being a man of science, I was only able to skim through it. Too many polysyllabic medical phrases I didn't have time to look up, but you read through this entire document, every word, and you believe it is accurate. You believe this shows without any shadow of a doubt that the blood on that gun belonged to Ms. Vaughn."

"I am one hundred percent sure the report is accurate and that the blood belongs to Ms. Vaughn."

Travis silently leafed through the report for ten seconds before looking up. "Well, I guess it's settled then. Thank you, Mr. Watson. No more questions."

Larry sat on the stand in stunned disbelief at the concession Travis had made. The judge and DA thought in overdrive trying to figure out what trap Travis had laid. The judge maintained a poker face, but Mr. Anderson's expression betrayed concern.

"Mr. Watson, you may step down. Mr. Foster, would the defense like to call any other witnesses?"

For the first time, a small smile escaped as he answered. "As a matter of fact, the Defense calls Dr. Morquist Levy, Chief Medical Examiner from Houston, Texas. Dr. Levy will join us by video conferencing this morning."

The DA immediately stood. "Objection, Your Honor. The defense has not disclosed this witness and his expected testimony to us. We have no idea of the qualifications of this witness."

"Your Honor, we did not receive any evidence at all until Friday evening, and I was able to speak to Dr. Levy only yesterday myself. I am confident we can establish his credentials, and I am also confident that the Court will be interested in what he has to say."

"Overruled. I'll allow his testimony."

The call connected, and Dr. Levy appeared on the screen. A thin man with thick glasses that magnified his eyes, he appeared with neatly combed dark hair that contrasted with his white-collared shirt and pale complexion. He had a name badge clipped to his shirt with a matching pen and pencil in his pocket. Overall, he gave the impression of a NASA scientist from the 1970s. He was quickly sworn in by the bailiff.

"Good morning, Dr. Levy. Thank you for joining us."

"Thank you for having me. This is my first time testifying in Montana."

"We're happy to have you. Can you please tell us about your qualifications?"

"Certainly. I am currently the Chief Medical Examiner for Harris County, covering the Houston metroplex. I have been a triple boarded pathologist for 27 years. I have performed thousands of autopsies and testified in 652 depositions and 471 trials. I have been the primary author on 67 peer-reviewed articles and co-author of 327 articles. Do you need more information?" He spoke in short, rapid sentences without pauses, effectively like an auctioneer announcing his medical credentials.

Travis chuckled. "I believe that's enough. Did you have a chance to review a report dated May 13 regarding an analysis of blood found on a weapon seized from Mr. Ramirez?"

"I did. The emailed report was received in my inbox at 10:04 am on Saturday, and I reviewed the report from 2:21 p.m. to 3:09 p.m. that same day."

"Overall, did you find the report to be of satisfactory quality?"

"Yes, the report comes from a nationally recognized lab known for quality."

"So you feel this report is accurate?"

"I hope so. One of my former students runs that lab now, and I would be shocked if her data was less than perfect."

"This report concludes that the blood on the gun is a perfect DNA match with the blood of Ms. Vaughn. Do you agree with that statement?"

"Based on the data in front of me, there is no doubt that the blood on the gun matches the blood of Ms. Vaughn to the highest levels of current technology."

"Well, let's turn our attention to the blood spatter on the gun. Can you please turn to page seventeen of the report which shows a close up photo of the blood on the gun. Do you have any thoughts on the blood patterns seen in this photo?"

"Objection, Your Honor. Witness is not qualified to speak on blood patterns." The judge looked at Morquist, who spoke before any other questions were asked.

"I maintain a certification in blood spatter analysis, have been the primary author on 14 papers and co-author on 52 additional papers regarding blood spatter evidence. I have examined 972 weapons for blood patterns and testified in court 518 times. My findings have never been erroneous."

The judge suppressed a smile as he said, "Overruled. Continue."

Travis picked up. "What can you tell us about the blood patterns on this gun?"

"The patterns are unusual for the facts of this case. Evidence indicates the victim was shot while kneeling at close range. This would mean a downward angle for the gun. Upon firing a high caliber gun such as a .45, the gun would be pulled up and to the left for a right handed shooter, exposing the right side of the gun to spatter. The gun would be pointed more horizontal, and the blood would travel upwards from below, so the pattern should be more vertical on the gun. This photo shows the blood parallel to the gun barrel, and I would expect it to be more perpendicular."

"But it is possible the shooter lowered the gun after firing instead of raising it?"

"Certainly a possibility, but very unlikely."

"Anything else about the pattern that seems off?"

"Yes. On the closeup, you can see the pattern is relatively consistent front to back. It is wider at the front and narrower at the back, but the lines are relatively straight. Usually, when you get blowback blood spatter from a close head shot, the blood has traveled rapidly and has created a different pattern than what is seen here. Normally, the pattern would show a clear point of impact with microdroplets spreading out in all directions from the impact. The majority will continue along the original axis, but some will splatter in all directions. We do not see that pattern here."

"So, is it your professional opinion that the blood pattern could have been caused by a close shot to the head at a downward angle?"

"It would be an unusual pattern for such a shot, and although unlikely, it is definitely possible the blood pattern came from that type of shot."

Travis shuffled his papers before looking at Morquist. "Dr. Levy, am I to understand it is your professional opinion that the blood is a 100% match with the victim, and that the blood pattern, although unusual, could have occurred when Ms. Vaughn was shot at close range while kneeling?"

"That is correct."

"Then I assume it is your professional opinion that the blood found on this weapon occurred when Ms. Vaughn was shot?"

"Absolutely not. I am 100% certain that the blood belongs to Ms. Vaughn, but I am also 100% certain that the blood did not get on the gun at the time of her murder."

The courtroom stirred, and the judge turned his gaze on the crowd to restore silence. Travis ignored the interruption and kept his momentum. "That is quite an extraordinary claim. Could you elaborate, please?"

"Sure. If you turn to page twelve of the report and look at the third footnote, I can explain everything." The DA rapidly flipped pages to find the footnote. "You will see the report notes the presence of three different chemicals in the blood sample. One of these chemicals is potassium EDTA, which is not found in the blood naturally. It is an anticoagulant used in blood tubes like this one." Morquist held up a lavender top tube. "A commercial lab such as this one does not use this chemical for any tests, and the only source of that chemical can be a blood transport tube."

"Isn't it possible the chemical was somehow transferred innocently during the testing procedure?"

"Impossible. Analysis of evidence like this would be done in a sterile environment with fresh gloves and fresh tools for every sample, and the blood of Ms. Vaughn would have been processed a week earlier and would have been in storage far away from the work area."

"Maybe this chemical was innocently transferred from another sample?"

"Again, not possible. If there was contamination from another sample, we would see a second set of DNA in the results."

"Dr. Levy, will you please state clearly for the court your interpretation of this report?"

"This report proves conclusively that the blood found on the gun came from a tube of Ms. Vaughan's blood at some point after her murder."

"Thank you, Dr. Levy. Your Honor, we ask for these charges to be dropped, and an investigation initiated into how this evidence was corrupted."

The judge turned his attention to the DA. "Mr. Anderson, how would you like to proceed?"

The DA looked at his team before deciding. "Your Honor, the prosecution requests a fifteen minute recess."

"Very well. Court is adjourned for fifteen minutes." He banged his gavel and left the courtroom.

. . .

Travis leaned back in his chair, opened a paperback book, and read without a care in the world. Alejandro leaned over. "What are you reading?"

"It's *Killing Floor* by Lee Child. Outstanding book."

"What's it about?"

"It's about a man who is wrongly accused of murder in a small town and has to prove his innocence."

"So it's like research for my case."

"Something like that. Here, take this copy. I've read it a few times, and I think you'll enjoy it."

"Thank you. Do you really think this will be all over today?"

"Son, it was over ten minutes ago. They're trying to figure out how to get out of this room with a sliver of their dignity intact. Look at them over there."

Travis pointed at the prosecution's table, which now included Larry Watson and the Sheriff, who had joined the DA and his assistant, and although their voices were low, clearly tempers flared.

The DA demanded in a harsh whisper. "Larry, I need to know right now if that guy is right or not. No bullshit. Give it to me straight."

"I agree with him that the pattern is unusual, but could be explained by a secondary transfer from a finger or clothing surface. The problem is the presence of potassium EDTA. There is no way to explain that unless we say the report was wrong."

"That would be a great idea if you hadn't testified under oath thirty minutes ago that every word in the report was true and accurate. Larry, how the fuck did that blood get on that gun?"

Larry sighed heavily before answering. "The only way that blood containing potassium EDTA could get on that gun was that it was taken from a vial in the lab and intentionally placed on the gun."

The Sheriff interjected. "Are you saying someone intentionally placed that blood there to frame this guy?"

"That's exactly what I'm saying."

The DA asked, "Larry, how did you miss that note in the report?"

"For Christ's sake. The damn report is twenty pages long and is always formatted the same way with the same footnotes. I didn't read them all the way through. I'll take the blame for this."

"No. The motherfucker who planted the blood on the gun is gonna take the blame and will have twenty years in jail to think about it. We have to drop the case. The evidence is tainted, and even with a recheck of the blood, there is enough doubt to run a train through my case."

Embarrassed silence prevented eye contact. "All right, folks. We're about to be the laughingstock of the legal community, but let's do the right thing."

The meeting broke up with five minutes left in the recess. They returned to their seats and tried to look busy perusing documents while avoiding eye contact. Finally, the bailiff called the court back in session, and the judge returned to the bench.

"Well, Mr. Anderson, how would the state like to proceed?"

The DA stood slowly and locked eyes with the judge. "Your Honor, the state would like to offer its deepest apologies to Mr. Ramirez. It appears that we have been the victim of a crime ourselves, as someone has manipulated evidence in this case. I have instructed the Sheriff to open an immediate investigation into how the perpetrator gained access to Ms. Vaughan's blood and to Mr. Ramirez' gun. I will instruct the lab to thoroughly scrutinize all of their security procedures to uncover how this was done and to make sure it cannot happen again."

"I am sure that the people of Montana appreciate your dedication to solving this new crime, but what specifically are you doing in the case of Montana vs. Alejandro Ramirez?"

"Your Honor, the state would like to dismiss all charges against Mr. Ramirez related to the murders of these seven individuals."

"Mr. Anderson, I would like to be clear that these charges will be dismissed with prejudice."

"Agreed, Your honor."

"Mr. Ramirez, please rise. On behalf of this court, I would like to apologize for the charges that were brought against you using false evidence. These charges are being dismissed with prejudice, which means that you are found innocent of the charges and can never be tried for them again. Mr. Ramirez, you are a free man. Court is adjourned."

The judge quickly made his way out of the courtroom as it erupted into congratulatory noise. Mamacita pushed her way to the front to smother first Alejandro, and then Travis, with bone crushing hugs. She whispered in his ear as she hugged him, "Thank you, Mr. Foster. You can eat and drink free at my place as long as you live."

Travis extricated himself from the hug. "Be careful what you promise. I can easily drink more than my normal fee."

Travis handed his copy of the book to Alejandro. "Enjoy the book and enjoy your freedom. We'll work on the wrongful arrest suit next week." Travis made his way out of the courtroom to many high fives and back slaps.

The DA and his assistant silently packed up their papers, still in disbelief at what had happened. The sheriff stared at the floor, wondering how he was going to get out of this mess. He was in charge of the investigation into how the evidence was altered, but the ripped bag he had produced at the evidence check-in was sure to be discussed. He was one of a few people who had access to both the gun and the lab samples. Even worse, he was going to have to explain to John and Tomas what had happened at the trial. With Alejandro free, he would have to reopen the investigation into the murders. He had two crimes to solve, and he was complicit in both of them. He needed to find a way out of this mess, and he wasn't confident that a solution even existed. He trudged away from the courthouse.

CHAPTER 25

Monday, May 16
10:57 a.m.

The Sheriff brooded in his private office after giving strict orders to hold his calls and to turn away visitors. The media circled, and he hadn't a clue what to say. He was startled when his door abruptly opened unannounced. "I told you! No visitors!"

"Sorry, I don't have an appointment, but we need to talk." John Felton stepped in and collapsed into a mismatched, stained chair across from the Sheriff. John wore a tan leather blazer to go with his jeans and clean cowboy boots. He gently laid his Stetson upside down on the desk. "You look like shit, Sheriff."

The Sheriff leaned back in his chair and released a heavy sigh. "Maybe that's because we're in a world of trouble."

John looked baffled. "We? What do you mean, we? We are not in trouble. You're in trouble."

The Sheriff sat up straight, and leaned cross his desk, narrowing his eyes. "Let me be perfectly fucking clear, John. We're in this together. My problems are your problems. If I go down for this, you're going down with me."

John returned his hard stare with a condescending smile. "Sheriff, you know the people we work for. You know what happens to people who fail them. We need to work together to find a way out of this mess."

The Sheriff sat back in his chair. "Well, if you have a story to explain how the evidence got altered and have a new suspect for the murders, then I'm all ears."

"Working on it. We're going to need to fabricate a story that the actual killer broke into the lab and smeared the blood on the gun before we raided Alejandro's house."

"That could work, but it would have to be someone with access to the lab who knew Alejandro was the leading suspect."

"I don't suppose you have any officers on the team who you're unhappy with?" John suggested.

"Don't even go there. I'm not sending one of my officers to death row."

John held up his hands up and stood, grabbing his hat as he turned to the door. "Okay, but you need to find a murderer who also broke into the lab and altered the evidence on Alejandro. We need a solution, and we need it fast. The people we work for do not tolerate failure."

"Have you heard from them today?"

"No. I was about to call them to tell them we're working on a solution. That'll buy us some time, but we need a scapegoat."

. . .

I headed into town around noon for lunch, landing at Marty's Diner. Again, Travis had a table and waved me over.

"Happy Monday, Travis. Celebrating something?" I asked as I pointed to his three empty beer bottles.

"Doc, you must be the most poorly informed person in this town. I am indeed celebrating the release of my client, and I have you to thank."

"Wait, Alejandro is free? How did that happen?"

Travis summarized the proceedings. "And that, my friend, is why I am celebrating."

"Glad to hear Morquist helped. Hard to imagine how a mistake like that happened."

Travis turned serious for a moment. "Today was no mistake, son. It's another example of the piss-ass excuse for the police department in this town fucking with evidence to cover for their buddies. Willing to throw that poor boy into a cell on death row for…" Travis stopped as he realized he had said too much. "Anyway, the case is over. I'll drink to that."

"So this sort of thing has happened before?"

"Forget I said anything. I'm an old babbling drunk. Look, here's our lunch. Let's enjoy these fries." Small talk unrelated to the case dominated the rest of our conversation, but the drunk ramblings of the old man continuously replayed in the back of my mind.

. . .

I left the house at eleven that night and called The BT on the way. He answered before I even heard it ring. "It's ready to go, Doc. I got an hour of tape from the cameras, and I'm ready to loop it when you say so. Text me when to start and when to stop."

"Thanks, The BT. Do me a favor and keep an eye on the live feed, and call the Sheriff if I get in trouble."

"No problem. I keep an eye on everything all the time. Be careful. There're two guards out tonight," He abruptly disconnected.

I drove to the same place I had parked last time, put on my equipment, and double checked the gear for Banshee. We hiked to the greenhouses, but once again paused on the way to admire the night sky. The cloudless display showcased the stars winking at me. "Banshee, we need to spend a night sleeping under these stars." Banshee tilted his head.

After forty-five minutes, we overlooked the greenhouses. The two guards, one sitting in a folding chair facing the greenhouse door and the other wandering the perimeter, looked lackadaisical, but they would have to leave for me to get into a greenhouse. I texted The BT to cut the live security feed and roll the looped tape. He texted back to tell me it was safe to move.

I checked Banshee's gear one last time and sent him away with the command, "SILENT." Banshee took off into the dark, and I watched his progress on my camera. He circled behind the greenhouses with occasional direction changes from me. When he was on the opposite side, I had him back up into the darkness where the light couldn't penetrate, then commanded, "STAY SILENT."

When the perimeter guard wandered within fifty feet of Banshee, I activated his speaker and whispered into my microphone. "Shhhhhh. He's close."

The guard instantly turned his flashlight toward the sound of my voice. I had Banshee silently move another thirty feet away from the greenhouse and activated the microphone, again. "C'mon, he's gonna see us." The guard definitely heard that one and called to his partner as he charged toward the voice. His partner jumped out of the chair and followed him into the darkness. I gave Banshee a command to return silently, then sprinted for the door of the nearest greenhouse.

In twenty seconds, I was inside and turned my light on. The first ten rows were some sort of fir shrub with a pungent pine scent that failed to overpower the distinctive odor emanating from the back of the greenhouse. Rows eleven onward comprised neatly lined marijuana plants, about twenty to each row, with at least fifty rows in this greenhouse alone. I took video and pictures and grabbed a sample before my exit.

This was the tricky part. If they were back, I would walk right into them. Hopefully, they were still chasing empty voices in the darkness. I cautiously pushed the door open a few inches. I didn't see anyone, and no one shot at me. I pushed it open a little further, and I saw their lights moving in the distance. Relieved, I stepped out and let the door go. Unfortunately, the door had a tension hinge, presumably to keep it shut during windy days. The moment I let it go, the door slammed, and the metal on metal clanged like a thunderclap in the night. I wasn't sure it could be heard at the main house, but the guards would identify the noise. They immediately turned their lights in my direction and ran toward me.

With stealth eliminated, only speed remained. I ran as hard as I could for the darkness away from the guards. I neared the edge of the floodlight's reach, when three round bursts from the AR-15's they were carrying encouraged me to run even faster and jerk randomly left to right. I made it to the line of darkness, as one guard unloaded a clip at me on full automatic. Bullets pinged the ground to my left, and I turned hard right away from the line of fire. They continued to shoot, but punched the dirt further away from me.

I stopped to focus my night vision and softly called for Banshee. He materialized from the darkness seconds later with his tongue hanging out of his mouth and his tail wagging. "You like these kinds of walks, don't you? C'mon, let's get outta here."

Our forty-five-minute walk to the greenhouse turned into a twenty minute jog back to the car. Banshee curled up in the front seat with his eyes closed, as I struggled to get my heart rate back to normal and pondered my next steps.

. . .

Back at the greenhouses, the two guards argued about what to do. Rogelio didn't tolerate failure, but lying to him was the scarier option. Finally, they decided to report it.

"It's late. This better be important," Rogelio answered.

"Someone tried to get into the greenhouses, but we scared them off."

Rogelio came fully awake. "I'm sending some men to relieve you, and then meet me in the security office." He called the bunkhouse and ordered four men to relieve the two guards. "I want every square inch of that area searched. Make sure no one is still around."

Rogelio hurried to the security office and had the guard pull up the video from the security cameras on the greenhouses. "Go back thirty minutes," he ordered. Six video feeds time stamped thirty minutes earlier appeared on the main screen. They showed different angles of one bored guard lounging in his chair and another wandering the perimeter of the greenhouses.

"Fast forward for me," Rogelio ordered. The tech sped up the feeds as they watched. The guard in the chair remained seated while the roving guard marched comically fast around the area. They watched the entire thirty minutes in less than a minute of real time that showed no evidence of abnormal activity.

"Go back an hour, and do it again." The tech dutifully cued up the video at the correct time and ran the tape forward again. Once again, a guard sat in the chair and the other walked the perimeter with no abnormal activity. Rogelio's concern swelled to alarm.

Rogelio had the two guards explain about investigating the voice, the slamming greenhouse door, and seeing someone run into the darkness. They had fired shots at him, but weren't sure if they had hit anyone, and then called Rogelio.

He dismissed the guards and called John. "Sorry to wake you, sir. We had an intruder at the greenhouses. I think you should come see this."

John swore before hanging up. In five minutes, he met Rogelio in the security office, wearing jeans, a wrong side out sweatshirt, and an extremely pissed off look on his face. "What the hell happened?"

"The guards heard some voices and went to investigate. While they were searching, they heard the greenhouse door slam shut and saw someone running away. They fired a bunch of shots, but don't think they hit him. He ran away in the dark."

"Did they get a good look at him?"

"No. They saw the back of him running away, but that's not the worrisome part. Somehow, they hacked into our security system and looped a video from earlier in the evening. We didn't catch anything on the security cameras."

John wearily sat down to think through the problem. "We got two folks working together with the expertise and foresight to override the security system. No way it's cops. They would have returned fire. Gotta be Doc snooping around again. How hard would it be to hack our security system?"

Rogelio shrugged his shoulders. "Probably not too difficult. It's a solid system, but we haven't done anything special to protect it. Never been a problem before."

"Well, it's a damn problem now. Get someone to look into how they accessed the system, then make sure it can't happen again. We need to increase the number of guards and expand the perimeter until we catch these assholes."

"What are we gonna tell Tomas?"

"For the moment, not a goddamn thing. We'll let him know after we catch the pricks. Get to work."

• • •

Halfway home, I remembered to call The BT to return the security video to normal. As usual, he picked up on the first ring. "Way ahead of you, Doc. Returned the video to normal as soon as you disappeared into the darkness."

"You were watching?"

"Someone has to have your back. You were doing great until that door banged shut. That's one of the things they teach in spy school, by the way. Don't let metal doors slam together during a covert insertion."

I welcomed his humor to release some tension from the last hour. "I must have missed that class. Thanks for the help with this. They doing anything interesting now?"

"Nah, they're wandering around acting tough and chasing shadows."

"Thanks again for the help. Get some sleep."

"Sleep? This is prime time for hackers. Get some rest and stay safe, Doc, and make sure to take care of Banshee. He's one cool dog."

CHAPTER 26

Tuesday, May 17
7:42 a.m.

After a brief sleep, Banshee and I hoped to meet Travis again for his advice over breakfast at Marty's Diner. As soon as we stepped across the threshold, Travis waved us over with the newspaper in one hand and a mimosa in the other.

"Good morning, Travis. Still celebrating your victory?"

"A single day of celebration after balancing the scales of justice in this town hardly seems adequate. Have a seat."

Banshee headed straight to Travis' side of the table. "I see this dog has more taste than loyalty," Travis commented, as he vigorously scratched his neck.

"True, but he'll be right back over here when the bacon arrives. Travis, I need your thoughts on a legal matter."

Travis looked at me curiously. "It's my policy not to work before ten unless I'm in court, but happy to lend an ear."

"Is this covered under attorney client privilege?"

"It is, but to be on the safe side, why don't you make this a story about your hypothetical friend talking to a hypothetical lawyer. Allows me to deny hearing anything if the need arises."

"Okay. Hypothetically, my friend and his dog were touring a large prestigious ranch, and he overheard a conversation not meant for them about a mysterious shipment leaving the ranch that night. My friend and his dog spied on that shipment and placed a GPS tracker on the truck, which delivered nursery supplies to a gardening business in Salt Lake City. My curious friend asked an associate to dig up financial records on the ranch and on the nursery, which showed large amounts of unexplained cash in both companies. My friend decided on another trip out to the ranch, and while his associate cut the feeds to their security cameras, he snuck into one greenhouse and found this." I showed him a picture of the marijuana plants on my phone.

Travis studied the picture for a moment while he sipped at his drink. "By my count, your friend has broken about ten different laws, but let's cut the crap. You figured out John is growing and distributing marijuana out of his ranch."

"You already knew about this, didn't you?"

"Of course I knew. First time we met, I told you this town has no secrets. I've been here my whole life, and for the first forty years, that ranch barely broke even. Suddenly, they became extremely profitable and set up a foundation to revitalize the town and buy half the property around here. You don't make that kind of money selling trees. He's basically set up a money laundering operation."

"Who else knows about this?"

Travis shrugged. "A lot of people suspect, but probably very few actually know anything. John keeps the ranch locked down tight."

"Why haven't you reported this?"

"I'm not law enforcement, and I have no direct knowledge of any wrongdoing. Besides, the money has really helped this town."

"Surely the Sheriff knows about it."

Travis scoffed. "I am fairly certain the Sheriff has a working knowledge of the activities on that ranch, but as I mentioned previously, the relationship between John and the Sheriff is complicated, and I am not at liberty to discuss it further."

I sat back in my chair. "This little town is full of secrets."

"There are many more skeletons in the town closet than you might imagine."

"Speaking of skeletons, do you think the ranch has anything to do with all those bodies found near their property line?"

Travis pointed his finger at me. "That, my friend, is the million dollar question to which even I do not have an answer. It's certainly possible, but I have no knowledge of any connection to those bodies."

"And if you did?"

"I would burn that ranch to the ground, metaphorically speaking. What are you going to do with this newfound knowledge that your 'friend' uncovered?"

"I feel like I should report it to the Sheriff."

"That would be unwise. The Sheriff is having a terrible week. He'd probably arrest your friend before he could say two sentences."

"Are you willing to share the information with the Sheriff while keeping me anonymous?"

"Easy enough to do, but you're poking a bear with a really big stick."

"Poke the bear for me. I'm pretty sure the ranch has something to do with all those dead bodies."

"Fine, I'll do it, but be careful and watch your back. Things are about to get real exciting in this town."

"No worries, Banshee has my back."

"That's a good thing. I think you may need him before all this is cleared up."

• • •

During his walk back to his office, Travis decided not to visit the Sheriff in person, as his presence would likely be unwelcome at the station after yesterday's events. He plopped down in his chair with a fresh bottle of beer in his hand and called.

"Sheriff, this is Travis. You have a moment?" Travis imagined the Sheriff turning red and seething with anger at the sound of his voice, and he wasn't far off.

"What the hell do you want, Travis?"

"I wanted to make you aware of a potential problem that has come to my attention."

"I think you've caused enough problems."

"Yesterday's proceedings are concluded, and that matter is closed. I want to make you aware of an issue that one of my clients shared with me recently."

"Any chance you can tell me which client?"

"Unfortunately, no. The client requested anonymity, and professional ethics require me to honor that. He discovered some interesting information about the Felton Forty."

The Sheriff debated whether to disconnect. "I'm gonna regret this, but go ahead."

"My client claims to have evidence that the Feltons are growing large amounts of marijuana on their ranch and distributing it in Salt Lake City." Travis waited in awkward silence.

The Sheriff closed his eyes and tried to concentrate on not having a stroke. He had awoken that morning sure that there was no way this week could get any worse, and it had just deteriorated exponentially. After a few calming deep breaths, he responded. "Did your client witness this firsthand?"

"He saw the plants with his own eyes and has firsthand knowledge of them being shipped to Salt Lake. He is not aware of a distribution network."

"You mentioned evidence. What does he have?"

"He has pictures and a sample he claims are from a greenhouse at Felton's ranch, but I cannot verify the source of either."

"How did he get those?"

"I did not get into any details of how the evidence was acquired."

"And your client will not come forward himself?"

"He wishes to remain anonymous, and I agree that would be best for his long term health."

The Sheriff sighed. "Thanks for sharing, Travis. Unfortunately, with secondhand information from an anonymous source and no produced evidence, there's not enough to get a warrant to search their place, but I'll be sure to make a note of this conversation and follow up if more information becomes available."

"I expected no less from you, Sheriff. I will also make a note of this conversation in my files. Good day, Sheriff."

The Sheriff turned his chair to gaze out the window at the town he had served for over twenty years. He had worked hard to build a safe, vibrant community. Sure, he had bent a few laws along the way, but always for the good of the town. When he first agreed to help the Feltons, he made it a condition that a percentage of the money had to be poured back into the town. It had worked so well that they had increased funds to the town as part of their money laundering strategy. The new hospital, schools, office buildings and housing were all paid for with Felton money. Hell, the office he was sitting in had been funded by their foundation.

Now, the scheme threatened to crumble around him. Bodies had been found, and that investigation was open with no suspects. The investigation into how the evidence against Alejandro was manipulated had begun, and now Travis had information about the marijuana operation. The Sheriff was in charge of all three investigations and intricately involved in all three crimes. He sat there for a long time, staring unseeing at the town and considered his options, eliminating them as fast as he formed them. Thirty minutes of reflection later, he still had no answers on how to escape this situation.

A half-finished lunch did nothing to improve his mood, as the Sheriff finally called John Felton. He had avoided it as long as possible, and John picked up on the third ring.

"Good afternoon, Sheriff. I hope you're calling with some good news."

"Actually, quite the opposite. We have another problem."

"Sheriff, we pay you for solutions, not problems."

"John, shut the fuck up and listen for a minute. I'm calling as a courtesy to let you know that Travis Foster knows about your little pot farm out there. He learned about it from an anonymous client. Has someone been snooping around out there?"

"As a matter of fact, someone has been out here. We caught a glimpse on tape, but no definite ID."

"This is now your problem. I've got too much shit to deal with related to the bodies and the Alejandro situation. I don't have time to deal with this as well. You need to figure out who it is and shut them up, or shut down the operation."

"You know shutting down is not an option. My partner would not accept that peacefully."

"I'm well aware of what Tomas would do. I don't want to know any details, but solve it, and solve it fast."

John stared at his phone after the Sheriff ended the call. Things had been going along smoothly for so long, and now everything was falling apart, including the Sheriff. He was fast becoming a liability. Decisions needed to be made quickly.

Tomas answered immediately. "Hola, John."

"We have an urgent problem that requires a solution."

"What is this urgent problem?"

"Whoever has been snooping around here talked to an attorney in town and told him about our operation. The attorney contacted the Sheriff, but didn't have any proof. The Sheriff can stall further questions for a time, but eventually this will come out."

"Are you suggesting we make the attorney disappear?"

"No. We need to eliminate his source. If we take care of who was snooping around here, then Travis has nothing."

"Are you sure who was spying on you?"

"It's got to be Doc and that damn dog of his. He has a history of sticking his nose where it doesn't belong, and all this trouble began when he came to town. Plus, he's friends with Travis."

"So, eliminate him, and the problem goes away."

"It's not that simple. He's a pretty high profile guy around here, and there's already a lot of unexplained bodies haunting this town."

"Then make it an accident, but make it soon. If the problem is not solved by you today, it will be solved by me tomorrow. Understood?"

"Okay. We'll take care of it."

"See that you do."

John texted Connor to meet him in his office. "I got a job for you, son. It needs to be done tonight."

Connor gleefully listened to the plan.

CHAPTER 27

Tuesday, May 17
8:44 p.m.

The ER had been quietly unremarkable, so I shouldn't have been surprised when a frantic, disheveled man brought in his pregnant wife with fifteen minutes left in my shift. We moved her to a stretcher, as she yelled the baby was coming.

I threw on some gloves as the nurses hooked her up to monitors and an IV. I turned to her husband to get a quick history.

"I'm Doctor Docker. What's your name?"

"Phil Lowry."

"Okay, Mr. Lowry, when did the contractions start?"

"About an hour ago."

"Is this her first baby?"

"Yes."

"Any problems with the pregnancy?"

"No, but the baby isn't due for another three months."

All activity seemed to halt in a momentary suspension of time as concern rippled across everyone's faces. "Are you sure the due date is in three months?"

"Yes, she is only 26 weeks pregnant."

"Mrs. Lowry, I'm Doctor Docker, and I need to examine you. Take some deep breaths and try to relax." I reached down to examine her cervix to see how dilated she was. Instead of a dilated cervix, I felt the crown of the baby's head.

"Mrs. Lowry, the baby is about to be born. Take some deep breaths and hold off pushing for a moment. Team, get the warmer on and a neonatal resuscitation kit ready."

CJ walked in at that moment. I was never so happy to see my night relief show up a few minutes early. She took one look at the serious faces. "Whattya got?"

"Twenty-six weeker about to be born in the next two minutes."

"You catch, and I'll set up resuscitation." CJ turned her attention to the resuscitation team and equipment.

"All right, Mrs. Lowry. Let me know when you feel the next contraction start. I want you to give a big push when I tell you, and then you're going to be a mom. You ready?"

"Yes, Doctor," she said through panting breaths.

"Are you having a boy or girl?"

"No idea, Doctor."

"We're about to find out." Her face scrunched up in pain as the next contraction started. "Deep breath and push for me. Push, Mrs. Lowry."

I felt the baby's head advance as she pushed. "One more push, Mrs. Lowry!" She gave a final push, and the tiny baby boy rested in my hands. Definitely a preemie, he weighed less than two pounds with paper thin skin. He fit comfortably into one of my hands.

CJ, ready with two clamps and scissors to cut the umbilical cord, whisked the baby off to a warmer in the room's corner. I made sure Mrs. Lowry physically tolerated the birth well, and then left her in the charge nurse's care. I turned my attention to helping CJ with the baby.

The nurses had already dried him and were placing monitors as CJ prepared to intubate. He gasped for air through lungs too immature to function properly. CJ positioned the laryngoscope to visualize the vocal cords, and then expertly slid a breathing tube the size of a straw into the trachea. Monitors confirmed the return of carbon dioxide from the tube, and the oxygen numbers improved. More importantly, his chest moved, and his horrible blue/gray color brightened to vibrant pink. CJ continued to ventilate the patient, as I checked circulation.

The pulse, a steady 120 at the moment, was good for a preemie, but I needed IV access to give medications and fluids. With no time for a peripheral IV, I prepared to place an IV in the umbilical vein.

I put on a sterile gown and gloves, cleaned the area around the umbilical cord, then unclamped it. The umbilical catheter slid into the largest of the three vessels, the umbilical vein. Good blood flow and easy flushing confirmed the catheter was in place. I secured it and asked for the nurses to push Mrs. Lowry's bed to the warmer.

"Mrs. Lowry, congratulations on your new son. He has to go upstairs soon, but you can say hello for a moment."

She tearfully stroked his cheek and his tiny arm, smaller than her finger. "He's so little."

"But he's strong. Don't let his size fool you. He is one tough little guy. What's his name?"

"We haven't decided yet. Maybe we will name him after you."

"Please don't do that. He deserves better."

Mrs Lowry insisted. "What's your name, Doctor?"

"It's AJ."

"No, your real name."

"I'll tell you, but it has to be our secret."

I leaned over and whispered in her ear, and Mrs. Lowry laughed. "You know, Doctor, maybe we won't name the baby after you."

The neonatal team arrived to transport the baby to the NICU, which would be his home for the next three months. Soon after, a nurse took Mrs. Lowry to the labor and delivery floor for her post partum recovery.

Suddenly, the empty ER fell silent again. "Nice timing on your arrival, Dr. Johnson. Good to have another pair of hands for that one."

"Always nice to start a shift with a burst of adrenaline. Anything else to check out?"

"Nope. The beds are empty, and the floor is yours."

"In that case, get out of here and get some rest. By the way, what's your real name?"

I leaned over and whispered in her ear, "It's a secret," and I led Banshee to the car.

• • •

I settled into my G Wagon, clicked Banshee's harness into the passenger seat belt, and pulled up some classic Bruce Springsteen on the radio. Thunder Road sang through the speakers as I eased out of the parking garage and turned toward home. A strong sense of accomplishment always accompanied the delivery and resuscitation of a newborn. Bringing a new life into the world refreshingly cleanses the death and injury we also see.

As I sang the last of the song, my car jolted violently, struck from behind, causing it to fishtail wildly. Instinct took over, as I counter steered while applying the gas to regain control. A heavy vehicle, the G wagon fought for traction as it swerved back and forth. I swung the wheel rapidly, decreasing the swerve each time, and after a few tense seconds, I had control of the vehicle again.

In the rear view mirror, a pickup truck turned its bright lights on and increased speed. My initial concern of an accident from an impaired driver escalated to alarm from an intentional attack by an aggressive driver. I punched the gas, and the 577 horsepower engine roared as my vehicle launched forward. The truck sped into me a second time, but my acceleration softened the impact, and I easily kept control of my car.

I considered my options. I could easily outrun any pickup, but the driver probably knew exactly where I lived. Time to switch from hunted to hunter.

I put a little distance between us and let off the gas. The truck accelerated behind me, and in the darkness, I could make out an older model red pickup, but I couldn't see the driver. When the truck closed within fifty feet, I floored the brake pedal. For a large vehicle, the G wagon stops quickly with its ceramic brakes. As I slowed, I watched the headlights grow in my rear view mirror and wondered what the driver would choose.

• • •

In the red truck, Connor's fury burned. He had waited for Doc to leave the hospital, then snuck up on him with his lights doused and hit him perfectly on the rear passenger side of his vehicle. The top heavy vehicle should have slid sideways and flipped into the ditch on the right or into the creek on the left. Somehow, he had regained control and accelerated away. Connor's orders were clear: make it look like a hit-and-run accident and make sure Doc died. After all the other times he had done this, no one had ever regained control of the vehicle after the first hit.

Connor stomped the gas pedal to the floor as both cars sped up. The high speed would make the accident more violent. Determined to catch him on this stretch of road, Connor fantasized about standing over a dead Doc when he registered his brake lights. At first, the action did not compute, as this was a straight stretch of road with nowhere to turn and no reason to brake.

Finally, his brain concluded that the car ahead of him was not merely slowing, but stopping. He mashed his own brakes to the floor, but he had reacted late, and his brakes were older. No way could he stop in time. Survival instinct overcame the mission, and he steered into the left lane to avoid slamming into the Mercedes. With his abrupt swerve and the truck's limited grip from locked brakes, he lost control, sliding by Doc on the left. The truck snapped back and spun around to face the Mercedes before coming to rest fifty feet in front of Doc's vehicle. While a stunned Connor processed what had happened, Doc lit up his truck with his glaring brights.

• • •

I watched the truck glide toward me in the rear view mirror. I didn't want a wreck, but the back of my vehicle was sturdy and full of nonessential parts. The truck would sustain damage to the engine compartment, incapacitating it. I braced for impact, but my concern shifted to amusement as the red truck slid by me on the left and spun out of control. It conveniently ended up facing me only fifty feet away, and I hit my brights. A visibly shaken Connor stared back at me.

Unsurprised to see Connor's face, I knew I had to lose him. I could outrace him, but that endangered other drivers. Instead, I switched to four-wheel drive and turned right off the road toward the creek. Depending on recent weather, Myer's Creek could be anything from a trickle to raging white water. Currently, about thirty feet wide and five feet deep with a steady, gentle current, the creek offered perfect conditions.

I eased my G wagon down the slope and entered the water at a steady five miles per hour, making sure that the engine could draw in air and not water. Air intakes for most vehicles are located under the hood, but the G63 had a snorkel, a tube that ran to the top of the vehicle to draw air into the engine from above. As long as the snorkel remained above water, none would get into the engine.

I eased into the deepest part of the creek, and the water level outside approached my shoulders. Plenty heavy to maintain a straight line in the gentle current, the four-wheel drive carried me across the creek. After twenty slow seconds, my G wagon climbed out of the creek and onto the other side like some prehistoric mechanical monster. Water drained off as I drove up the gentle slope on the far side of the creek. I turned in my seat to watch Connor's next move.

. . .

Furious, Connor watched the Mercedes try to escape slowly across the creek. Without a second thought, he accelerated down the slope and splashed into the creek, which drove water into the engine compartment. The engine sputtered briefly.

Once he lost forward momentum from his sudden entry, Connor pushed the gas pedal to the floor, hoping to cross the creek quickly. The engine responded by opening all its valves to suck in more air to produce acceleration. The problem was that the valves could access no air, only water. The submerged air intakes could produce no power, and the engine drowned. With one last sputter, it died in the deepest part of the creek. Connor slammed his hands down on the wheel in frustration, as a smiling Doc waved goodbye, abandoning him in the creek.

. . .

I probably shouldn't have waved, but the sight of Connor stranded in the middle of the creek amused me. I reached over to scratch Banshee, unimpressed by all the excitement, as we listened to Jungleland on the way home. I arrived ten minutes later and inspected my vehicle. Largely cosmetic, the limited damage showed only on the bumper and on the rear quarter panel. Annoying, but nothing a talented mechanic and insurance dollars couldn't repair. I called the police to file a hit-and-run report, stating that the erratic red truck had headed toward Myer's Creek. I decided to not mention Connor's involvement. I figured if it was a Felton truck, they would trace it to him, and if not, Connor would produce about a hundred witnesses to back up his fake alibi, anyway.

Inside the house, I double checked all the locks on the doors and windows before I set the alarm. I left the shotgun by my bed and the Glock on my night table, making sure both were loaded. I commanded Banshee to "GUARD." His ears perked up as he immediately took off to patrol the house. He would sleep with one eye and both ears open all night. I went to sleep comfortably, knowing no one would get by Banshee.

. . .

A wet Connor arrived back at the ranch forty minutes later after a phone call to Rogelio and a short swim. John waited for him.

"What the hell happened?"

Connor grabbed a towel from the bar and vigorously dried his hair. “I hit him at a pretty good speed, but he kept control. That G wagon has more weight on it than I thought.”

“How did you end up in the creek?”

“He took off, and I followed him. He made it through, and I bogged down.”

“Did he see you?”

“Definitely. The motherfucker waved at me as he left. I’m gonna kill that son of a bitch.”

“No, you’re not. We had one chance to make this look like an accident. He’s probably already reported it. You sure the truck is clean?”

“Yeah, I stole it from the Last Chance Bar parking lot. Probably hasn’t even been reported yet, and I wiped everything down.”

“Okay. I need to call Tomas. He’s gonna be pissed.”

John called Tomas, briefly explained what happened, and then spent another minute saying “okay” and “yes, sir” before ending the call. He turned back to Connor and Rogelio. “Tomas will be here tomorrow afternoon.”

CHAPTER 28

Wednesday, May 18
7:00 a.m.

Banshee and I arrived with warm donuts for my morning shift in the empty ER. My first patient didn't check in until after eight.

"Good morning, I'm Doctor Docker. What's going on today?" The female patient in her early twenties exhibited shallow breathing.

"I think I broke my sternum."

"That's not a very common complaint. Tell me what happened."

"I was coaching a cheer team last night, and we tossed this girl in the air. She was supposed to land flat in our arms, but she landed sideways and her elbow hit the middle of my chest. Hurt like a son of a bitch last night and even worse this morning. I googled my symptoms, and I think I have a broken sternum."

"Don't believe her, Doc. She's a drama queen." The new speaker entered the room and planted herself on the other side of the bed. I looked back and forth between them. "I presume you are her twin?" Redheads and identical in every feature, right down to the light blue eyes, the patient's sister answered.

"I'm Hannah, and we're not twins. I'm adopted. Our parents spent a long time looking for someone to match Jessica, here."

"Don't listen to anything she says. She's a smartass. Yes, we're twins," Jessica said.

"I'll just assume your dad has high blood pressure and gray hair."

"And probably an ulcer," Hannah chimed in.

"Back to business. I need to do a quick exam, and then we can get a chest X-ray. Probably won't show a broken sternum, but I want to make sure the ribs and lungs are okay."

"So how do we treat it, if it's broken?" Jessica asked.

Before I could answer, Hannah started chanting, "Rest, ice, and ibuprofen. Rest, ice, and Ibuprofen." I looked at her and she just shrugged. "Dad tells us to use rest, ice and ibuprofen every time we get hurt."

"Your dad sounds like a pretty smart guy."

Hannah rolled her eyes. "Don't tell him that. He's already convinced he's a doctor."

"In any case, let's get the X-ray and make a plan." They started arguing about which injuries hurt more before I left the room. It must have been quite the adventure raising those two.

. . .

Kirsten stopped by around lunch time carrying a couple of white styrofoam containers. "Got time for a lunch break?" she asked.

"Depends what's in that container. If it's meatloaf, the answer is no."

She peeked inside. "Nope. Looks like they put a grilled cheese sandwich and fries in this one."

"What about the other one?"

She peeked into the other container. "Looks like another grilled cheese and fries."

I raised my eyebrows in surprise. "Dr. Jenkins, have I converted you to my ways?"

"Let's just say your childish behavior is rubbing off on me."

"I would prefer to be rubbing on you."

"Maybe later. I only have a few minutes before my next surgery."

We went to the break room and enjoyed our gourmet lunch. Banshee showed off every trick he knew, earning a French fry and a smile from Kirsten for each one.

"Got any plans this evening?" I asked as we finished up.

"Nope, it's a pizza and Netflix kind of night."

"How about I bring the pizza, and we can have a pizza and Netflix and chill kind of night?"

"I got a better idea. How about we chill first, eat the pizza and watch Netflix, then chill again?"

"A two chill night sounds like a challenge, but worth the effort. Five o'clock?"

"Five o'clock works fine. I gotta go." She gathered up her trash and leaned over for a quick kiss on my cheek. "See you later. Love you."

We both paused as she waited for my reaction to her use of the L word for the first time. I leaned in to hug her, as I whispered in her ear, "Love you, too."

. . .

Tomas arrived at the ranch at lunchtime and sat down with John, Connor, and Rogelio. "I am unhappy with your inability to solve this problem. I do not tolerate failure. I assume this Doctor made a police report about the incident last night."

John answered. "He did, but he didn't mention Connor's name, so he probably doesn't know it was us."

"Idiot. Of course he knows it was you. He's been poking his head around here, and then someone tried to run him off the road. Who else would try to run over this Doctor?"

Connor spoke up. "It's not my fault. His truck was heavier than I expected."

Tomas turned his steely eyes toward Connor. "Earlier today, I had to decide whether to have you put into a barrel and buried alive. It would be wise for you to remain silent and let the elders speak."

Connor gulped as Tomas turned his intense gaze back to John. "Another attempt on his life will attract too much attention with so many bodies in this town already. We are not going to kill this Doctor, but we will discredit him. When we are done with him, no one will believe him, no matter what he says."

Tomas spent five minutes explaining the plan. "We go tonight."

They nodded in agreement. Connor practically salivated with anticipation.

. . .

The rest of the afternoon saw a steady flow of easy patients. In between, I thought about my relationship with Kirsten and when our dating had transformed into love. I'm not normally a fall-in-love kind of guy. I had enjoyed plenty of relationships in the past, but they were usually a mutual agreement to hang out together and have fun. None had potential for a long term relationship, or God forbid, marriage.

After the idea of marriage popped into my head, it wouldn't leave, which was strange, since I had spent thirty-eight years not thinking about it at all. Marriage implied settling down in one place, and kids, and schools, and minivans, and PTA meetings. Maybe even twin girls. Nothing inherently wrong with any of those ideas, but I associated none of them with my own life. I was destined to move on to a new town after three months to experience a new set of adventures.

At four o'clock, I checked out, finished my charts, and went home for a quick shower before heading to Kirsten's. I arrived a few minutes after five, and Kirsten greeted me wearing a sweatshirt and shorts with wet hair, fresh from the shower herself.

"C'mon in. I was going to put some lotion on."

"Perfect timing, as always. Fortunately for you, I am certified in lotion application."

"That's good news. Some of these body parts are hard to reach." She slowly stepped into the bedroom, slipping off her sweatshirt and shorts as she walked.

. . .

A half hour later, a well-moisturized Kirsten fought to catch her breath. "Well, that was the most intense lotion application I've ever experienced."

"I warned you I am an expert."

"I'll never doubt your abilities again. You know what all that activity makes me want?"

"Round two?"

She punched me in the arm. "No, it makes me want pizza. And then round two."

We ordered pizza, threw on our clothes, and straightened up enough so that we didn't look like we had rolled around in bed. We settled on the couch and browsed through movie options.

"You know, about what I said earlier today, I'm not sure why I said it. Did it bother you?" Kirsten asked while I scrolled through the movie options.

"It didn't bother me so much as caught me off guard."

Kirsten smiled. "I guess the middle of the ER was not the best place to announce my love for you."

"The middle of the ER is rarely a good place to announce anything."

"Why do you like emergency medicine so much?"

"Unpredictability. I could be reading a book, and the next moment, resuscitating a trauma victim. You're always one moment away from chaos in the ER."

"You like chaos?"

"I like the challenge of chaos. The job is to tame it, and bring order that yields the best outcomes for the patients."

"What about your job as a traveling ER doctor with a new contract every three months? Don't you get tired of moving?"

"It's an adventure for Banshee and me to go to fresh places and meet new people."

"I asked you before. Do you do it because you are running away from something or because you are seeking something?"

"Maybe a little bit of both."

"What are you seeking?"

"I'll know when I see it, and then it'll be time to settle down."

"I guess I'll have to work on convincing you to extend that contract."

"You're doing a damn fine job so far. Now, what movie are we going to watch?"

"I feel like some action and drama would be appropriate for the evening."

"How about *The Bourne Supremacy*?"

"Which one is that?"

"The one where he is minding his own business and Treadstone sets him up, so he has to go kick their asses."

"Doesn't his girlfriend die in that one?"

"Yeah, but he makes them pay for it. Go get the pizza at the door, and I'll get it set up."

. . .

Two hours and one pizza later, the movie was over, and we were both stuffed. "I have to get going. I have to be in the ER early tomorrow."

"Not yet. We haven't had dessert."

"Did you magically bake a cake while I was watching the movie?"

"No, I had something else in mind. Best dessert ever."

Twenty minutes later, Kirsten curled on top of me. "I hope to God you don't have a third course planned for this evening. I'm not gonna be able to work tomorrow."

Kirsten laughed as she rolled off me and threw on a sweatshirt. "Maybe some other time, but I have to work tomorrow, too."

She walked me to the door, still wearing only her sweatshirt.

"I hope you don't have nosy neighbors. It would be scandalous to let them see you dressed like that."

Kirsten threw open the door, walked onto the porch, and laughed. "I have the nosiest neighbors around, and I'm sure my scandalous behavior will be the talk of the town by morning. But you know what? I don't care, because I do love you, and I hope you find what you're looking for right here."

She threw her arms around my neck and stood on her toes to give me a long, sensuous kiss and her neighbors a long look at her perfect backside. The kiss finally ended, and I gave her a gentle pat on her exposed ass.

"I think I may have found it already. Now get inside before someone calls the cops." Kirsten was still on the porch smiling as Banshee and I headed for the G wagon. She blew me an exaggerated kiss, turned toward the door, raised her sweatshirt and gave one last shake of her hips as she went inside.

"Banshee, what do you think about spending a little more time in Montana?"

. . .

Connor watched the scene unfold from down the street. Doc was so smug about that dog and his nice car, and that little whore shaking her ass for everyone to see. Let's see how smug he was later tonight.

He called Tomas on the phone. "Doc left, probably headed home."

"Let's give him time to get home and settled. Leave the area and be in position in thirty minutes. Don't mess this up, or you will sleep in a barrel tonight."

Connor drove off to find some fast food. Anticipation made him hungry.

CHAPTER 29

Wednesday, May 18
8:47 p.m.

Kirsten stepped out of the shower, put on a bathrobe, and curled up on the couch with the latest book by Daniel Silva. She planned to read for a few minutes while her hair dried, but her thoughts kept going back to Doc. Something exciting was happening there, and she really wanted him to stay and looked forward to learning everything about him, including his actual name. She giggled as she realized she still did not know what AJ stood for. She would ask him again in the morning.

. . .

Tomas called Connor. "Are you in position?"

"I'm ready."

"Remember to wear your gloves, and you must not be seen. Wait at the back door until I let you in."

"I know. I'm not an idiot."

Tomas could argue that point, but ended the call instead. The boy was a liability, but he kept John under control.

Tomas parked his car down the street. Dressed as a delivery man, he carried a large envelope and wore a baseball hat, glasses, and a small pillow stuffed into his half untucked shirt. He appeared in the failing light as a chubby, near-sighted, slow-moving delivery man, a far cry from his normal svelte and well-dressed appearance. He lumbered to the door and rang the bell.

Engrossed in her book, the doorbell startled Kirsten. She pulled her robe tight and shuffled to the door. A quick peek out the window revealed a delivery man with an envelope. She called through the door. "Can you please leave it on the porch?"

"No, ma'am. I need a signature. It's some sort of legal documents."

Kirsten sighed, and double checked the tie on her robe. She had already put on enough of a show for the neighborhood earlier. She opened the door.

The delivery man held out the envelope, and as she reached for it, he raised the other hand to point a gun at her. "This is a robbery. Do what I say, and you won't get hurt. Be quiet and back slowly into the house."

A shocked Kirsten slowly backed into the entryway. She racked her brain for options and found none. She was barely dressed and had no weapons, and the stranger was already shutting her door with the gun still centered on her chest.

"Don't even think about it," Tomas said. "Walk slowly to the kitchen."

Kirsten turned around to comply. "My jewelry is in the bedroom. Take whatever you want."

"We'll get to that. Stay calm, and everything will be ok."

In the kitchen, he had her stop by the island. "I need you to turn around slowly with your hands in the air."

Kirsten put her hands above her head and slowly turned around. The gun pointed directly at her face, inches from her eyes. Her entire world focused on the opening of the barrel, fearing the bullet that could race into her brain before she even processed what was happening.

Which is why she never saw his other hand lurch forward with an eight inch knife toward her lower chest. Tomas held the knife palm up with the blade sideways. He aimed to the side of her sternum, at the area between the fifth and sixth ribs. He briefly felt the knife scrape bone and feared he had hit only her rib, but it glanced off and plunged deep into her chest. Sharpened to a razor's edge on both sides, the knife easily cut through the soft tissue. Two inches in, the tip of the knife encountered the left ventricle of the heart, still beating, unaware of the attack, then opened a one inch wide hole to sever nerves that coordinated the electrical activity of the heart. The knife continued its journey to exit the aorta, almost completely severing it.

The results were catastrophic. In under a second, the heart stopped beating, and blood filled her chest cavity, depriving blood to her vital organs, including her brain.

Kirsten never had time to understand what happened. Her brain momentarily processed pain, but by that time, she was already fading. She had only a second of clarity that she was dying before darkness overwhelmed her.

Tomas' attack was perfect, a testament to his years of violent experience. He slid the knife out and carefully placed it in the envelope. A gift from Javier many years ago, he would clean and sharpen it for the next time.

He lifted Kirsten onto the kitchen island. The heart stopped pumping so quickly that the chest cavity contained most of the bleeding. He closed her eyes and offered a brief prayer for her soul. The irony of praying for someone he had murdered escaped him.

He opened the back door and motioned for Connor, ready to play his part. "Where is she?"

"Change of plans. She was about to scream, and I had to stab her. She is dead." In fact, this had been the plan all along. Connor had been told he was to assault her first, but Tomas would not let that happen, and he still needed Connor angry.

"What the fuck? That's not the plan! I was supposed to have some fun with the bitch before doing her."

"Relax, plans change. We still have work to do." Tomas led him into the kitchen, where the island displayed Kirsten's body with her robe hanging open. Connor tore the robe open, completely exposing her. His gloved hand reached for her chest, and Tomas slapped it away.

"Do not disrespect the dead."

"What? She's fucking dead, man. She won't care."

"You fucking imbecile. This needs to be a crime of passion, not a chance for you to grope a dead woman." Tomas grabbed the largest knife from the block on the counter with his gloved hand and gave it to Connor. "If you are angry with her, now is your chance to show it. Stab her."

Connor took the knife and looked at Kirsten lying there, naked. He recalled all the times she and every other beautiful woman had rejected him. He held the knife over his head and hacked into her chest. He pried it out and struck her again and again, lost in the moment, as rage consumed him.

Tomas smiled as he watched. He needed a crime of passion, and Connor definitely played his part. He silently counted the knife strikes, and after the seventeenth, he grabbed Conor's arm. "Enough. Give me the knife."

Tomas placed it in a plastic bag he had produced from his pocket, while Connor stared at the body, oozing little blood, since the heart had already stopped. Color had already drained from her, and her chest and abdomen were covered with ripped wounds. Her face remained intact, eyes closed, as if she had peacefully slept. Connor turned away.

Tomas had Connor replace his dirty gloves with clean ones, and then did the same for himself with the dirty gloves stuffed into another plastic bag. Tomas cast a disgusted glance at Connor. "Go find me her phone."

. . .

The Sheriff reclined in his favorite chair to watch a basketball game, when his cell phone rang. Who the hell was calling him at this hour, and why did people always call in the final two minutes of the game? He paused the television and looked at his phone, surprised to see Kirsten's name lit up on the screen.

"Good evening. To what do I owe the honor of this call?"

A male voice answered. "Sheriff, this is Tomas. Listen to me carefully. I need you to put on your uniform and drive to Kirsten's house. No lights and sirens. Drive normal, and I will explain everything when you get here."

"Hold on. What the hell's happening? Let me speak to Kirsten."

Tomas' voice hardened. "Sheriff, put your uniform on and come over here. Now. Drive normal, and do not attract any attention. Do not speak to anyone. Have I made myself clear?"

"I'll be there. But if anything has happened to Kirsten..."

"Sheriff, let me remind you who you really work for. Any threat you make pales in comparison to the violence I can bring to you. I will forget your last statement, but do not challenge me again." Tomas broke off the call.

The Sheriff stared at the phone as Kirsten's name faded from his screen. His chest tightened to the point of nausea as he grappled with a horrible foreboding about what he would find at Kirsten's house. Too deep in partnership with these people, he had no way out and had gotten Kirsten caught up in his mess. He put on his uniform as directed and stumbled to his car, all thoughts of the basketball game forgotten.

. . .

Ten minutes later, the Sheriff parked in front of Kirsten's house, hitched his belt, and climbed the stairs to the front door, which opened as he approached. Connor passed the Sheriff, avoiding eye contact. The Sheriff watched him walk into the dark street without saying a word.

"What the fuck is going on, Tomas?" The Sheriff demanded inside the house.

"Our situation has become unacceptable with the threat of exposure too high. Unfortunately, difficult decisions had to be made."

"Where is Kirsten? Where is she?"

"She is dead, Sheriff. I am sorry, but it was necessary. She did not suffer at all."

"You son of a bitch!" the Sheriff reached for his gun, but Tomas, prepared and faster on the draw, pointed his gun at the Sheriff's face with one hand, while the other prevented the Sheriff from drawing his own weapon.

"I understand your anger, but do not direct it at me. This whole situation was caused by that Doctor. He is the one snooping around. He is the one who involved your daughter, and he is the one who is going to be blamed for her death."

The Sheriff stared hard at Tomas for several seconds before releasing his gun and collapsing in a nearby chair.

"Many things still need to happen tonight. We know Doc was here this evening, and we need to get the story straight to pin this on him."

"I want to see her." The Sheriff rose from his chair.

"I will take you to her, but the scene is not pretty. We had to create the illusion of a crime of passion. The injuries you see occurred after she was already dead. She did not suffer at all."

Tomas directed the Sheriff toward the kitchen. The Sheriff trudged slowly, dreading the scene ahead of him, but knowing he had to see it. He stopped in the doorway, as if blocked by an invisible wall. Sprawled nude on the kitchen island with the harsh LED lights making her fair skin a ghostly white, Kirsten's chest and abdomen gaped with ravaged wounds, and blood pooled on the counter beneath her, dripping silently down the side of the island in multiple streams.

His shoulders shook as he sobbed at the sight of his daughter. Finally, he turned his back on the kitchen and returned to a seat in the living room. Tomas waited patiently until he regained his composure.

"What the hell was Connor doing here?"

"His involvement guarantees cooperation long term from other parties."

The Sheriff looked up and held eye contact with Tomas. "I don't want him involved in this."

"As long as things go well tonight, his involvement will never be discovered. Besides the two of us, only John is aware of what happened."

"I should burn you and this whole mess to the ground."

"That is an option, but you would also destroy your life and the lives of those you still love. Focus your anger on the doctor. It is because of him that all of this is necessary."

The Sheriff thought hard for a few moments. "How is this going to work?"

Tomas leaned forward in his seat, happy for the acquiescence. "I called you earlier from Kirsten's phone. You will say that Kirsten called you. She told you she had a nasty argument with Doc, and that she was scared because he had threatened her. You decided to come over and check on her and found her dead. You will go out to your car and call it in on the official radio. When your team arrives, you will process the scene as you normally would any murder scene. Because of the call from Kirsten, you and a team of officers will go over to Doc's house to question him and search his place. He should allow it, since he had no part in this. It is important that you search his car, and when you do, you need to place this on the back floor of the vehicle." Tomas produced the bag with the bloody knife and laid it on the table in front of the Sheriff. "If you do this, Doc will be found guilty of this murder and discredited as a witness to anything he discovered about the ranch."

The Sheriff picked up the bag and turned it over in his hands. He finally looked at Tomas and nodded. "Okay. I can do it."

"Bueno. Time is of the essence. You must make the call."

"I need to say goodbye to my little girl first." The Sheriff steeled his shoulders and walked back into the kitchen, circling the counter until he was near her head. He leaned over and stroked her hair, as he gave her a last kiss on the forehead. "I'm sorry, sweetie. I never meant for this to involve you."

He straightened up, dried his eyes, and staggered to the front door, with Tomas following. At his car, Tomas handed him the bagged knife. "Remember, place the knife in his car." The Sheriff contemplated the knife in his hands, checked back his nausea, and tossed it into the passenger seat. He called the station as Tomas walked into the night.

. . .

Within twenty minutes, most of the police force arrived on site. The murder of a prominent doctor who was also the Sheriff's daughter meant all hands on deck. Police cars blocked both ends of the street, and yellow tape outlined a wide perimeter.

The Sheriff stopped everyone from entering until the crime scene forensics arrived. He called his team together. "Kirsten was stabbed multiple times. She's dead, and the house is clear." This pronouncement produced expressions of grief and anger from his team, but the Sheriff held up his hand for silence.

"Kirsten called me earlier this evening, saying she and Doc had spent the evening together, but it ended in a fight, and Doc had threatened her. I came over to check on her and found her already deceased."

"Let's get the motherfucker!" One deputy yelled and others joined in.

The Sheriff again held up his hand for silence. "No one wants the murderer more than I do, but we do this by the book. No vigilante shit. I'm going over to question Doc, and I'll take officers with me. The rest of you secure the scene until the evidence team gets here. I want every inch of this house scoured for evidence. We're going to question Doc and search his place if he allows it. If not, we'll bring him in for formal interrogation and get a warrant. No mistakes."

The Sheriff wearily fell into his car, and his four chosen officers followed in two more police cars. More officers cleared a path for them through the growing group of neighbors. Among the small crowd, Travis Foster missed nothing.

CHAPTER 30

Wednesday, May 18
9:53 p.m.

Sitting on the couch in shorts and an old gray t-shirt, I jolted from scanning Twitter on my phone when the doorbell rang. Banshee growled from his end of the couch, and I told him to relax while I went to the door.

I found a stern Sheriff and four other officers glaring at me.

"Doc, mind if we come in for a moment?"

"What's this all about?"

"It's better if we talk inside."

I tried to imagine why five officers would be at my home this late at night and assumed it had something to do with my interactions with Connor. After a brief pause, I held the door open. "Come in."

I led the group to the kitchen table. They declined my offer of drinks, as the Sheriff sat down across from me and the other officers spread out around the room, casually surrounding me. Banshee sat at my side and watched the tense group.

The Sheriff sighed. "Doc, there's no easy way to put this. I just came from Kirsten's house, and she's dead."

Time suspended as I processed his sentence beyond my comprehension as tears filled my eyes. Only moments ago, we had laughed over dinner and a movie and talked about our future together. "What do you mean? She's dead? What happened?"

"She was murdered."

"Murdered? What do you mean, murdered? How? Why?" Suddenly I realized why five officers surrounded me in my kitchen. "Holy shit, Sheriff, I'm sorry. Your little girl…" Tears, again.

The Sheriff brushed off the comment and continued. "I have a few questions. Do you mind if we record this conversation?"

I nodded my assent, and the Sheriff continued as a deputy turned on his phone recorder. "You were over there this evening, correct?"

I fought to regain focus and concentration, although I still wept. "Yes. We spent the evening together. Dinner and a movie."

"When did you leave?"

"About an hour, an hour and a half ago." A deputy took notes on the conversation.

"She was fine when you left?"

"Yeah. She was…perfect. We had a great evening together. Do I need a lawyer?"

"I don't know. Do you need a lawyer? We have reports that you two had a fight, and that you threatened her before you left."

I stood up, and all the officers leaned in. Banshee quietly growled. "That's insane. We had a great evening together. We talked about our love, our future together, and about extending my contract to stay here longer. We've never fought."

The Sheriff nodded. "Since you were the last one to see her alive, we need to clear up a few things. Do you mind showing these officers the clothes you wore this evening, while I take a quick look at your car? If everything looks good, we can move on to other leads, but we need to clear you first."

"Sure thing. The car's unlocked in the garage. I can show you my dirty clothes, if you want."

The Sheriff looked at his team. "You two go with Doc and look at his clothes. Don't touch anything. I'll take a quick look at the car, and then we can be on our way."

I led the two officers up to my bedroom, with Banshee following.

. . .

Alone in the garage, the Sheriff put gloves on before opening the back door of the car. The otherwise spotless gray interior harbored only dog hair, as if woven into the fabric. He reached under his shirt for the bagged bloody knife and carefully removed it. Without further thought, he casually flipped it onto the passenger side floor in the backseat. It bounced once before settling on the carpet, flinging small droplets of blood, Kirsten's blood, in all directions. The intruding fact choked the breath from his tightening chest.

The Sheriff removed his dirty gloves, carefully placed them in the bag, and sealed it, making sure no blood stained on the outside, and then tucked it back into his shirt. He donned fresh gloves before taking a picture with his phone of the little scene he had staged.

Without further consideration for the life he was about to ruin, the Sheriff returned to the kitchen.

. . .

Underwhelmed by my dirty clothes, the officers stoically shunned my attempts at conversation. My mind had cleared from the initial shock, and I had a thousand questions for the Sheriff, who I heard in the kitchen. To my surprise, the Sheriff stood waiting with his cuffs in his hands, as two officers reached for their guns.

"AJ Docker, I am placing you under arrest for the murder of Kirsten Jenkins. Put your hands on the counter."

I complied, and a deputy advanced to frisk me over Banshee's low growl. I ordered him to relax as the Deputy finished.

The Sheriff pulled my hands back behind me and locked the cuffs in place. "You have the right to remain silent..." He read me my rights and asked if I understood them. Too stunned to mumble an affirmative, I grappled with my surreal predicament when the doorbell rang.

The Sheriff looked at a deputy. "Answer that and get rid of them."

The Deputy opened the door, and loud voices in the hallway approached. The Deputy failed to hold Travis back. "Sorry, Sheriff, he pushed by me."

Travis immediately absorbed the scene of the five adrenalined officers crowding my kitchen and of me in cuffs. "I assume my client has been read his rights."

"Of course he has, Travis. What the hell are you doing here?"

"Protecting my client." He turned to me. "Don't say a damn word to anyone. I'll meet you at the station. Understood?"

"Yes, sir. Can you take care of Banshee for me, please?"

"Of course." He called for Banshee, who approached tentatively.

"FRIEND." In response to my command, Banshee sniffed him briefly and obediently sat next to Travis.

"Leash and food are in that cabinet."

"I'll take care of him. Sheriff, please allow my client to get dressed before you take him down to the station."

The Sheriff nodded at a deputy. "Grab a pair of his jeans, shoes, and socks from upstairs."

"And a sweatshirt, please," Travis added.

All five officers watched as I changed out of my gym shorts. Apparently, they worried I would fight to escape, but I barely had energy or brain power left to get dressed in this nightmare. Finally, they led me outside with the cuffs secured tightly.

Travis gave me one last warning. "Doc, not a single word until I get there."

I nodded, leaned down to give Banshee a kiss on the head, and ducked into the back of the police car.

"Travis, I'm gonna need you to leave my crime scene," the Sheriff commanded.

Travis scanned the room before returning his gaze to the Sheriff. "No funny business this time."

"Fuck you, Travis. Get out of here."

Travis grabbed the leash and the dog food before calling Banshee. "Let's go, boy. We got some work to do."

The Sheriff watched them leave. "Okay. Let's get out of here and seal the house until the evidence team gets here. Gonna be a long night."

• • •

The trip to the police station blurred past, with my mind stuck on replay. Kirsten was dead. They think I killed her. I didn't kill her. Kirsten was dead...

Still dazed as my cuffs were removed and my clothes exchanged for dark blue scrubs, boxers, and sandals, the absurd thought that the scrubs felt comfortable except for "Inmate" across the front and back flitted through my mind. Finally, my cell door clanged shut, followed by the buzz of an electronic lock, the sounds of surrealism transitioning to stark reality.

I sat in jail accused of murdering the woman I loved.

Appreciative of the quiet time alone, my mind finally shifted into an analytical mode that I used to solve appalling, complex problems that presented in the emergency room. First rule, set emotions aside. Second, focus on what you know. I knew only three things: Kirsten was dead; the police thought I killed her; and someone else did it.

I took stock of my surroundings. About eight by eight feet lit by dull yellow ceiling lights filtered behind dirty, thick plastic, the concrete cell with one wall of bars afforded no privacy. A bed bolted to the floor offered a thin gray blanket and a pillow more appropriate for a small dog. A toilet behind a three foot wall had a brown stained sink beside it. At least the facilities were moderately clean, and the absence of a second bed prevented the possibility of a roommate.

The room reeked of fear, anxiety, and frustration, or maybe that was me.

I stretched on the bed, closed my eyes, and replayed the details of what had happened at my house. The Sheriff arrived with four other officers, so he expected trouble. He seemed anxious, but his daughter had been murdered, precluding any normal demeanor. He was calm until he went out to the garage. When he came back, he angrily arrested me. Therefore, he found something in the car that connected me to the murder.

I mentally reviewed the contents of my car and couldn't imagine a connection to a murder in there, but I still did not know how she died. I finally determined I didn't have enough information to make any intelligent deductions and discontinued further thoughts for the moment.

Compartmentalization is an important skill in the ER. Whether watching a car accident victim take their last, futile breaths or evaluating a child with multiple fractures from an abusive father, patients' needs had to be met. The medical care team had to stay composed and be able to take care of every other patient thereafter, no matter how upsetting or complex their conditions might be. Eventually, shifts ended. If all the emotional baggage from every shift weighed medical professionals down, two weeks would crush them. So we learned to wall off the hard parts and clear our minds. I concentrated on clearing space in my head for my pending ordeal.

The door buzzed, and two guards entered. "On your feet, your lawyer is here. No need for cuffs, if you cooperate."

I glanced at the 450 pounds of angry police officers squaring off in the doorway and managed a small smile. "I'll cooperate."

They each grabbed an arm anyway and led me down the hall to a concrete interrogation room with only a table and two chairs. Travis, with his papers spread across the table, occupied one chair.

"You sure you're okay with no cuffs?" An officer asked.

"Thank you, Officer. I'm sure I'll be safe in here. I'll knock when we're done."

The officer nodded and left the room, the door buzzing behind him. Travis held a finger to his lips for silence. He walked to the camera in the corner nearest him, unplugged the power, and put a black bag over the lens. He repeated the process for the second camera.

"A little paranoid?" I asked with a small smile.

"Definitely, but I want to make sure I'm paranoid enough. They're not allowed to listen or watch, but caution is the better part of valor in this case. Okay, everything is now under attorney-client privilege." He sat back expectantly to wait for me to talk.

"What happened to her?"

"She was stabbed."

My eyes watered as I thought of her bleeding out from a stab wound. "Why are they coming for me?"

"The Sheriff says he received a phone call from Kirsten, saying you threatened her after a fight."

"Bullshit. We didn't fight, and she would never call her dad. She could barely stand the guy."

"They also found a bloody knife in your car."

Silence hung between us as I processed this new information. "I didn't do it."

"I know."

I looked at him quizzically. "How can you be so sure?"

"A guilty man proclaims his innocence first and then asks what evidence is against him. An innocent man asks what happened first and proclaims his innocence later."

My anger swelled. "Someone killed her and is setting me up."

"It appears that's the case, and we both know who's involved."

"The Feltons."

"Definitely, but everyone will have alibis for last night. We know why they did it."

"To shut me up."

"But we need to prove how they did it, and more specifically, who did it."

"Okay, how do we get that proof?"

"That's my job, while you get to rest in here. Now, start by telling me everything you did yesterday, from the moment you woke up to the moment you walked in this room. Don't leave anything out."

I spent thirty minutes reliving my day. I almost broke down when remembering that last little flirty dance she did for me on the porch as I left, the last time I would ever see her. Travis took copious notes. When I finished, he tucked his notes into his briefcase.

"Don't say a word about this case to anyone. It's okay to talk, but not about the case. Do you need anything?"

"A better pillow."

Travis laughed out loud. "They bought that pillow about fifteen years ago, and the city budget doesn't provide for a new one for another five years. I'll see what I can do. In the meantime, I brought you a gift." He reached into his bag and brought out a paperback book. "It gets pretty boring in that cell, and reading will help the time pass."

"Seriously? *The Fugitive*?"

"Seemed appropriate subject matter. I'm going to get you cleared of this, Doc, without the need for you to jump out of a bus."

"And get the guys who really did this?"

"You have my word. Get some rest. Gonna be a long few days."

He banged on the door, and the guards escorted me back to my cell. I lay down on the bed and opened my book.

CHAPTER 31

Thursday, May 19
7:47 a.m.

I slept better than expected given my situation. I put my book under the pillow to prop it up enough to keep my neck from cramping, and the guard checked on me every hour, but I quickly learned to ignore him. I definitely gained a better understanding of how zoo animals must feel.

My day started with fifty push ups and fifty squats. About the time I finished, another guard showed up with a tray of breakfast tacos, orange juice, and coffee, again, better than expected.

As I finished, the Sheriff appeared in front of my cell, looking down on me. "My men treating you okay?"

"Yes, sir. Quiet night with no problems."

The Sheriff stared, like he wanted to say more, but finally turned and left without another word. I wouldn't have been surprised at harsh treatment as the supposed murderer of his daughter, but he remained professional. I finished breakfast, put the tray aside, and sat down to read with my attention divided between the book and my current situation.

A little later, the guard escorted me to meet Travis, who disabled the cameras again as Banshee jumped up to greet me.

"Morning, Doc. Get any sleep last night?" Travis's radiated his intelligence more brightly than usual.

I tried to answer as Banshee showered me with kisses. "Wonderful. When I get out of here, I'm gonna look for a pillow like the one in my cell. Not sure where you find a thin, flat, scratchy pillow, but that's my mission. Thanks for bringing Banshee."

"I think the Sheriff worried Banshee was part of a plot to break you out, but I told him he's for emotional support. Frankly, I'm surprised the Sheriff allowed him to visit."

"Is he being good for you?"

"He's been by my side the entire time. It's been fun trying out various commands and seeing what he knows. He's better trained than most lawyers."

I gave him another pet and a hug. "He's a smart boy. Thanks again for bringing him by. What's going on with the case?"

"Nothing new, yet. The autopsy is today, but I don't expect any surprises. We know you had sex with her that evening, and we know she was stabbed multiple times. I doubt the coroner will find anything else, but you never know. They have the knife found in your car, and it matches the kind she had in her kitchen. Blood types match, and I expect the DNA to match as well."

"That doesn't sound promising."

"No, but there are some things in your favor. They tore your house and car apart, and didn't find any evidence of blood anywhere else. Strange to have that much blood at the scene and on the knife, but none anywhere else in the car or on your clothes."

"Strange enough for reasonable doubt?"

Travis shook his head. "Maybe, but not for sure. You might have been extra careful not to get blood on anything."

"So I was extra careful about not getting blood on anything, but threw the bloody murder weapon in the back of my car and forgot about it?"

"Well, you spent the evening over there, and the Sheriff reported a call from his daughter saying you threatened her. She was found dead soon after, and the murder weapon was found in your car."

I paused for a moment. "We don't actually know the Sheriff received a call from her."

"Phone records will show whether a call took place, for how long, and what time."

I stood up and paced, which often helped me to think more clearly. "But we have no idea what was said. We only know a call occurred between two phones. We don't even know for sure who was on each phone."

"Go on."

"The Sheriff claims she called him and said I threatened her, but there is no way that happened. I never threatened her, and we left on great terms, and even if she had been concerned, she wouldn't call her dad, even though he's the Sheriff. Therefore, the Sheriff is lying about the phone call."

"We have no way to prove that."

I continued my train of thought, undeterred by his interruption. "If he's lying about the phone call, he might be lying about other things." I paced some more. "The bloody knife couldn't be in my car when I left her house, because she was still alive. I came straight home and parked in the garage. No one had access to that garage."

"Someone might have snuck in while you took your shower."

I laughed and pointed at Banshee. "A fucking mouse couldn't have entered that garage with him around. They would have had to open the garage door or sneak through the house, and Banshee would have alerted me. The only person who could have planted it was the next person to enter the garage, the Sheriff."

Travis stared at me as he simmered, unsurprised at the possibility of this scenario. He quietly watched me pace and listened for more revelation.

"It makes sense. The Sheriff has to be in on the plot against me. I can prove it."

"How can you prove it?"

"Think about it. We're in a small town, and I'm accused of slaughtering the Sheriff's daughter. At the very least, you would expect them to claim I 'resisted arrest' and rough me up some. I should get harsh treatment from everyone here, but instead I'm treated like a VIP with a cell to myself. No one has laid a hand on me. I got a hot breakfast, a book and a visit from Banshee. You don't do all that for the guy who killed your daughter. You make his life a living hell."

"He certainly had the means and opportunity to set you up, but what about motive? Did he kill her, or is he covering for the killers, and why would he do either? Without motive, we have nothing."

"Since I'm locked up in here, it's up to you to find a motive."

Travis rubbed his chin as he ruminated. "There may be a link to all of this."

"Tell me what you're thinking."

"Too soon. Let me do some digging. I've got work to do, and I need to give Morquist a call. I want him to review everything."

"Before you go, ask the Sheriff to come in here. I want to test out my theory."

"Be very careful, Doc. This is a dangerous game. He banged on the door and asked them to get the Sheriff.

A minute later, Sheriff Stein was standing in the doorway. "Is there a problem?"

I answered before Travis spoke. "No problem, Sheriff. I wanted to see if it was okay for Banshee to spend a few hours in the cell with me. Travis is gonna be gone all afternoon."

The Sheriff looked from Banshee to me. "I know what that dog can do. If he causes a problem or threatens my men, he's going to be turned over to animal control."

"He won't be a problem."

The Sheriff scowled. "Then I'll allow it. Anything else?"

"No, sir. Thank you."

The Sheriff nodded and left, closing the door behind him. Travis smiled at me. "I believe you may be on to something, Doc. Remember, no talking to anyone about the case. I'm outta here."

"C'mon Banshee. I got lots of interesting smells for you to investigate."

. . .

As I read the last few chapters of my book, the door outside my cell clanged open. I didn't even look up, as I had already learned to ignore the frequent guard checks. A fresh voice interrupted my reading.

"Well, don't you look comfy."

I found a smiling CJ standing with a brown paper bag smelling of lunch in her hands. She had chosen jeans and red heels with a matching red silky blouse and was the friendliest food delivery person I had ever met.

I held up my sad pillow. "This pillow died about ten years ago, so I have been using Banshee as a pillow while I read." Banshee was up and stretching as his nose led him over to CJ. "You here to break me out?"

"Definitely sounds like fun. I could dig a tunnel to the middle of your cell and help you escape."

I pointed at her shoes. That might ruin those shoes."

She laughed as she kicked up her foot. "Don't be silly. Heels are for planning an escape. The actual digging requires cowboy boots and this cute pair of overalls I bought last week. While we're planning your freedom, I figured you might want some lunch. Grilled cheese and fries for you and some chicken nuggets for Banshee." She handed the bag through the small opening in the bars.

"How did you know Banshee was in here?" I asked as I unpacked the food.

Her smile and laughter engulfed her as she answered. "You still don't get it. Small town, USA. All anyone is talking about is this case. If you started doing pushups, half the town would know it within five minutes." She turned serious. "How you doing in there?"

I sighed through a weak smile. "Hanging in there. A bit of a change from my usual lifestyle. By the way, I probably won't make my shift tomorrow. I would have called, but they took my phone." I snacked on the fries while I fed chicken nuggets to Banshee.

"We got it covered. Don't worry about the ER. We'll take care of things until you get back."

"I thought you were here to fire me."

"I know you can't talk about the case, but I saw you and Kirsten together. No way you did the things they claim. So I am going with innocent until proven guilty, and when this gets dismissed, you still have a job."

"Appreciate the vote of confidence."

"Public opinion is you are innocent, at least three to one."

"Those are pretty good odds. Hopefully, I can get that ratio on my jury."

"We'll see. Anything I can do in the meantime?"

"First of all, thanks for the food. If you have a moment, I'd really appreciate a new book."

"What are you reading now?"

I held up my copy. "*The Fugitive.* Travis has a sense of humor. I wanted to see if you would buy me a copy of *The Bourne Supremacy* to read next."

"Sure. I can run over to the bookstore and be back in fifteen minutes."

"Great. Two other things. Do you mind taking Banshee with you? He needs the exercise, and the Sheriff has his leash, and if you find me a pillow in better shape than this," I said, holding up the tattered mass, "You will be my favorite person ever."

She laughed at the sad pillow. "I got sweaters fluffier than that thing. Happy to do it. Let me get his leash."

We finished our fast food, and the guard returned with CJ to let Banshee out. She clicked him onto his leash. "C'mon boy. Let's go run some errands." I watched as he happily bounded out the door with CJ.

Immersed in the last pages of my book, I was surprised when they returned so quickly.

"Sorry it took so long. Banshee was excited, and I let him run around the park for a few minutes. I'm happy to report that all the squirrels have been safely chased into their trees."

With his head down and his tongue hanging out the side of his mouth, Banshee reluctantly sauntered back into the cell. CJ held up my book and a new pillow. "You'll be happy to know that both were thoroughly searched and contain no weapons or secret messages. Although I have to admit, the idea of helping in a jailbreak is growing on me."

The guard shook his head as he locked the door again.

"Let me know if you need anything at all. The guards have my number and said they would call if you ask." Her eyes watered. "I'm so sorry this is happening. Kirsten was such a beautiful person, and you two were perfect together. I don't know who did this, but we need to get them and get you out of there."

I reached out through the bars to hold her hands. "Thank you. It means a lot to have your support, and thanks for the pillow and book."

She squeezed my hand. "Why did you want that particular book?"

"It's the one where the bad guys come after Jason, frame him for a murder, and kill his girlfriend."

"That's awful. How does it end?"

"He hunts down the guilty parties."

"Enjoy your book."

"I plan to."

• • •

Travis came by that evening with dinner for Banshee and me. "Hope you don't mind. It's another grilled cheese and fries." Banshee sniffed excitedly at the bag.

"Thanks for this. You can never have too many grilled cheeses. Where are we on the case?" I put the chicken nuggets on the floor and Banshee happily attacked them.

"About where we were yesterday. Autopsy is complete, but I haven't seen any reports yet, and DNA on the knife is still pending. Something is off, though."

"What do you mean?"

"There's no outrage from the Sheriff. He's investigating the murder of his daughter, but he's being calm and polite, like he's helping an old lady cross the street. Hell, he really is treating you more like a resort guest than a prisoner."

"No offense to the Sheriff, but this is a pretty shitty resort."

"It's a five star resort compared to the next place they'll send you. Speaking of which, I'm gonna ask for a continuance, which will keep you locked up here for the weekend."

"And that's a good thing?"

"Better than the alternative. If we argue tomorrow, we have nothing to argue with for bail. It's likely the judge will deny it, and if that happens, you'll be moved to county while awaiting trial, and that puts you in with the general population."

"You know, my cell is looking pretty comfy at the moment. Will delaying the hearing until Monday make much difference?"

"It'll give Morquist time to review the evidence and see if he can poke any holes in the case. And it'll give me more time to dig up dirt. The goal is to get you bail, so you can be free while awaiting trial."

"Anything I need to do tomorrow?"

"Stand there, look pretty, and don't say a damn word. I brought a suit and tie over from your house. They should let you shower and shave in the morning before you head over."

"That's a good thing. I'm getting a little ripe in here. You mind walking Banshee before you leave?"

"No problem. Get some sleep tonight, Doc. I need you looking fresh in there tomorrow."

"I've got a good book and a new pillow. I should sleep like a baby."

CHAPTER 32

Friday, May 20
8:03 a.m.

I woke refreshed and excited about my outing, although I had to endure a court proceeding. I was doing okay in the cell, but the mere thought of fresh air tasted sweet. After breakfast and a much too brief shower, I dressed in my suit. They cuffed my hands in front of me to prepare for transport.

"Is the dog joining us today?" the officer asked.

"He is supposed to." I failed to add by whose authorization.

The officer shrugged. "Makes no difference to me as long as he behaves." As usual, Banshee had won over the hearts of those around him. They led me outside to a police car for the brief journey, and a crowd of about fifty people awaited the spectacle, including photographers and reporters from various media outlets. I tried to maintain a stern countenance, but I knew Banshee's smile would steal the show. I took deep breaths, savoring the fresh, fragrant breeze.

At the courthouse, another group of photographers and the curious awaited. In a holding area for prisoners, they unlocked my cuffs. I sat by a window that showcased the sky and inhaled more fresh air. I promised myself never to take for granted the intoxicating comfort of fresh air again.

After only a few minutes, they escorted me to the courtroom. If last week had set a record for the most people in the courtroom at one time, today's crowd clearly broke it. With every seat occupied, folks stood like matchsticks two and three deep along the perimeter. Nervous energy electrified the crowd with whispered comments and subtle gestures in my direction. I scanned the crowd to find CJ, offering a reassuring smile from the third row behind my table. From the other side of the room, the Feltons glared at me. Opinions of the rest of the crowd seemed split. I had a feeling most of the smiles were for Banshee, though.

Travis sat at his worn, bare table, that held only a chipped coffee mug, which I imagined contained a fair bit of Bailey's. His clean, crisp suit contrasted with his usual rumpled appearance. The District Attorney and an assistant busily conferred and moved stacks of paper around their table.

The bailiff addressed the court. "All rise. Court is now in session, Judge Morestrand presiding." The judge climbed onto his dais and looked out over the court, and his eyes narrowed on Banshee before he took his seat. "We are here today for the bail hearing in the case of the State versus Augustus Julius Docker."

I winced as my full name echoed throughout the court. There was a reason I went by AJ. I glanced over my shoulder to catch CJ stifling a smirk.

"Before we begin, I see that the defense has an extra member at their table," the judge said as he nodded at Banshee.

Travis stood for his response. "Yes, Your Honor. Banshee is a highly trained emotional support dog for my client and a hero of this city. His disarming of a school shooter and saving the lives of our children is well documented."

The judge nodded. "I'll allow it as long as he behaves. That goes for the rest of you as well. You are spectators here to observe the judicial process, but you are not participants in that process. Any outbursts or disruptions will not be tolerated. Mr. District Attorney, you have the floor."

The DA rose swiftly. "Thank you, Your Honor. The state is charging Doctor Docker with first degree murder in the death of Kirsten Jenkins, and we request no bail because of the heinous and vicious nature of his crime. We believe he is a threat to the community and a flight risk."

The judge turned his gaze to Travis, who slowly stood. "Your Honor, the state has not produced a single bit of evidence linking my client to this murder. Holding him without bail on such a serious charge in the absence of evidence would be a grave injustice."

The DA held up some papers. "We have the victim calling her father, the Sheriff, saying she was threatened by the accused, and we have the murder weapon found in his car."

Travis shook his head as he spoke. "What you have is hearsay, an alleged conversation between the victim and her father that cannot be corroborated. They might have been talking about anything, and the conversation could have been with anyone. Also, DNA analysis attempting to link that knife to the murder scene is incomplete. An alleged hearsay conversation and a knife that may have nothing to do with the scene is no basis for withholding."

The indignant DA countered. "That knife is a perfect match to the set found in her kitchen."

"Possibly. It also perfectly matches eighty-seven other knife sets sold in town in the last year. It turns out that knife set is one of the most popular available at Target. Your Honor, may I suggest a reasonable compromise? It appears that information vital to the case is not available at this time, but should become available over the weekend. If recent history in this court has taught us anything, it's that hasty decisions based on incomplete information may result in a gross miscarriage of justice. Therefore, I propose we hold off on any decisions until Monday. Hopefully, information will become available that will provide clarity in this case."

The judge turned his gaze toward the DA, who after last week's defeat, preferred a simple no-bail win. Conceding to the inevitable, he agreed. "Prosecution agrees to continue proceedings on Monday."

Judge Morestrand nodded. "These proceedings will continue Monday at nine o'clock. Defendant will remain in custody. Court is adjourned." He banged his gavel and left the bench.

Travis leaned in. "I'll bring you another book for the weekend." Banshee proudly led our group out of court and back to my cell, where he collapsed to sleep on the cool, gray floor.

. . .

John Felton met with the Sheriff behind an abandoned gas station outside town. The Sheriff arrived ten minutes late, angering an already frustrated John.

"What the hell was that this morning?" John asked before the sheriff exited his car.

The Sheriff took his time standing up and arranged his belt before replying. "Good morning to you as well, John. Now, what was your question?"

"Don't fuck with me. I need to know you have everything under control, so we don't have another fuck up like last week. I don't have to remind you what's at stake here."

The Sheriff drew himself to his full height and approached John until he was only inches away, towering over the smaller man. "I'm perfectly aware of what's at stake, and let me be clear. If you ever threaten me again, I will snap your little pencil neck and deal with the consequences later. No one has sacrificed more than I have."

John took a step back and held up his hands defensively. "Apologies. The stress is getting to me. Do we have things under control?"

"Everything is fine. The DNA on the blood will come back as a perfect match for Kirsten. The knife is a perfect match to the set in her kitchen. The call logs will back up my story of her calling me. By

Monday, he'll be locked in a state facility without bail, and nothing he says will be taken seriously."

"What about the autopsy?"

"It shows she died from knife wounds. DNA will prove she slept with him. The story is foolproof."

"So was the story for Alejandro last week."

"Don't remind me. I still need to find a scapegoat for those other bodies."

"Tomas will help us come up with someone, preferably one who is killed while trying to abduct a hiker walking on that trail. Stay focused on Doc for now. We need him locked up and discredited."

"Tell Tomas everything is fine," the Sheriff stated as he collapsed back into his car.

John watched him pull away in a cloud of dust and dreaded contact with Tomas.

CHAPTER 33

Saturday, May 21
7:48 a.m.

Travis called Dr. Levy first thing in the morning. "Good morning, Doctor, and thank you for agreeing to help me."

"No problem. Happy to help. No way Doc did this. Hopefully, I can find some answers for you."

"I hope so, too. I know he didn't do it, but I can't prove it yet. What should I send you?"

"I need all crime scene photos, the autopsy video and photos, and all lab reports."

"I have all of that, but it's a lot of information. You sure you can get through it this weekend?"

"Based on my experience, it should take a few hours to get through all the material. I will call you at two o'clock your time tomorrow with my conclusions. If there is anything to find, I'll find it. If I haven't found it by two, it doesn't exist."

"Thank you. I'm sending a link to the information now. Let me know if you need anything else, and thanks again for doing this."

"Happy to help. Doc is good people and would be there for me if I needed him. Goodbye."

Morquist disconnected as Travis mused. "I need a miracle, Morquist. A miracle."

. . .

As I perused the end of *The Bourne Supremacy*, Travis stopped by with lunch. "I hope you guys aren't tired of grilled cheese, fries, and chicken nuggets."

Banshee and I eagerly sat up as salty goodness wafted into my cell. "No, sir. That's a meal for champions." I opened the container for Banshee as he impatiently thumped his tail. "How goes the lawyering?"

Travis sat in a folding chair outside my cell. "Could be better. Got the info to Morquist, and hopefully, he can find something interesting. He's one strange dude."

I gulped down a bite of sandwich before answering. "Definitely strange, but possibly the smartest person I've ever met. If there is something to find, he'll find it."

"He said so himself. That DNA will come back this afternoon, and if it matches her blood, they have you with the murder weapon, which added to the Sheriff's word about your threatening her, is more than enough to deny you bail and hold you for trial."

I savored the still hot fries. "So, what can you do before Monday?"

"While Morquist reviews the evidence, I'm going to walk the neighborhood and see if anyone saw anything. Police talked to everyone on the street, and so far no witnesses, but I'll knock on some doors to see what I can find. Do you need anything?"

"I could use another book, and Banshee needs a walk."

"I'll take him over to the bookstore and find something good."

The guard came for Travis and Banshee, and I devoured the rest of my lunch and returned to my book. Twenty minutes later, a happy Banshee greeted me, followed by Travis. They let Banshee in the cell, and Travis handed me a book. "Seemed the most appropriate."

I looked down at the title, *Falsely Accused*. I laughed with gratitude. "This will do nicely."

Travis nodded and left to go talk to Kirsten's neighbors while I curled up with Banshee to finish my book.

. . .

At three o'clock the report came in, and Larry Watson reviewed it, making sure to read everything, including the footnotes. When he was sure, he called the DA. "The blood on the knife is a 100% DNA match for Dr. Jenkins' blood."

"No mistakes this time?"

"No mistakes. I read everything twice. It's a perfect match for her blood."

"Fresh blood? Not planted blood from the lab?"

"Pure blood with no contaminants."

"Good work. Make sure a copy gets over to Travis. I would love to see his face when he gets that report."

The DA hung up and called the Sheriff. "The blood on the knife is a perfect match for your daughter's. We got him."

A subdued Sheriff replied. "Thanks for letting me know. Will be good to get this behind me."

Stein sat in silence and sipped whiskey. Unsurprised by the results, he knew that the bloody knife would be the final nail in Doc's coffin. For the thousandth time, he considered telling the truth, and for the thousandth time, he passed on the chance. He reluctantly called John and spoke before he uttered a greeting. "The blood is a DNA match. They'll get him on Monday." He hung up before he had to suffer the sound of John's voice and threw his phone aside. He poured another glass of whiskey and tried to forget the last week.

. . .

As Travis trekked through the neighborhood, he checked his emails between houses. He opened a new one from Larry Watson to see the DNA report on the blood from the knife, a perfect match for Dr. Jenkins' blood. No surprise. He forwarded it to Morquist in the hope he worked some magic on it and knocked on the next door.

A kindly old lady answered immediately. "Travis, what are you doing out there in the afternoon heat?"

"I wanted to see if you had a free moment to talk, Esther."

"Of course I have time to talk to you, Travis. Come in and have a seat. I have some cold lemonade in the fridge."

A cool lemonade sounded good, especially with a splash of vodka.

CHAPTER 34

Sunday, May 22
2:00 p.m.

Dr. Levy called precisely on time. "Good afternoon, Doctor Levy. Punctual, as always."

"Good afternoon. I have completed my review of the evidence, and there are a couple of interesting findings." Morquist explained his observations in excruciating detail, while Travis took copious notes, as he struggled to keep up with his rapid speech.

When Morquist finally paused, Travis asked if there was anything else.

"Not at this time. Unless more evidence becomes available, I cannot testify to anything beyond what I've already described."

"And you're willing to testify live at the hearing tomorrow?"

"Of course."

"Good, then this is what we're going to do." Travis outlined his strategy and then refined it with Morquist.

Travis ended the call and poured himself another drink before he reviewed all the evidence. He replayed his strategy in his head and refilled his glass multiple times until he convinced himself that he was ready. Content, he proceeded to the jail.

. . .

Feeling antsy in my cell, I exercised several times a day, read my books, and napped, as there wasn't anything else to do in my concrete and steel cage. I couldn't imagine living like this for the rest of my life. Even a sad eyed Banshee looked at me imploringly. "It's okay, bud. You're out of here tomorrow. Only question is whether I get to join you."

The outer door suddenly banged open, and Travis walked briskly into the room. On further reflection, he stumbled. It appeared Travis had been hitting the bottle pretty hard today. He collapsed in the folding chair outside my cell with a silly grin.

"How is your day going, Doc?"

"Apparently, not as well as yours. You celebrating something?"

Travis held up a finger to his mouth. "It's a secret."

"Does this secret involve me?"

"Very much so."

"Are you going to share it with me?"

Travis shook his head vigorously. "Nope." He pointed around him as he continued, "These walls have ears."

I didn't doubt the police might listen to this conversation, even though it was privileged, but I felt like I deserved to know more. "How about a little hint?"

Travis beckoned me forward as he leaned in closer to the bars. He misjudged the distance and hit his head solidly on the bars. The blow seemed to focus him a little as he beckoned for me to move closer. When we were both next to the bars, he whispered, "You're going to be a free man tomorrow. Guaranteed."

I asked how, but he shook his head with his finger over his lips. "Just act normal. Tomorrow, you don't have to say or do anything. Just sit and let me do the rest. Trust me."

I leaned back and tried to muster more trust in this crazy old inebriated man in front of me. His eyes twinkled over his grin. He winked before turning on his heel, almost falling, and then weaving his way out the door. For some reason, I did trust Travis.

I sat back down on the bed, and Banshee laid down next to me with a loud sigh. “I know, boy. One more day. One more day.”

. . .

The Sheriff observed a clearly inebriated Travis leave the station and thought to himself that the poor guy had given up. Kirsten’s ghost seemed to squeeze his heart, and he turned back to his paperwork in an effort to escape.

CHAPTER 35

Monday, May 23
7:53 a.m.

Refreshed and ready for battle after some pushups, squats, and a breakfast taco, I changed into my suit. Outside, another crowd watched as I walked handcuffed with Banshee beside me to the police car. A short drive and another gauntlet of photographers later, I sat restlessly in the holding area to await the hearing.

Travis asked the guards to give us a moment of privacy, as I took in his rumpled appearance, a sharp contrast to his perfect suit on Friday. He noted my disapproving gaze and commented, "It's all part of the act, son. Make them think they have the advantage when we cannot be defeated."

"We can't?"

"Not by a long shot. You'll be a free man in an hour, and the town will talk about this day for years to come. I promise."

"Still not gonna tell me your secret?"

"All in good time. You go out there and look pretty. No matter what happens, keep a blank face." He turned his attention to Banshee to scratch his neck. "And you be a good boy out there."

Travis left, and I paced anxiously in the tiny room until the guards called for me. My hands were sweaty as I entered the overflowing courtroom. Once again, CJ gave a reassuring smile from her seat behind Travis, while the Feltons glared at me from the other side of the room. I sat down for a moment before the Bailiff called out. "All rise. Court is now in session. Judge Morestrand presiding."

The judge swept into the room and took his seat on the bench. He glanced at the overflowing room and at the four guards stationed around the perimeter. He turned his attention to the parties in front of him. "Are we ready to proceed with the bail hearing for the defendant?"

Travis and the DA nodded.

"The State may present its argument."

The DA stood rapidly and articulated. "As mentioned on Friday, the State is charging the defendant with first degree murder, premeditated, and will seek the death penalty. We believe the defendant is a flight risk and a danger to society and should be held without bail pending trial. We call our first witness, Sheriff Stein, to the stand."

Sheriff Stein, in full dress uniform, took the stand and was sworn in.

"Sheriff, I apologize in advance for the directness of the questions, as the victim is your daughter, but it is necessary." The DA paused for a moment as Travis shuffled papers.

"Can you tell us, in your own words, what happened on the night of Wednesday, May 18?"

The Sheriff took a deep breath. "I was home watching a basketball game after work, and I received a call from my daughter on my cell phone. This was about 7:15. She said that she had an argument with Doc, and before he left, he threatened to hurt her."

"Did she say how he threatened to hurt her?"

"No, only that he threatened her. She wanted me to come by and talk to her about it. So I put on my uniform and drove over to her home."

"Did you go immediately?"

"I spent a few minutes finishing a sandwich before heading over. It was probably about twenty minutes after the call when I arrived at her home."

"What did you find when you arrived?"

"I rang the doorbell and knocked on the door, but there was no answer. I tried the door and found it unlocked, so I entered."

"Were you entering as her father or as the Sheriff?"

"I was entering as her father. I walked in and called out but got no response, so I looked through the house. When I got to the kitchen, I saw her body. She was…" The Sheriff paused as his eyes glistened with tears.

"It's okay, take your time."

The Sheriff gathered himself. "She was lying on the island, naked, with multiple stab wounds. Fresh blood was still draining from the wounds. It was obvious she was dead, but I walked over to check on her, anyway. She was gone. No pulse. Eyes staring at the ceiling."

"What did you do then?"

"I'm not really sure. I stood there for some time, trying to understand what had happened. I couldn't believe she was gone. Finally, I made a quick search of the home for anyone else, then I went outside and radioed the station to let them know we had a homicide. Then I waited by my car until the other officers arrived. Once the scene was secure, I took four officers over to Doctor Docker's home to question him, since my daughter was worried about him."

"What happened when you arrived at his house?"

"He acted surprised to see us and let us in. I explained what had happened and asked if we could take a quick look around his house. He agreed to let us do so, and some officers went upstairs while I went to the garage. When I opened the back door of his G wagon, the bloody knife was clearly visible on the floor. At that point, I returned to the kitchen, arrested Dr. Docker, and read him his rights."

"Thank you for sharing that information today, Sheriff." The DA spent another ten minutes clarifying details of the Sheriff's testimony, and Travis spent the time looking through various files. He didn't object to any of the leading questions posed by the DA. Finally, the DA finished.

"Your witness, Mr. Foster," the judge stated.

Travis looked up from his papers as if confused by what was happening. "Your Honor, the defense has no questions for the witness at this moment, but would like the right to call him later, after our witness testifies."

The judge allowed it. Next, the DA called Larry Watson, who was sworn in.

"Mr. Watson, can you tell us about the night of May 18?"

"Yes, I was notified of a homicide, and I arrived at the scene at 9:39. The house was secured, and no one was inside. Only the Sheriff, who found the body, had been inside, so it was a pristine crime scene. I put on my protective gear and entered the home, taking pictures of everything."

The DA spent several minutes going through the photos of the kitchen, including graphic pictures of the body. The breasts and genital area were blurred to maintain some sense of decency, but the exhibition of violence profoundly affected the courtroom. Dead silence reigned as Larry described the wounds.

"There were a total of eighteen stab wounds to the chest and abdomen area. It is likely that wound number twelve in this photo was the cause of death." He pointed to a wound over the left chest wall.

"Was there any other relevant evidence found at the home?"

"There was this knife block," as a picture of the kitchen was put on screen, "which shows one of the eight knives missing. Otherwise, we found no other significant evidence at the scene."

"I understand you were called to a second scene that evening as well."

"Yes, after we finished up at the victim's home, we made our way over to the defendant's house, where a bloody knife was found in his car."

"And you processed this scene as well?"

"Yes. You can see here a picture of the knife as it was found in the back seat of the vehicle, clearly covered in blood. We collected it under sterile conditions and brought it back to the lab. The knife was a perfect match for the knives in the kitchen. The blood from the knife and from the floor of the car were both tested for DNA, and results indicated a perfect match for the victim's DNA."

"Were there any fingerprints on the knife?"

"Only Dr. Jenkins' smudged on the handle."

"Based on the totality of the evidence and your experience, what did you determine from all the evidence collected?"

"It is my professional opinion that the knife found in Dr. Docker's car came from the kitchen of Dr. Jenkins and was the murder weapon used to kill her."

The crowd murmured, as the DA declared he had no more questions. The judge gaveled them to silence. "Mr. Foster, surely you have some questions for this witness?"

Travis stood slowly. "Indeed, I do, Your Honor. Mr. Watson, can you tell me where else the victim's blood was found in my client's home and car?"

"No blood was found anywhere except on the knife and in the backseat of the car."

Travis leafed through a report. "It looks like you tested his clothes, the rest of his car, and most of his house for blood. Surely you found some other trace of blood somewhere besides the backseat of his car?"

"No, sir."

"Does that seem a bit unusual to you?"

"Not at all. He could have been extremely careful not to get blood anywhere else."

Travis had a puzzled look on his face. "Am I to understand, your expert opinion is that my client was so meticulous that he avoided getting a single drop of blood anywhere on himself, on his clothes or on his belongings?"

"Yes, sir."

"But that same man who was so meticulous, callously tossed a bloody murder weapon on the gray carpet in the back of his car, and left it there? That sounds like the act of a careless man, not a meticulous man."

Larry was squirming in his seat. "I can only say what evidence we found."

"And what evidence you didn't find. To reiterate, you believe the blood and knife found in my client's car were a perfect match for the blood of the victim and a missing knife in her kitchen, and that this knife was the murder weapon?"

Larry was baffled that Travis seemed to make a case against his client. "Yes, sir," he stammered.

"In that case, I have no further questions for this witness." Travis returned to the files on his desk, as the judge and DA looked on in silence. Finally, the DA spoke. "The prosecution rests, your honor."

CHAPTER 36

Monday, May 23
9:52 a.m.

"Mr. Foster, would you like to call any witnesses?"

A sleepy looking Travis disappeared as an energetic Travis rose to his feet. "The defense would like to call Dr. Morquist Levy to the stand."

Morquist appeared virtually on the screen and was sworn in. "Dr. Levy, will you please tell the court your background that makes you an expert in these proceedings?"

Morquist was about to answer when the DA interrupted. "If it pleases the court, the prosecution is familiar with Dr. Levy and will stipulate that he is an expert in forensic pathology."

"Fine by me. We can skip the preliminaries and move straight to the heart of the case. Dr. Levy, did you have a chance to review any evidence related to this case?"

"Yes. I reviewed 371 photographs, a 51 page autopsy report, 84 pages of various other reports, and three videos, totaling thirteen minutes and forty-three seconds."

"And were you listening earlier to the testimony of Mr. Watson?"

"Yes."

"Mr. Watson testified the knife found in Dr. Docker's car was a perfect match for the ones found in the victim's kitchen. Do you agree with that statement?"

"Based on everything I have seen, I agree the knife found in the car is a perfect match for the knives found in her kitchen." The DA was listening intently.

"I see. Mr. Watson also testified that the blood on the knife and on the floor of the car was a perfect DNA match for the victim's blood. Do you have any thoughts about that?"

"I am in one hundred percent agreement that the DNA on the knife and in the car is a perfect match for the victim's DNA."

"Mr. Watson seems to believe this knife was the one missing from the kitchen block in the victim's kitchen. Thoughts?"

"It is certainly possible someone else might have a similar knife, but with the victim's fingerprints on the knife, and one missing from her kitchen, it is almost certain that the knife came from her kitchen."

"To summarize, it is your expert opinion that a knife from the victim's kitchen was used to stab her, and that same knife was found in my client's car, covered with the victim's blood. Is that accurate?"

"That is accurate."

"Am I correct it is your testimony, based on your expert opinion, that the murder weapon used on Dr. Jenkins was found in my client's car?"

"That is incorrect."

Travis paused. "I'm confused. You said this knife stabbed Dr. Jenkins."

"That is correct, but it didn't kill her. Another knife was used to kill her. There was a second knife used at the scene that is not in evidence."

This produced generalized chaos in the room that took a full minute to restore. Finally, Travis resumed.

"Dr. Levy, you made the extraordinary claim that there was a second knife at the scene, and that knife actually caused Dr. Jenkins' death. Would you elaborate, please?"

Morquist pulled up a picture of the body. "There are eighteen stab wounds on the victim. Seventeen of these are vertically oriented, while only one, number twelve in this photo, is oriented horizontally. Wound number twelve is unique."

"For example?"

"First, we have the horizontal orientation. Next, we have the width of the wound. This wound is 2.3 centimeters wide. The other wounds were all caused by a knife that is only 1.9 centimeters wide. The kitchen knife is exactly 1.9 centimeters wide. It is too narrow to have caused wound number twelve."

"Any other differences?"

"Yes. Wound number twelve was caused by a double sided blade. You can see at autopsy that both edges of the wound were cut cleanly. The other knife wounds were all caused by a knife with a single blade. Finally, this knife wound was clean and deep. The horizontal orientation allowed the knife to pass cleanly between the ribs. There is a slight scrape on rib number four, but not enough to slow the knife. It was likely done by a person holding the knife in the left hand, standing directly in front of the victim. It passed cleanly through the chest wall, traveling seven inches upward into the left ventricle and aorta. Death would have been instantaneous. The knife was removed smoothly, with no further damage on the way out."

"Have you seen knife wounds like this before?"

"Rarely. This is a knife wound from a professional, designed to instantaneously incapacitate and kill. It is likely that Dr. Jenkin's heart stopped before she was even aware of what happened."

"And what about these other seventeen wounds? How are they different?"

"As I mentioned, a different knife was used, most likely the one found in the car. The knife was swung from above repeatedly into the chest and abdomen. The cuts were sloppy with tearing at the edges and clearly occurred after she was already deceased. We know this because of the lack of clotting or bruising at any of these incisions. The angles indicate it was done by a person holding it in the right hand, standing near the patient's right hip, while the patient was laying flat."

"It is your professional opinion that wound number twelve occurred from a double sided knife held in the left hand while the patient was standing and administered in a professional manner to cause instant death. And the other seventeen wounds were sloppy wounds by a different knife held in the right hand and administered after she was dead while she was lying down. Is that correct?"

"That is correct."

"No further questions."

The DA stood to address Morquist. "Dr. Levy, you have made some extraordinary statements here today which I would like to review." The DA spent fifteen minutes peppering Dr. Levy with questions, but couldn't get him to alter his testimony at all, effectively solidifying it. After the ever calm Morquist repeated his conclusions word for word a fourth time, a clearly frustrated DA gave up and dismissed the witness.

The judge turned his attention back to Travis. "Any more witnesses before I make my ruling?"

Travis smiled as he replied. "We would like the opportunity to ask Sherif Stein a couple of quick questions." Sheriff Stein returned to the witness stand and was sworn in again. "Once again, Sheriff, my apologies for these difficult questions during this trying time."

The Sheriff nodded for him to proceed.

"We have heard your testimony previously about how you visited the home of the victim after a phone call from her, and how you found her body. Let's turn our attention to the investigation. Did your officers interview anyone after the murder?"

"My officers interviewed everyone who lives on that street about the events of that night."

"Any chance they missed anyone?"

"Every single household was interviewed by an officer, and the results are all in the file."

"Did those interviews reveal anything interesting or any information relevant to the case?"

"None of the neighbors witnessed any abnormal activities on the night of the murder."

"And no one heard anything?"

"Correct. No one heard anything that night."

"I see. Would you say that the neighborhood where Dr. Jenkins lived was a safe neighborhood?"

"Very safe."

"No violent crimes previously reported in that area?"

"None that I can think of."

Travis turned to his table and retrieved a pile of papers. "Sheriff Stein, I have here a list of 911 calls from this neighborhood. Would you believe there were seventeen calls to 911 from her street in the last year?"

The Sheriff looked puzzled. "That doesn't sound correct to me."

Travis waved the papers. "It's all right here. In fact, sixteen of those calls came from Ms. Esther Combs, who lives directly across the street from the victim."

The Sheriff laughed out loud at the last statement.

"Am I missing something, Sheriff? Is there some humor related to the distress of Ms. Combs that I do not understand?"

"Forgive me. Esther, Ms. Combs, is a very nice elderly lady who lives across the street from my daughter's house. She is retired and spends most of her free time working in her yard. She calls 911 whenever someone's dog defecates on her lawn, and it is not picked up."

Travis let a chuckle run through the crowd. "And do you send an officer out to her house each time she calls?"

"We send an officer and make a report. She makes us pick up the droppings as 'evidence,' but mostly I think she wants us to clean the lawn for her."

Another chuckle arose from the crowd, and even the judge smiled. "Has there been any progress made in apprehending the dastardly dog droppings villain?"

"I am sad to report that the villain is still on the loose."

"How does Esther feel about this?"

"She's pretty angry. I make it a point to avoid her around town, or she will bend my ear."

"I actually spoke to Esther on Saturday over a nice glass of iced lemonade. She spoke of her frustrations about the repeated violation of her yard and the inability of the police to do anything about it. She's so frustrated, in fact, that she took matters into her own hands. She bought two security cameras a couple weeks ago and had them installed on the front corners of her house under the eaves, so they couldn't easily be seen. Those cameras are motion activated and record to a cloud where the images are permanently stored. Were you aware that Ms. Combs had security cameras in her front yard?"

A suddenly serious and nervous looking Sheriff replied, "No."

"The images from these cameras are remarkably clear, and Dr. Jenkins' front porch is clearly visible in the background. Would you like to see the images that were captured last Wednesday?"

"Objection, your honor." The DA was out of his seat and approaching the bench. "The state was not made aware of this recording prior to this hearing. We have had no opportunity to review it, or even verify its authenticity."

"Your Honor, the original video remains on the cloud server with all the appropriate time stamps to verify its authenticity. I understand the State has not had a chance to see this video yet. No one, except myself, has seen this video, but I assure you, it will explain many things and prevent the State from making a grave mistake."

The DA stared at Travis, who held his gaze, as the judge pondered his decision. The crowd was completely silent, waiting for a decision.

"A man's freedom and life hang in the balance. I'll allow the video." The crowd squirmed with anticipation. Travis nodded subtly at the DA, who, after a moment, nodded back and returned to his seat.

The Sheriff fidgeted as Travis plugged the thumb drive into the projection system. He took the controller and addressed the court. "This video segment runs from four o'clock to ten o'clock last Wednesday. As I mentioned, the camera is activated by motion. Some of the video is passing cars or pedestrians irrelevant to this case."

Travis pressed play, and the first time stamp at 4:54 p.m. showed Doc's car parking in front of Dr. Jenkins' house. The excellent quality clearly detailed her house. Doc and Banshee walked to the front door, where Kirsten welcomed him inside with a kiss.

The next few clips revealed a few cars and pedestrians who had activated the camera. The crowd silently watched the video.

At 6:14 p.m., a brief clip showed a pizza delivery and Doc's acceptance of it at the door. At 8:12 p.m., Doc stepped outside the front door with Banshee. Kirsten escorted him onto the porch, wearing only a large sweatshirt. Clearly, they were laughing and enjoying each other's company. Kirsten gave him a quick kiss, and then flirtatiously flashed her bottom at him, which he playfully slapped. She blew kisses to him as he got in his car and left.

At the table, Doc wiped tears from his eyes as he wept, watching his last moments with Kirsten. He had replayed it in his head a thousand times, but the video seared his heart. On the stand, the Sheriff transitioned from nervous to resigned. His eyes watered as he watched his clearly happy daughter flirt with Doc.

At 8:47 p.m., a delivery man approached the house and rang the doorbell. Kirsten answered, wearing a robe, and the man pushed his way into the house and closed the door. A collective gasp arose from the audience.

At 9:07 p.m., the Sheriff arrived at the house. As he slowly approached the front door, Connor Felton walked out with his head down without saying a word to the Sheriff. The Sheriff ignored him and went inside.

The last clip at 9:17 p.m. showed the Sheriff exit the front door, followed by the delivery man. They walked to the Sheriff's car, where the delivery man handed him a plastic bag. The Sheriff looked at the bag in his hands, shifted his gaze back to the house, and threw the bag in his passenger seat before sitting down and picking up his radio.

Travis turned off the video, as the judge banged his gavel to restore order to the unruly crowd. "Quiet! I will not have this in my courtroom.

One more outburst, and the room will be cleared." The judge stared across the room until stunned silence prevailed.

Travis spoke softly. "Sheriff, please tell the court what really happened that night."

Looking down, the Sheriff finally spoke. "Kirsten didn't call me that night. She was already dead, killed by Tomas Escamillo, the man dressed as the delivery man, and Connor Felton stabbed her afterwards."

"This is bullshit!" Connor yelled from his seat.

The judge banged his gavel again. "Silence, young man."

Doc noted the rising tensions and leaned over to whisper in Banshee's ear. "ALERT." Banshee sat up straight and turned his attention to the crowd. His whole body tensed up and quivered.

The Sheriff continued. "The Feltons have been growing marijuana and selling it to Tomas. I'm on the payroll and have been covering for them for years, but it was never supposed to get violent. It was only supposed to be selling marijuana and everyone making a few extra bucks, but then it escalated. When some of the men stole, they were eliminated. When those tourists stumbled on the operation, they were eliminated. I didn't have a choice. I was forced to cover up those murders, and then Kirsten's." The Sheriff broke down and sobbed.

Travis approached him. "Tell the rest of it, Sheriff. Tell them why you had to protect the murderer of those tourists and of those men found off the hiking trail."

The Sheriff focused on Travis and dried his eyes. "I protected the murderer because he's my son. Twenty-three years ago, I had an affair with Carol Felton, and Connor was born. No one knew except John, Carol, and me. Connor killed all those people. My son killed those people."

Connor stood up and yelled, "You fucking liar!" He reached down to an ankle holster on his left leg, grabbed his .38 caliber revolver, and raised it to point at his father.

Banshee bunched his back legs, sprung forward one step, jumped onto the bannister, and launched at Connor's gun, like a streaking ball of fur over the heads of the seated crowd.

Unaware of the beast hurtling at him, Connor focused only on aiming his gun at his father's chest. He acquired his sight, steadied the barrel, and smoothly pulled the trigger in rapid succession, sending two shots roaring to the witness stand.

As Connor turned his attention to his next target, he noted only a blur in his peripheral vision before he felt the pain. Banshee clamped down on his wrist with the full force of his jaws, crushing muscles, ligaments, tendons, and nerves. The hand lost function, and the gun dropped to the floor. Banshee's momentum carried him past Connor, but he held onto the wrist, jerking Connor off his feet, and with a sickening crack, snapping both bones in his forearm. Still, Banshee held on.

With his left arm burning with blinding pain, Connor could see only dark eyes boring into him as sharp teeth gripped his wrist. Connor screamed.

CHAPTER 37

Monday, May 23
10:17 a.m.

My stunned surprise intensified with searing anger as I watched the video of Kirsten's dad talking to her murderers and calmly tossing the bloody knife in his car. I resisted an overwhelming urge to strangle the Sheriff as he confessed. Like everyone else, I did not know that Connor, his illegitimate son, had ruthlessly hacked away at his half sister's naked chest.

As I struggled to control my anger at the Sheriff, I had forgotten about Connor, but Banshee hadn't. With a swift leap and an almighty growl, Banshee launched himself over the crowd as Connor raised his gun. Banshee flew to neutralize the threat, but too late. The thunderous firing of the weapon echoed throughout the courthouse as people screamed and crouched on the floor. Banshee's teeth gripped Connor's wrist and disarmed him, but the bullets had already fled the gun. I whipped my head around to see Sheriff Stein's incredulous stare at the blood blooming across his shirt.

I called for Banshee and hurried to the Sheriff's chair. Banshee leaped back over the bannister to my side, and I ordered him to guard me, as I turned my attention to the Sheriff's oozing wounds.

I ripped open his shirt to see two holes in the left chest only an inch apart, one pouring out bright red blood and the other bubbling with dark maroon. I applied pressure on the wounds, although I knew my efforts were futile. He had taken a direct hit to the heart and would bleed out no matter what I did, but I held the pressure anyway and saw infinite sadness in his eyes.

"Hang in there, Sheriff. We're gonna get you to the hospital."

"I think you're lying to me Doc, which is okay, since I lied to you." He winced in pain. "Never meant for this to happen. Promise me one thing, Doc."

"What do you need?"

"Promise me they'll bury us together. Me and Kirsten."

"I promise, but you hang in there. You keep fighting."

His voice was faltering. "No more fight, Doc. Time to rest. Time to apologize to Kirsten."

I felt his last heartbeat, and then nothing. The blood stopped flowing as I took my hands away.

"What do you need?" CJ had rushed to help me.

I turned to her. "Nothing. Two shots to the heart. He's gone."

CJ, no stranger to death, nodded in acceptance. I looked at the clock and turned back to the Sheriff to close his wide open eyes. "Godspeed on your journey, Sheriff. I hope you find peace. End of watch at 10:18 a.m."

The judge watched the attempted resuscitation. "Thanks for trying, Doc. Dr. Johnson, can you please go tend to that idiot Connor, while I restore order in here?"

CJ complied, while the judge banged his gavel at a record decibel level. "Order! Listen up! I need this room cleared immediately of everyone except legal counsel and law enforcement. Make your way out the doors calmly and safely." His authoritative voice effectively filed the crowd through the double doors.

On the floor, Connor writhed, clutching his wrist. Two officers stood over him as CJ called for a medical kit to bandage his wounds before transporting to the hospital. An officer read him his rights as she bandaged his arm.

With the court emptied, the judge addressed the lawyers. "I am taking a five minute recess. Be in those seats when I return." The judge turned to me. "Follow me, Doc." I stood up, and a guard moved to follow us. The judge waved him off. "That won't be necessary."

The judge held the door to his private chambers open for me and Banshee, since my hands were covered in blood. I stared in awe at a dark wood-trimmed office devoted to law and fishing. The shelves supported hundreds of law books, and the rest of the office displayed fishing paraphernalia, including historical art, rods, reels, and lures. A mounted king salmon well over four feet long frozen in mid-leap covered the open wall behind his desk.

Likely used to speechless responses from first time visitors, he shrugged his shoulders. "I like to fish when I'm not doing this." He pointed to the salmon. "That one took an hour to reel in and cost a fortune to have it mounted and delivered from Alaska." He rummaged in a drawer and pulled out a trash bag. "In here." He motioned to his private bathroom.

He held the bag open while I carefully got the blood soaked jacket, shirt and tie off without ruining his floors, leaving me in a bloodstained undershirt with bloody hands and arms. He got the sink started for me. "Get cleaned up, and I'll meet you outside."

I scrubbed the blood from my hands, watching the red rivulets slowly turn to pink, and then eventually to clear. I looked into the exhausted eyes reflected in the mirror, and all the emotional trauma washed over me at once. Kirsten's death, the trial, the confession, and the second violent murder. I splashed water on my tearful face and dried it, composing myself. I turned to Banshee, who still had Connor's blood on his snout. I scrubbed him until we were both presentable.

The judge, resting at his desk, threw me a t-shirt. "This is the only clean thing I have around here." I unfolded the blue shirt and saw the writing in big, red letters: "Don't judge the size of my fish!" The judge shrugged, "Let's get back. It's not actually proper for me to be in here alone with a defendant, but then again, a lot of rules have been broken in my courtroom today." I put the shirt on, followed the judge, and took my place at the defense table next to Travis.

The judge banged his gavel from the bench. "Court is back in session. Sheriff Stein was a good man who made terrible mistakes. May he rest in peace." The judge nodded toward the body, which remained in place for the crime scene technicians.

Before he continued, Travis spoke. "Your Honor, I would like to apologize to the court. I had no expectation that the video would provoke this violence. I..."

"No apologies necessary. You did your job and provided critical information that led to the truth, something that has been sorely lacking of late. Without truth, there can be no justice. The court extends its thanks to you for a job well done."

The judge smiled down at Banshee. "The court would be remiss not to recognize the heroic actions of Banshee. His speedy and decisive disarming of the shooter prevented further injury. You are certainly welcome in my courtroom any time." I whispered a command for Banshee to bow, and he stood and faced the judge, then dipped his head to the floor while curling one leg underneath him.

The judge clapped in approval. "Someday, you're going to have to show me all the tricks that dog can do." His visage turned serious again, and he addressed the DA. "I assume you have a statement for the court?"

The DA stood and straightened his tie. "Yes, Your Honor. Based on the new information provided by the defense, the state would like to drop all charges against the defendant."

"To be clear, you request to dismiss the murder charge against Augustus Julius Docker, with prejudice, and to expunge the charge from his record?"

"Yes, Your Honor."

"Thank you, Mr. Anderson. You may be seated." He turned his attention to me. "Dr. Docker, please rise. The state has dismissed the murder charge with prejudice. That means you are innocent in the death of Dr. Kirsten Jenkins and can never be tried for that crime again. Furthermore, all records of those charges against you will be removed from the public record. On behalf of the court, I would like to offer my sincerest apologies for recent events. It is unfair that you were publicly identified as a killer. It is unfair that you were incarcerated for five days. Most tragically, you were denied the opportunity to grieve properly for the loss of one whom you clearly cared for. The court does not have the power to undo the wrongs of the past, but I do have the power to make sure justice is served moving forward. Dr. Docker, you are a free man. Court is adjourned."

Travis hugged me as the gavel banged one last time. I motioned for the door. "Let's get out of here."

Travis had already packed his papers into his worn black briefcase. "Agreed. Crime scene technicians have a lot of work to do, and God knows I need a drink. Let's head over to my office."

A sizable crowd of media and onlookers waited for us outside. "How we handling this, counselor?"

"Let me do the talking. You stand there and be quiet, and try to look smart in that t-shirt.

We both looked at my t-shirt and burst out laughing, a much needed tension release. It took a moment to regain our composure, and we strode into the bright sunlight with Banshee at my side. The media hustled to get in front, and the crowd pushed in behind them. Travis held his hands up to ask for quiet, and eventually the crowd settled.

"I am happy to announce that Dr. Docker has been cleared of all charges in the tragic death of Dr. Jenkins. While we are ecstatic at this just result, this is not a time to celebrate. The hearing uncovered many disturbing facts about this town and ultimately led to the death of our Sheriff by another act of senseless violence. That's all I have to say for now."

Reporters hurled questions at us and pressed further inward. I gave a hand signal to Banshee, and he barked loudly. The press immediately scampered backward.

I bent down to calm Banshee. “Please give him some space. He’s still a little high strung from the activities in the courtroom earlier.” Most of the press had witnessed his attack on Connor, and magically, a clear path to Travis’ office emerged for us.

Travis whispered as we walked. “Damn dog has more uses than a Swiss Army knife.”

I patted Banshee’s head as we trudged on our way.

. . .

Travis headed straight for the bar in his office, threw me a can of ginger ale, and grabbed a bottle of vodka before collapsing into his chair. He put his feet up on the desk and drew a long swig straight from the bottle.

“Skipped my morning mimosa today,” he explained.

“You do pretty good work sober. You should try it more often.”

“Nah. I get grumpy when I’m sober too long.” He took another sizable swig.

“Travis, when did you know the truth?”

“I spoke to Esther Saturday afternoon during my walk around the neighborhood. I asked if she had any security cameras, and she told me all about her problems. Turns out the cops asked her if she saw anything and left. Never asked her about cameras. Everybody knows Esther is half blind and probably couldn’t see people on her own porch very well. She didn’t know how to access her account for the cameras, so she spent the rest of the day finding her password, and when I returned in the morning, she still didn’t have it. So I helped her reset her password, which meant finding her email login. I couldn’t even access her account until Sunday afternoon.”

“The challenges of a small town lawyer.”

“Indeed. One of the few times I wished I had an assistant. I finally got the video copied and sent to myself. I had no idea who the delivery guy was, but it was pretty obvious Connor and the Sheriff were in on it.”

“Did you know the Sheriff was Connor’s real dad?”

Travis leaned back further in his chair. "I always suspected. The timing was right with the affair and his divorce, and the relationship between the Sheriff and the Feltons was always so odd. Everyone knows Connor is a psychopath, and the Sheriff went out of his way to make sure he never got convicted of anything serious. Not many reasons for a small town Sheriff to put up with a kid like Connor."

"Still hard to believe."

"Yeah, but it explains why the Sheriff would protect him after Kirsten's murder. His son was all he had left after she was gone."

I shook my head. "This whole thing has turned into a Greek tragedy."

"This is only the beginning. Connor will get the death penalty for murdering the Sheriff. The Feltons are gonna get nailed for trafficking drugs and for the other murders. The ranch will go out of business."

"That's a pretty big deal around here."

"Oh, it gets much worse for the town. Remember, John owns half the commercial real estate around here, and his foundation has funded a ton of projects, but all those funds are dirty drug money. The town is going to have to reconcile what to do about that. Thankfully, that's not my job."

I held up my ginger ale in a toast. "You should stick to what you're doing. You're pretty damn good at it. I owe you my life."

"I'll drink to that, but I'll drink to almost anything. All I did was talk to some people. What are your plans now?"

"I haven't really thought about it. I spent most of the weekend planning how to survive in a real jail. I guess I'll go home and get cleaned up, then check to see if I still have a job."

Travis stood up. "Good plan. Come with me. We need to go get your vehicle."

. . .

We walked to the police station to find a skeleton crew of a few junior officers, the others probably working the crime scene at the courthouse. Travis strutted inside like he owned the place.

"Listen up. My client needs the keys to his vehicle."

The officers glanced nervously at each other. "I'm not sure we can do that, sir."

Travis approached to within a foot of the officer. "Let me clarify. My client, who was wrongly arrested and wrongly charged with murder, who was framed by your boss, who is considering whether to sue this department, and whose dog disarmed the actual murderer in court, would like his vehicle. Now!"

"I'll have it brought around to the front right away." He motioned for another officer to get the car.

I spoke up. "I want to get some things from my cell."

The officer shrugged toward the prisoner area. I stepped through my open cell door one last time. All weekend I had imagined living my life in a small cage, wasting away in oblivion. Banshee whined. "Don't worry, buddy, we're going home."

I picked up my three books, fluffed up my new pillow for the next guest, grabbed the old, ratty pillow, and threw it in the trash can on my way out.

Travis and I watched my G wagon roll to a stop. I opened the door and Banshee hopped into the passenger seat. I glanced into the back seat to find that the carpet had been cut out where the Sheriff had thrown the knife. Travis shook his head. "Gonna add that to the city's tab."

"Can I give you a ride somewhere?"

Travis grinned mischievously. "No, I think I'm gonna head over to the diner and enjoy my celebrity status for a little while. All the ladies will want to have a word with me."

"Well, enjoy. I'm going to get a hot shower. Thanks, again, Travis." I held out my hand.

Travis shook my hand. "You're welcome. Let's never do this again."

I watched him walk down the street, waving and greeting everyone. A small group followed him, hoping for the latest gossip. Travis looked like the pied piper of Waterford.

Banshee squirmed in the front seat. I leaned in to hug him. "You're getting a bath when we get home."

Banshee stuck his head out the window and collected smells all the way home.

. . .

I promised myself never to take for granted standing under a hot shower without an armed man watching me. I gave Banshee a good bath as well, freeing both of us from jail scent.

I grabbed a Diet Coke and climbed into the Adirondack chair on the back porch. Banshee took off into the yard to replace the smell of shampoo with that of dead leaves on his clean coat. I reveled in the sun with the fresh breeze on my face. I closed my eyes and savored the aromas of flowers and a hint of wood smoke. I felt the grain of the wood chair on each fingertip. I opened my eyes and focused on a flock of birds circling lazily in the sky.

My eyes watered as I contemplated how close I was to losing all of this and how Kirsten could never again experience it. The birds blurred through my tears as I cried uninhibitedly for the first time in years. I sobbed for lives lost and freedom gained. I cried for the tragic life of the Sheriff, who sold his soul and sacrificed his daughter to save his son, only to be gunned down by him. Mostly, I ached for Kirsten, a victim of senseless violence who lost everything. I was the one who got her involved. I was responsible for her death, in a way. I would carry that burden forever.

Eventually, my tears dried, and I wiped the stinging salt from my eyes, and decided to get my life back in order. I whistled for Banshee, who bounded to my side, tongue lolling out of the side of his mouth. "C'mon boy. We need to go see if I still have a job."

. . .

Nervous to see how I would be greeted, I strode through the double doors of the hospital emergency room and was met with applause from the staff, as well as a few back slaps, with everyone happy to see me.

CJ emerged from her office to see what the ruckus was about, and her face lit up when she saw me. She hurried to hug me. "Welcome back! I knew you were innocent!"

"Does this mean I still have a job?"

"Hell, yes, you have a job! I'm too old to cover your shifts."

I pointed to the trauma room at the end of the hall with a deputy standing outside the door. "I assume that's Connor in there?"

"Yeah, Banshee did a number on that wrist. Broke the radius and ulna and tore half the muscles and tendons. He's going to the OR in a few minutes. Gonna be a long recovery, and he probably won't ever get full function back to that hand." She scratched Banshee's ears as she gave the update. Banshee beamed. Whether he reveled in the ear scratch or in the report on Connor was indiscernible.

I shrugged. "Actions have consequences. You fire a gun around Banshee at your own risk."

"On a more logistical note, you good to work your shift tomorrow, or do you need some time off? You can take as much time as you need."

"Thanks, but I'll be here. Rather be working than sitting at home alone."

"Cheer up, you're not alone. Come by tonight around six. It's family pizza night, and you and Banshee are invited to join us."

I tried to wave off the offer. "I don't want to be a bother."

"No bother. It's family and friends pizza night. Besides, my kids are dying to meet Banshee. See you at six?"

"We'll be there. Thank you. For everything."

I chatted with a few more people, and the operating room team came to collect Connor for surgery. They wheeled him in a stretcher, half drugged with his arm bandaged and with two deputies following. Hard to believe how much suffering this one man had caused. I turned my back on him and walked out with Banshee at my side.

CHAPTER 38

Tuesday, June 14
11:44 a.m.

I sat down to lunch at Marty's Diner when CJ walked in, looking for me and Banshee. As usual, she looked fantastic, sporting a pink blazer over a blue t-shirt. She greeted Banshee first with a scratch behind the ears.

"You're such a good boy, aren't you?" She turned to me. "What's up, friend? You asked for the meeting."

I pointed at the menu. "Order something and then we'll talk." CJ decided on a burger and onion rings to go with my grilled cheese and fries. Banshee would have to settle for grilled chicken.

"What's on your mind, Doc? Another crime ring need taking down here in town?" Her eyes twinkled.

"No. I'm hopeful my crime fighting days in Montana are over. In fact, I think my days in Montana are quickly coming to an end."

Disappointment shaded her eyes, but CJ understood. "Time to move on?"

"I'm afraid so. It's beautiful here, but too many tough memories. I plan to finish my contract and move on."

"I'm not surprised, but I will miss you. We would love to have you here full time. You have an open offer on the table if you ever feel like coming back."

"Thanks. I appreciate it. I may take you up on that someday."

Travis smiled from the entrance, and I waved him over to our table. "Pull up a chair and join us."

"I don't want to interrupt your lunch."

CJ jumped in. "Join us, please. Doc's planning to leave Montana for fresh adventures."

Travis shook his head. "Not surprised. It's been a complicated time for you here."

"Enough about me. I need an update on everything Felton related."

Travis leaned back in his chair and sighed. "I'll give you the condensed version. As you're well aware, Connor has been charged with capital murder of the Sheriff, as well as of the other seven people he shot in the woods. Seems he was smart enough to leave photos of all his poor victims on his phone. Even had them saved in a file called 'Trophies' under his favorites."

"Glad they could get into his phone," I observed.

Travis laughed. "It was a real challenge. Apparently, his password was 1-2-3-4."

CJ shook her head. "I didn't know he could count that high."

Travis continued. "Needless to say, Connor is well and truly fucked. Not even Morquist could set him free. The prosecution offered Rogelio a deal to testify against the Feltons to avoid murder charges, but he still faces the drug charges. Rogelio is telling the state everything he knows."

"Were they able to identify the other victims?" CJ asked.

"Yep. Rogelio identified all of them. The five men worked at the ranch and were caught stealing product. John told them to move on, but Connor took them out to the park area and shot them. Since John knew it, he has been charged with the murders as well as drug trafficking and money laundering. Convictions for Connor and John are pretty much guaranteed."

"Be careful. They said the same thing about me. What about the couple buried out there?"

"Bad luck. They were hiking through the ranch, smelled the weed as they passed the greenhouses, and stopped to partake. They were seen walking away, and Connor hunted them down."

"So, what happens to Carol and the ranch?"

Travis laughed. "Carol is a survivor. She denied any knowledge of the drugs, money laundering, and murders. Says she spent her days out there drunk and high on pain pills and doesn't remember much. It's about the most iron tight alibi imaginable. She's already filed for divorce. The feds seized the ranch due to interstate money laundering. They expected Carol to fight them, but she hates the ranch. She worked a deal to give up all claims to it in return for immunity and a onetime payment of two million dollars. The feds are now the proud owners of a 40,000 acre ranch."

An incredulous CJ scoffed. "Carol's walking away with two million dollars?"

"That's right. Makes sense all around. The feds own it free and clear and can auction it off whenever they want, and Carol has enough money to drink away her remaining years."

"I don't think her liver can handle another two million dollars of liquor," I noted.

"The key is moderation," Travis said as he sipped his beer.

"Okay, here's the big question. What happens to the foundation?" CJ asked.

Travis sighed. "That's what we've been working on. Technically, the money is dirty, because it came from drugs and money laundering, but a lot of it was used for good things, like the new hospital and court room. The feds initially wanted to take it all back, but we explained that would lead to years of legal fights and bankrupt the town, so we reached an agreement. All the business assets owned by the foundation would be turned over to the government and sold to private investors, and the government would keep that revenue. All the money currently in the foundation, and all the non profits controlled by the foundation, will remain in place with a new board overseeing the funds."

I whistled. "Someone is going to be in charge of a lot of money. I hope they use it wisely."

"I will certainly do my best to spend it wisely."

Genuinely happy for Travis and the foundation, I laughed. "You're in charge of the foundation now?"

"My new job is executor of the Waterford Foundation. I get to spend the next few years spending other people's money."

CJ hugged him. "Congratulations! They couldn't have chosen a better person for the job."

"I agree. The town is lucky to have you in charge. One last question though, any word on Tomas, the guy who killed Kirsten?"

Travis leaned forward with hard seriousness darkening his eyes. "Officially, they are still looking for him. He's dropped off the grid. Feds think he may have snuck into Mexico."

CJ and Travis studied my reaction with compassion. I wanted the feds to find him, but I wouldn't get Kirsten back either way. I missed her so much my chest ached. I raised my Diet Coke. "To Kirsten."

CJ raised her lemonade and Travis his beer as they said in unison, "To Kirsten."

We clinked our glasses together and drank. Somehow, the shared memory of her brought fleeting solace.

"So, Doc, CJ mentioned you were moving on. Where are you headed next?"

I scratched Banshee's ears. "Banshee's always wanted to see Las Vegas. Isn't that right, boy?"

Banshee barked excitedly at the mention of his name.

"Las Vegas, it is."

. . .

In the back of a rusty, beat up, white pickup truck, five workers sighed with relief as they crossed the border into Mexico. The truck drove into town, and at the first traffic light, a lone figure stepped out and walked away. Tomas already planned to rebuild his business, and now thought only of revenge.

THE END

ACKNOWLEDGEMENTS

For anyone considering a visit to Waterford, I am sorry to inform you it is purely fictional, but many other idyllic small towns in Montana would be happy to host you.

The school shooting scene was extremely difficult to write. As a work of fiction, I had the opportunity to save all the students' lives. Sadly, that is not the case in actual school shootings, despite heroic efforts by first responders.

CJ is loosely patterned after a good friend who is emblematic of everything good about emergency medicine. Words do not do justice to her charisma and positive energy, but they can capture the scale of her shoe collection.

Travis is my favorite character, and I have no idea where he came from. His role grew as I wrote. Hopefully, we will see more of him.

I took the liberty to shortcut the legal processes to help the story flow more smoothly. Many talented writers share stories with more accurate legal depictions. I'm just a doctor trying to keep my main character out of jail for the next book.

As always, many thanks to everyone who made this book possible. Jo Lane provided developmental editing, and as always, her suggestions only made the story better. My wife, Tamara, provided valuable editing feedback, and I actually listened to about 90% of it. A smarter man would have listened to all of it. Finally, none of this would be possible without the help of my agent, Cindy Bullard at Birch Literary, and Black Rose Writing. Their efforts bring stories out into the world, and make it a better place.

ABOUT THE AUTHOR

Gary Gerlacher is a pediatric emergency physician who trained and worked in multiple Texas emergency rooms before opening his own pediatric urgent care clinics. His thirty years in medicine have focused on expanding access to high quality care for all children, and his stories give a unique view of the inner workings of the emergency room. He has three adult children and currently resides in Dallas with his wife, Tamara, and two rescue dogs. To stay up to date on future books, visit GaryGerlacher.com.

ALSO FROM GARY GERLACHER

AN AJ DOCKER THRILLER

LAST PATIENT OF THE NIGHT

GARY GERLACHER

NOTE FROM GARY GERLACHER

Word-of-mouth is crucial for any author to succeed. If you enjoyed *Faulty Bloodline*, please leave a review online—anywhere you are able. Even if it's just a sentence or two. It would make all the difference and would be very much appreciated.

Doc and Banshee continue their adventures in *Sin City Treachery*, available in Spring, 2024.

Thanks!
Gary Gerlacher

Made in United States
North Haven, CT
13 April 2024